SHOvv ME MERCY

PAUL VINER

Published in the UK in 2023 by Fursaken Tails Publishing

First edition published 2023

Paperback ISBN 978-1-9162601-3-9
eBook ISBN 978-1-9162601-4-6

Cover design and typeset by SpiffingCovers

This book is dedicated to my beloved family. Thank you for all of your support. I know that I never say it, but I love you all xxx

CHAPTER ONE

The metropolis's normally bustling streets were for once eerily quiet, and devoid of the usual hordes of those horrible, raucous two-legged street dweller things.

Mother Nature appeared to have been riled, and she was unleashing her full wrath and fury on the grimy, bleak city.

She offered no sympathy to the few plucky, bedraggled mortals who bravely, or foolishly, scurried about below her, who now found themselves in the throes of being battered senseless by the violent storm, that she had swept across the country from the Aegean Sea.

A few hours earlier, a glorious sun-kissed spring day with a baby-blue sky, had blessed the city. Bars and cafés, for the first time in months, had been able to fling open their doors. Their pavement terraces had bustled with artists and socialites, allowing the ambience of the day to be kind to their skin, while discussing current affairs and putting the world to rights, over a cooling afternoon beverage or two.

There was at least one positive outcome from Mother Nature's vast deluge of rain. It had dissipated the pungent stench that pumped mercilessly from the exhausts of the hundreds of vehicles that clogged the asphalt jungles roads. Every hour of every day, the man-made products derived from crude oil lined the already overflowing pockets of the oil barons, and added even more toxic, deadly chemicals to the city's ever-increasing pollution, wrapping itself around the inhabitants' bodies like a second skin. The deadly poisonous particles floating in the filthy, contaminated air that involuntarily invaded the locals' lungs and stung their eyes had for now at least been washed away, and the city had taken on the refreshing scent of rain.

"For pity's sake, why won't you just clear off and leave me alone?" one of the Earth Mother's victims howled out angrily.

She was at her wit's end. Physically, her body had been ravaged. Mentally, she was stuck in a perpetual state of confusion, her emotions fluctuating from fury to fear in the blink of an eye. In her anguished, confused state, she believed that she was the sole intended target of the storm.

"What are you bloody looking at?" she snapped angrily at any of the two-legged street dwellers, who had had the audacity to glance over at her as they hurried, hunched up against the driving rain, down the soiled streets.

Her attempt at strutting about indignantly, with her head held high and lips curled back, exposing two rows of menacing, fanged teeth, had all been to no avail. In fact, her act of defiance had been a smokescreen. If she let the truth be known, in her current condition she was in no fit state to fight the feeble, evil, two-legged street dwellers, let alone the immense power of her tormentor.

For the first time in her life, she had to concede defeat. She glanced back to where she believed her antagonist was hiding. Feeling degenerated, she lowered her head, then slowly retreated from what she perceived would have been a bloodbath.

Her paws slopped clumsily across the sodden footpaths of the side streets. With the weight of the world bearing heavily down on her shoulders, she trudged back towards her temporary home.

What a waste of time her scavenge for food had proven. Rather than satiating her hunger, she had ended up soaked through, scared stiff, and to make matters worse, she was still starving.

She huffed as she passed the small café, the one whose kindly owner would throw her any scraps of food she had leftover at the end of the day. Annoyingly, it was closed, so no food today. Adding to her frustration, the metal security grill had been pulled down over the small porch, denying her somewhere safe and dry to rest awhile.

For once, the wooden bench near the café had none of those horrid things sitting on it.

"That'll have to do for now," she thought to herself.

A sudden painful twinge caused her to wince as she crawled beneath the wooden slats. Hopefully, at least she could get a moment's respite from the billowing rain that bombarded her emaciated flesh.

As she lay trembling on the drenched paving slab, her saturated, flea-ridden fur danced wildly as the biting wind howled through it.

She shuffled from side to side, trying to get herself into a more comfortable position.

"Sod it, I give in," she grunted to herself.

A sudden sound startled her. She bumped her head on one of the bench's wrought iron supports as she spun around to see where the noise had come from.

A small aluminium bistro table from a coffee shop up the road had found itself involuntarily caught in a sudden gust of wind, and it bounced noisily down the street.

She let out a huge sigh of relief.

"Phew."

The shock of the sudden noise caused her heart to start to pound as fast as a rock band's snare drum, as if it wasn't already beating fast enough as it was.

The bench just wasn't providing her with any protection from the storm. She slowly crawled forwards. Huge, pebble-like raindrops pelted down on her face and stung her eyes. She blinked, trying as best she could to clear her vision. She carefully looked all around. Once happy that the coast was clear, she dragged her body from under the bench. She shook herself, a wiggle that snaked down her body from the tip of her nose to the tip of her tail, displacing the water that had penetrated her top coat. What a waste of time that was, within seconds she was saturated again.

As she was about to set off, something caught her eye.

Was this the moment she feared? Were they preparing to attack her? She looked for somewhere to hide. Across the road, she spotted a darkened alleyway.

"Thank goodness," she thought to herself. "Damn, what if it's a dead end? I'd be cornered with no means of escape."

She was streetwise and knew every trick in the book that she herself would use if the boot was on the other paw, and she was the huntress.

Surely this couldn't be this waif and stray's final moments on Earth?

Although in agony, she knew that she needed to get to the safety of her temporary home as fast as she could.

She was one of life's natural born fighters; it wasn't in her nature to take the easy option and curl up and submit.

She gritted her teeth and started to run as fast as she

could towards the main road that crossed the centre of the city. She recoiled from the vehicles that sped past, saturating her even more – if that was at all possible – as they hurtled through the large puddles that had accumulated in the potholes.

She ducked as a flash of lightning illuminated the dark grey storm clouds that danced like a corps de ballet to the storm's thunderous drum across the sky above her.

She had to stop and catch her breath.

Her decrepit, sodden body found itself suddenly illuminated by the flickering, garish neon lights from a raucous strip joint. She looked over at the awning covering the main door.

"That'll do nicely. I can rest under there."

She started to move towards the stanchions holding the purple velour ropes that stood guarding the sodden, threadbare VIP red carpet.

"Oi, scram, clear off mutt!" yelled the bouncer.

He was standing at the main door, smoking a crafty roll-up, and sipping at a large JD and coke that one of the strippers had bought him. Up until now he'd had a boring evening and hadn't yet been given an excuse to slap or kick any of the drunken punters out. A bit of mindless violence towards a street dog would really cheer him.

She was in enough discomfort as it was, best to avoid getting into a fight with him and potentially receiving a swift painful kick from his size ten, steel toe-capped boots.

Without warning, she was abruptly struck by a sudden burning sensation from deep within her. To try and relieve the pain, she doubled her body up, then, without any warning, she vomited.

"Dirty bleeding hound!" yelled the bouncer.

She gave a final defiant bark of "Get stuffed porky" before turning to walk, as she was now in far too much pain to run back to her home.

Mother Nature took aim, and then hurled another barrage of burning spears of fire through her veil of dense storm clouds.

As the fiery javelins rained down, one billion volts of blinding white light illuminated the dark slate sky. For a brief second, the depressive metropolis found itself engulfed in a wondrous light show.

For an encore, she erupted another explosion high up in the atmosphere. A wonted, ear-piercing sonic shock wave followed, rumbling like a freight train, as it reverberated around the densely populated bleak edifices.

Sodden black and tan fur covered the scraggy body of the forsaken German Shepherd being stalked by the ferocious storm. Simply trying to walk was painful, to add to the throbbing pain in her stomach, her laboured strides were hindered by the infected ulcerations and weeping open sores that covered the pads of her paws.

She was no stranger to pain. As a street dog, it was sadly one of her most frequent and unwelcome acquaintances. In her two short years, it had reared its ugly head repeatedly in many of its various agonising guises.

Bevan, the name given to her by her late mother who had sadly shuffled off this mortal coil just a year earlier, knew all too well the anguish of locking jaws with a fellow street dog in a territorial fight. For Bevan, this was an all too regular occurrence for her, trying to survive on the lawless mean streets. She regularly received well-directed kicks from the dreaded, evil two-legged street wayfarers. The vile beings who thought nothing of hurling a jug of boiling water over her as she begged for scraps of food from the punters overindulging at one of the city's many street cafés. Her body sadly bore many scars.

Over the last few days, her appetite had become ravenous, forcing her to take even more risks in trying to source a paltry meal.

Her pain rapidly intensified, luckily she was nearly at her hideout.

CHAPTER TWO

Bevan dragged her weakened body down the filthy alleyway to the disused tradesman's entrance of an old building where she had recently set up home. At least it would offer her some protection from the unrelenting weather.

For the last few days, she had had a strange, overwhelming urge to make herself a comfortable bed, something she had never done before. She had ripped open carrier bags left outside charity shops and stole some of the donated clothes. Sadly, her freshly made bed was now drenched through.

Her nose went into overdrive, bombarded by the putrid miasma that had been exaggerated by the rain. The vile stench of vomit and decaying food repulsed her. She recoiled in disgust when she got an eye-watering waft of ammonia; the alley also doubled up as an impromptu toilet for late-night revellers.

Bevan managed to find a small dry area of grimy cobblestones, just out of the reach of the pelting rain.

Something startled her.

The flickering red 'Exit' sign, hanging above the rear door of a building just along from her hideaway, enabled her to make out the form of dozens of vile, disease-ridden agouti-coloured vermin, with their hairless snakelike tails, closing in on her.

Their wild eyes remained firmly fixed on the large dog,

potentially their next meal, as they swept in rhythmic motion, like a brown wave of raw human waste breaking towards the shoreline.

They had been driven out of the antiquated brick-lined sewerage system after it had become overwhelmed by the vast, sudden deluge of rain.

They scampered about in front of Bevan, hissing through their razor-sharp incisor teeth.

Bevan sat up and shuffled her body so that she could see them better. They had her cornered.

They let rip a barrage of high-pitched squeals. The rats were hungry and did not fear the large beast.

Bevan was too weak to run. Although heavily outnumbered, she knew that she had to fight back.

Through her discomfort, she growled and snapped at them. Her eyes darted from side to side, watching for any sudden movement from the vile things grouped in front of her.

The largest buck led the attack and scurried forwards. As he got close enough, in one swift, fluid movement, Bevan lunged her head downwards and grabbed him by the nape of his neck. He didn't have time to shrill as her sharp canine teeth slid into his scrawny flesh. The small bones in the vermin's neck easily succumbed to her powerful jaws.

She shook her head from side to side, then flung the lifeless body onto her bed of stolen clothes. Bevan retched, trying to clear her mouth of the flea-ridden, bitter-tasting fur that had been torn from the rat's body.

The rest of the mischief backed away.

Bevan let out a loud bark.

Another rat foolishly took its chances and scuttled

towards her.

Again, Bevan thrust her head forwards. The rat knew it was a stupid move trying to attack the dog alone; he stopped and turned to escape but was too slow. Bevan caught him, snapped her teeth together and severed his head.

It took one more ferocious bark for the rest of the swarm to flee. She picked up and slung the decapitated rat towards the bins, then dragged the pile of soaked clothes, with the other dead rat still on top, away from her doorway.

"Sod it. Just my bloody luck," she groaned to herself.

The sudden exertion caused her discomfort to get worse. She slumped to the ground, gasped for air and then drew her hind legs up towards her belly.

Bevan closed her eyes. Mentally she needed to prepare herself to confront whatever fate awaited her.

Ba-dum ba-dum ba-dum.

The harmony of her slow rhythmic heartbeat, pounding away in her chest, reverberated around in her head.

She had an uncontrollable urge to thrust. Suddenly, as if they had a mind of their own, her hind legs shuddered, then involuntarily kicked out.

A searing pain overcame her. She felt that she needed to expel every single one of her internal organs from within her body.

She gritted her teeth as a straw-coloured liquid dribbled from her body. She howled as her vulva was stretched to its limits.

Bevan took a deep breath and clenched her stomach muscles.

She gave one almighty push.

For a few moments, she lay panting heavily.

She closed her eyes and then let out a huge sigh of relief as the pain slowly subsided. She lifted her head and looked behind her.

Close to her hind legs lay a tiny puppy, covered in a transparent membrane.

Bevan's natural maternal instincts kicked in; she knew exactly what she had to do.

She bent her neck and shifted her head towards the little bundle, before very gently nudging the little pulsating bubble sac with her nose. She then carefully tore open the membrane with her teeth.

The pup remained motionless. Bevan began to lick it, stimulating the pup into taking its first gasps of life from outside the security of her body.

She smiled as she snuffled her snout into her pup's tummy.

The puppy's inert state soon changed, and its muscle tone was quickly established, allowing for its first exploration of its new environment, seeking contact with its mum for warmth, comfort and eventually, food.

As they lay there together, Bevan's moment of serenity was rudely interrupted.

A stabbing pain in her stomach made her wince. Again, she felt the urge to expel something from her body. Mercifully this time the pain was not as agonising as what she had just endured.

With a gentle push, a green fluid-filled pouch discharged from her vulva.

She bit through the umbilical cord that joined her pup to the life-giving placenta, which had kept it alive for the last sixty or so days.

Bevan hadn't eaten anything for days and was starving; she picked up and devoured the green organ.

The little pup, devoid of sight and hearing, snuggled tightly into the warmth of its mother's belly and instinctively found a nipple.

Bevan's eyes would momentarily close, allowing her, for the briefest of moments, to lapse into some much-needed sleep. She was exhausted from the ordeal of giving birth and the trauma she had endured in trying to escape the storm.

Thirty minutes passed before Bevan had the urge to push again. She picked her firstborn up by the scruff of its neck and moved it higher up her body for its own safety.

Her contractions could cause her legs to kick out and didn't want to run the risk of harming her puppy.

It didn't take too long for another little foetal sac to make an appearance. As before, she went through the birthing, tearing open and cleansing process.

Bevan was now the proud mother of two gorgeous puppies.

An hour passed before the contractions started again. No longer was she fearful of the pain, she took comfort in the knowledge that soon she would have yet another beautiful bundle of joy.

Bevan looked admiringly down at her family. She knew her nomadic, violent life was now about to dramatically change forever.

A cast iron downpipe ran down the wall close to where Bevan and her puppies lay.

She had a raging thirst and managed, without disturbing her pups, to manoeuvre herself close enough to take some essential licks of refreshing, cold rainwater from a small crack in the rusty pipe.

She had a two-hour respite before the contractions returned with a vengeance.

Bevan soon found herself delivering her fourth pup, however, just before the foetal sac made its appearance, it tore open.

There was no movement from her fourth-born puppy.

Bevan frantically ripped the pouch away from the pup's mouth and nose and chewed through the cord.

Panic-stricken, she licked the puppy's face; there was still no sign of life, her pup wasn't breathing. Bevan started licking with more urgency, but still nothing.

"Please no!" she howled out in despair.

In a state of panic, she started instinctively nudging its belly with her muzzle.

Suddenly, the helpless little puppy spluttered into life. It gasped as it filled its lungs with its first lifesaving intakes of breath.

"Phew, that was close," Bevan thought to herself.

She licked her fourth born clean, then it too slowly clambered up and snuggled tightly into her.

It was still raining, although thankfully the thunder and lightning had now subsided. The normal pungent stench of the alleyway had now been displaced by the fresh aroma of petrichor.

Bevan was exhausted.

To protect her pups, Bevan ate their defecated bodily waste. The aroma from the faeces could easily attract unwanted attention from another street dog.

As exhausted as she was, her pups would need to take milk from her every two hours. Somehow, she would now need to try and eat three times as much food as usual for her to be able to produce enough milk for her litter. No small feat for a street dog who already struggled to scavenge enough scraps for her own needs as it was.

CHAPTER THREE

The puppies' daily requirements from Bevan had become an exhausting, relentless onslaught.

For the first week, they had spent all their energy on sleeping, eating and defecating.

In between feeding and cleaning them, Bevan had tried as best she could to take short naps, and also to somehow find food for herself.

She had learnt that the high-pitched beeping sound, combined with the stench of diesel and shouting from the two smelly street dwellers meant that she needed to quickly move her pups. Their hiding place would be noisily dragged away, banged up against the large grey truck, lifted, emptied, then wheeled back. The fetid stench that filled the air for a few minutes after the truck had driven off repulsed Bevan.

It's funny how dustcarts all over the world reek the same. The decomposing contents of the remaining garbage juice, or leachate, penetrates deep into the steel metalwork, and the foul-smelling malodour remains forever more.

Physically, the puppies had changed beyond all recognition.

They had progressed from shuffling across the ground on their bellies to crawling. In fact, the firstborn had even attempted to take its first intrepid steps. It would have to patiently wait another week before it could walk, albeit with a wobbly gait.

Their eyes, with their hazy greyish-blue colouring, were slightly open; in a few days they would be fully open. It would take another six weeks or so for them to have fully developed sight, and for their eyes to take on the distinctive brown colouring, characteristic of their breed.

As of yet, their teeth had not started protruding through their gums, a welcome relief for Bevan who still had weeks left of nursing them.

The remnants of their umbilical cords had dried up and fallen off.

While her pups were sleeping, Bevan would conceal them as best she could under an old woollen blanket she had found.

Now came the time that she dreaded the most, she had to leave them and head off to try and scavenge food for herself.

Luckily, close to the doorway that she had made her home, were the refuse bins belonging to the small fast-food takeaway on the corner.

The millions of olfactory receptors in her nose homed in on the semi-edible discarded food waste. Although this proved to be a short-term lifesaver, she required more health-beneficial nutrients than the bins could provide and was now having to take far greater risks in acquiring food.

She feared constantly for the safety of her family. She knew only too well that they were too young to survive, even for just a day, on their own.

She dreaded the thought of them being discovered and massacred by a starving, cannibalistic street dog if she should succumb to ingesting poisoned food. Food that has been purposely and cruelly spiked with rat poison or shards of glass and left in a prominent place for a street dog to find.

This was the method being increasingly used by many of the homicidal two-legged city dwellers to euthanise as many of the ever-increasing stray canine population as possible.

Sadly, this was the horrific fate that Bevan's dear ma had succumbed to just a year earlier.

Bevan could only look on helplessly for three arduous days, as her matriarch lay dying in piercing agony right in front of her.

For seventy-two long, painful hours, her frail body haemorrhaged blood from every orifice. Her respiratory organs slowly failed, causing her breathing rate to have fluctuated between laboured and heavy.

As her life ebbed away, she was subjected to a series of violent muscle tremors and brain-damaging seizures. Gradually, one by one, her vital, internal organs collapsed. Her death was slow and excruciatingly painful, but mercifully for her, in the end, it came.

Bevan needed to eat to survive. She prayed for her pups' sake that her body did not become one of the rotting corpses, devoid of skin and riddled with thousands of burrowing maggots that she encountered daily.

She did all that she possibly could to avoid getting too close to the decomposing, perished ex-street dogs. Their lifeless eyes scared her, some gazed aimlessly skyward, and others appeared to stare straight at her, their deathly glare piercing Bevan's soul.

Their carcasses often lay stacked up in piles, gathered together by the city's municipal workers, waiting to be carted off and incinerated. The once-proud dogs' decaying bodies now filled the air with the repugnant stench of rotting eggs, although somehow, there was also a sickeningly sweet scent mixed in.

The street dogs' demised corpses were a constant gruesome reminder of the harsh reality of the lives they had once tried to live. Nomads who had roamed the streets of the despicable, unforgiving city that they had once called home.

These pitiful lifeless souls' bodies were sadly exactly how Bevan remembered her dear mother.

CHAPTER FOUR

The pups were approaching two months old and were now looking like German Shepherds. Their black and tan markings clearly showed through their soft puppy fur, and at last their ears had started to stand erect.

The doorway was no longer safe enough for the developing young family to remain holed up in.

For Bevan, trying to keep her animated pups quiet, and to not yelp out in excitement every time a two-legged street dweller passed their lair, was no easy task. The puppies' inquisitive minds were like sponges, continually absorbing the strange new sights, smells and sounds of the dangerous world that they lived in.

"Please, just for once, try to stay quiet my darlings," Bevan barked in a hushed voice at her pups.

She knew that winter would be arriving very soon. She urgently needed to find a secure, dry place for her family to call home, to protect them from the onslaught of the brutal approaching conditions. Winter's bitterly cold toothy bite and increased spells of wetter weather could prove fatal for her young pups.

Bevan poked her head out from behind the bins and scanned the area for any imminent danger.

She gave her pups a final command to stay put and quiet before heading off to try and find a permanent place of refuge.

With her eyes peeled, and nose to the ground, Bevan set about scouring the surrounding area. Sadly, she couldn't find anywhere locally that was suitable.

She needed to cast her net slightly further afield and headed off towards the wasteland, situated not far from the alleyway where she and her pups currently lived.

She hadn't been looking for long when she discovered an old workman's shed. Annoyingly, it was right next to the city's main central railway line.

On first inspection from her vantage point, it appeared to be free of any occupants.

She moved in closer.

The wooden hut's door, held on by one solitary hinge at the top, hung precariously and gently swung in the breeze.

Bevan circled the shack a couple of times before cautiously venturing inside.

She sniffed all around, checking for any signs of territorial scent marking. A strong urine stench would have defined that the hut had already been claimed by a fellow street dog.

Bevan would then have been forced into a ferocious territorial fight if she wanted to claim it for her family.

She detected a few faint aromas left by the previous canine inhabitants. The ghostly reminders of yet more forsaken souls who had also once sought sanctuary within the decaying structure.

She squatted and overmarked the fading scents with small amounts of her own urine. Bevan had made her claim. The shack was now officially her family's new home.

"Oh well, it's not perfect, but beggars can't be choosers. It may be a decrepit wreck, yet it smells a lot better than the bins, offers some protection at least from the wind and rain, and will be far safer than the alleyway. For now, it will have to do," she thought to herself.

Discarded, rusty tools lay scattered hazardously across the floor. The dank, musty air reeked of engineering oil and grease, the man-made products derived from fossil fuels that would have once been used to help maintain the city's train tracks.

The main structure was derelict. The timber frame and panels were riddled with woodworm. Most of the roof's slate tiles had been stolen years ago, and the tatty felt lining struggled to offer any form of protection from the elements.

The solitary side window had been vandalised, and vicious shards of glass lay strewn all across the floor.

Crossing the train tracks was a treacherous task. Not only did she have to be careful of the trains that hurtled past, but Bevan also had to avoid getting her paws trapped in the gaping splits in the heavy wooden sleepers or cutting herself on the razor-sharp edges of the fasteners that held the tracks in place.

The rails were constantly covered in raw sewage, from where the commuter trains holding tanks had been emptied before pulling into the main station. The potential of her contracting sepsis from an infected open wound was just another everyday hazard that she faced.

As happy as she could be with her new home, she ran back across the wasteland and bolted up the alleyway.

Bevan breathed a sigh of relief when she reached the bins and could hear her pups shuffling about behind them. She looked all around to ensure that she hadn't been followed, before squeezing between two of the bins.

She didn't want to run the risk of trying to lead all four of her pups to the shack, so she decided it would be safest to take them two at a time.

Now she had to make a gut-wrenching decision, which two of her pups to take first?

She decided to take her second born, the most sensible of the four, and her last born. Bevan knew that this would be the most difficult journey she would have to make.

"Right you two, wait here quietly for me. I'll be back as soon as I can for you."

The two pups being left behind nodded.

"OK, it's time. Stay as close to me as you can."

Again she checked that the coast was clear, before leading the two pups on the treacherous journey towards their new home.

"Come on keep up."

"Leave that alone."

"Stop shouting."

"Don't eat that."

Bevan had to keep on stopping, herding her pups together, and giving them commands. They had never ventured this far before and were both overwhelmed by the strange new world and everything that surrounded them.

Eventually they arrived at the shack. Bevan was exhausted, but she needed to get back as quickly as she could to the other two.

"I hope they listen to me," she thought to herself.

"I won't be long. Please, make yourselves at home. Do not, under any circumstances, venture outside, and please stay very quiet my darlings."

Bevan checked that the coast was clear.

"Two down, two to go," she thought to herself as she ran back to her other pups.

Luckily for Bevan, the second two pups were more obedient and remained close to her on the trip.

Once they were all settled, Bevan set about trying to make the shack feel a bit more homely.

She found a couple of discarded hessian sacks and dragged them to a draft-free corner. Although damp, the old gunny sacks, with their distinct musty lanolin, and wheat grain aroma, would at least provide an air of comfort and warmth for her pups.

Bevan poked her nose out of the door and scanned the area to see if she had been spotted by another street dog making her claim to the den.

"No one is to step outside. Do you understand me?" she barked at her pups.

None of them responded.

"Do you understand me?"

Her pups, who were laying snuggled up on the hessian sacks, begrudgingly nodded.

"Good. Now once more, stay here."

Although exhausted, there was no time for Bevan to relax. Yet again she had to venture off to try and scavenge some food for herself.

She hadn't long left when one of the pups playfully nipped the tail of one of his siblings.

The dog who had been bitten retaliated but bit the wrong pup by mistake. Furore broke out, three of the pups piled off the sacks and bundled into each other.

The smallest, last born pup, a little girl, kept well out of harm's way and remained on the sacks.

She knew there was no way that she could join in with the rough and tumble play fighting with her siblings. For her, merely trying to walk was difficult.

The scrap ended as quickly as it had started. Panting heavily, with their tongues hanging out, the three elder dogs looked over to where the smallest pup was lying.

She did her utmost to avoid any form of eye contact with them.

The older pups sat and stared at her.

Their heads tilted inquisitively to one side. They looked each other up and down, then back over at their little sister.

What was going on with her front legs? They looked down at their own, then back at the little girl's.

Bevan entered the lair, breaking the awkward silence that had ensued.

Gripped firmly in her teeth was a large joint of rib-eye beef she had managed to purloin for herself.

She had stalked a butcher's van along the main road as it made its deliveries to some of the local restaurants. Luckily, the driver had left the rear doors open when he had to carry a heavy box of venison into one establishment. Bevan took her chances and grabbed the first thing she could get her teeth on.

She dropped the lump of beef and shook her head.

"Look at the state of you all."

The dishevelled pups shuffled uneasily, not knowing what to say. Tufts of freshly torn-out fur hung from their mouths, and even more lay strewn across the floor.

"I'd only been gone for a little while and you have already managed to trash the place."

Bevan turned her head away from her pups and smiled

to herself. She wasn't angry at them, in fact, she was pleased they had settled in so quickly, but she still needed to remind them exactly who was boss.

She licked her lips as she prepared to settle down and gorge on her feast.

Just as she was about to take her first bite, she looked up and noticed four hungry pairs of eyes glaring at her.

Bevan tutted and shook her head.

"I'm really looking forward to the day when you lot can take care of your dear old mum," she grumbled as she tore off and chewed a few small lumps. Bevan dropped the chunks in front of her pups, who wasted no time in devouring the bloody flesh.

The pups had been weaned for a few weeks, and their ever-increasing appetites were proving a tall order for Bevan to fulfil.

She finished her meal, licked her paws clean and then checked that the coast was clear outside.

"Right darlings, stay close to me. It's time for us to all go out and do a wee before bedtime."

Once they had relieved themselves, Bevan ushered her pups towards an old bucket close to the shack that was full of rainwater.

"Right, quick drink, then back inside."

Once they were all ready for bed, Bevan poked her head out of the den for one last time, scoured the surrounding area for any obvious threats, then she slumped down with her exhausted pups on the gunny sacks.

Bevan then gave each of them a goodnight kiss. Although she always gave a sneaky extra kiss to her last born, her special little girl.

CHAPTER FIVE

It was the middle of winter, and the sky had now taken on a permanent dove-grey hue.

The pups, to Bevans's dismay, had matured, in the loosest of terms, into a pack of boisterous, constantly hungry, furry little bundles of inquisitive fun. They had grown accustomed to the vibrations and thunderous sounds of the trains that constantly hurtled past their home.

However, Bevan's family were no longer the only residents of the desolate wasteland.

Countless dogs had moved close by, after being forced to flee the city's central tourist areas, only a mile or so from where Bevan had made her home.

The strays of Sofia had initially tried to integrate and become part of daily life within the city, just like the pigeons in Trafalgar Square or the Barbary macaques of Gibraltar.

Having been pushed, due to the ever-increasing numbers of the population, to near starvation, they were now wreaking havoc.

Sofia's residents found themselves being randomly attacked as the strays became more brazen, out of desperation, in their attempts to find food.

The final nail in the coffin for the street dogs was when an overseas visitor was viciously attacked by a pack of dogs as she walked through a park. Her consequent hospitalisation for the life-changing injuries she sustained went viral when her family uploaded images of her bloodied wounds on a travel blog.

The fact that a tourist had been attacked could potentially have a dramatic detrimental effect on the city's economy; millions of leva were earned every year from tourism.

As a result, the mayor declared that the city's main tourist areas must, by any means necessary, be cleared of the 'bezsto panstveni kucheta', or 'unowned dogs'.

Dogs were now being ruthlessly hunted down and massacred.

Every day, Bevan found herself having to fight off more and more displaced dogs, who found themselves, as she once had, in desperate need of shelter.

Once they had received a swift bite or two from the protective mother, they limped away, with their tails firmly between their legs, and resigned themselves to finding a far less salubrious home of their own. Wooden crates, old oil drums minus their steel lids lying on their sides, a burnt-out car, you name it, if it offered any form of protection from the harsh elements, it was utilised.

Bevan had chosen well; the trackside location where she had set up home was situated close to a regular source of food. Every evening, waste was thrown out of the many local hotels, bars and shops. Up until now, she had had the pickings all to herself. The meagre scraps were now having to be ruthlessly fought over.

CHAPTER SIX

Christmas Day, and the countries of the Peninsula of Haemus were enduring one of the worst winters on record. During the previous week, the weather had turned extremely cold, daytime temperatures struggled to get above -10.

Exhausted, Bevan headed off on her daily quest to scavenge whatever food she could. Her task was made all the harder by the bleak, arctic conditions.

Along one of the alleyways close to the train lines where she lived was the tradesman's entrance for one of the more elitist food establishments.

As luck would have it, the kitchen door had been propped open so that the morning's food waste could be brought out and thrown into the restaurant's steel wheelie bins.

On any other day, these alone would have provided a good source of food for her, but not today.

The warm air from the kitchen rose as it hit the bracing cold, however, Bevan's nasal passages were sent into overdrive. She pointed her nose upwards and sniffed, it didn't take long for her to home in on the delicious, mouth-watering aroma of a feast. She hunched down and moved closer towards the door.

Bevan poked her head in. Like a fireball, the immense heat of the kitchen hit her square in the face. She backed out, shook her head, then slowly moved forwards and peeped in again. She scoured the kitchen, trying to find exactly where the glorious redolence was coming from.

An array of pots full of vegetables simmered away gently on gas hobs. Roasting trays full of crispy potatoes, sausage meat stuffing balls and pigs in blankets, sat on counters, waiting to be placed onto platters and served.

At the far end of the kitchen stood the head chef, hollering angrily at one of the waitresses. She had only just finished taking out the starters, and the main course was almost ready to be served.

Bevan couldn't believe her eyes, she needed to do a double take. Sitting on the main counter, lined up next to the service hatch, was a selection of freshly cooked meats.

There they sat, resting on their silver platters, allowing their natural juices to reabsorb into the meat fibres, waiting to be carried into the dining room and placed onto the oak side table. Or were they sitting there waiting for Bevan to take her pick?

In his moment of glory, in front of his adoring audience, the chef would sharpen his carving knife on his still, and then ceremonially carve large slices of the selection of freshly cooked meats.

The waitress took off her apron, screwed it up and slung it at the chef, then she stomped off. The kitchen's swing door almost flew off its hinges as she barged through it.

"Bloody amateur. I'll make sure you never work in a kitchen in this city again!" the chef shouted after her.

"Get stuffed, porky!" came her reply, to the amusement of the diners.

The chef grabbed the bottle of red wine he was going to use to make the gravy and took a huge slug from it.

It was now or never.

Bevan checked that the coast was clear. Luckily, the kitchen assistant was outside, hiding behind the bins, trying to shield himself from the bracing wind while having a crafty cigarette.

She ran into the kitchen and flitted straight to the back. She leapt up, putting her front paws onto the stainless-steel counter.

In front of her sat a leg of lamb that had been marinated in mint sauce, a gammon joint cooked in cider, a side of beef roasted in ale and mustard, and the star of the festive feast, a large golden, glistening turkey.

Bevan licked her lips. There was no time for her to stand there drooling over the selection, she needed to act quickly and pick the one that she wanted.

Her keen sense of smell broke down all the components in the selection of meats laying in front of her. She recoiled from the mustard and mint that covered the beef and lamb joints, the smell of apple on the gammon, with added star anise, and cloves of garlic repulsed her.

She was drawn to the natural aroma of the plainly cooked steaming bird.

Momentarily mesmerised, she stood on her hind legs, licking her lips and salivating at the golden roasted skin, glistening under the kitchen's heat lamps.

The body of the turkey was far too big for her to get her mouth around. She slid her bottom jaw into the cavity from where the innards had been removed and clamped her top jaw firmly onto the spiny backbone. Slithers of the crispy skin and delicate white meat were scraped off by her teeth. The turkey turned out to be far heavier than she had expected.

She let go of the bird, swallowed the delicious pieces of meat, then she tried to get a better grip.

Her teeth easily sank into the soft flesh, filling her mouth with its freshly cooked juices.

With the cumbersome bird gripped between her jaws, she leapt down from the worktop.

The still warm fowl's greasy limbs flapped from side to side in unison with Bevan's running momentum, as she began to make her escape, which was going to be difficult, to say the very least.

Bevan dodged her way back through the kitchen towards the door.

A drumstick and wing flew off. Although disgruntled that part of her family's meal had been lost, undeterred, she kept running.

The chef, who had calmed down and turned his attention to finishing the accompaniments to his meal, heard the sound of claws scampering across the tiled floor of his kitchen.

He turned and couldn't believe his eyes at the sight of a large dog running away from the serving counter.

"*Sacre bleu!*" he yelled.

He had spent two years working in Paris, and for an added air of sophistication, tried occasionally to speak in French.

He needed to serve the delights of his morning's labour to his awaiting diners, and there was the main star, hanging precariously from the mouth of a scavenging, thieving street dog; just a pool of meat juices remained where the turkey had once lay.

"Jerry, Jerry, where the bloody hell are you?" he screamed out to his assistant chef.

There was no reply.

"*Chienne, chienne!*" he hollered out in French, hoping the diners wouldn't understand. There was still no response from Jerry.

The chef grabbed a large wooden rolling pin and gave chase, clumsily stumbling and wobbling across his kitchen.

Luckily Jerry, the commis chef, had now finished his cigarette and was heading back into the kitchen to help with the finishing touches of the meal.

"What the bleeding hell?"

He couldn't believe the commotion that had ensued in the few minutes he had skived off.

With the doorway now blocked by Jerry, Bevan spun around.

Jerry joined the chef in trying to catch the dog, or more importantly, the turkey.

They kept blocking her escape route, by standing at the ends of the narrow galleys, frantically waving their arms and shouting.

Hearing the furore, one of the diners left his table and popped into the kitchen. He couldn't believe his eyes at the sight unfolding in front of him. He tutted, shook his head, went back into the dining room and told his wife they'd be better off trying to find somewhere else to eat.

Bevan kept twisting and turning through the maze of counters, trying to make her escape.

Jerry went back and frantically tried to close the back door, but nylon cable ties had been used to secure it open. The only way for him to prevent the scavenging beast from escaping was to form himself into a star shape in the doorway.

The head chef was still chasing Bevan around the

kitchen.

She was far too agile and determined. Even with the additional weight of the bird, that still somehow miraculously still hung from her mouth, she easily outran him.

With the doorway once again blocked, Bevan diverted back into the kitchen.

Jerry left his post and grabbed the first thing that came to hand, a roasting tray containing boiling hot oil from the countertop in front of him. The metal tin was searing hot, he yelled out in pain as it scorched the palms of his hands and fingers. He launched the tin and scalding hot oil in the direction that Bevan was running in. As the metal tray crashed onto the floor, splashes of boiling fat hit her; the pain made her wince, causing her to grasp the bird even tighter, her teeth cracked through the fowl's backbone.

The two men, in a pincer movement, chased her to the back of the kitchen. The head chef, the fatter of the two, was by now huffing and puffing.

Bevan seemed to be trapped. She glanced behind her and saw that the door was now unguarded. She took her chance and then bolted towards it.

Jerry sprinted after her. Midway down one of the galleys, he slipped in the puddle of oil that had come out of the tin he had thrown at the dog.

Like a slow-motion scene from a slapstick comedy sketch, his legs flew skywards and his body followed. It was certainly not to Olympic standards, but his involuntary backward flip resulted in him crashing to the floor, cracking the back of his head on the ceramic tiles.

"I've split my bloody head open!" he screamed out, trying to stem the flow of blood with his burnt hands.

"Get up you bloody fool!" shouted the chef, who had now caught his breath and was back in full pursuit.

Retrieving the turkey was far more important to him than helping his assistant, lying bleeding on the kitchen floor.

Bevan bolted out of the door, with the chef in hot pursuit.

He made a pathetic attempt at chasing after the fleeing dog that was scarpering up the alleyway.

Unfortunately for him, years of overindulgence, and being a glutton for the fat-laden meals he conjured up, prevented him from being in any fit state or shape to run.

Within just a few yards his stubby little legs gave up on him. Begrudgingly he had to give up the chase.

In a fit of rage, he hurled his rolling pin in the direction that the dog was running in. The heavy wooden kitchen tool bounced off the ground behind Bevan.

He was livid. He screamed and shouted words of abuse at the fleeing dog. Then, like a spoiled brat, he pulled off and threw his grubby, sweat-covered head chef's hat onto the ground and stomped on it.

He knew there was nothing more that he could do. Grumbling away to himself, he stood with his grimy hands on his fat hips. His face glowed as red as a ripe tomato, and a plume of steam rose from his sweaty bald head.

He watched in dismay as the dog disappeared off into the distance with the fruits of his labour, the prized Christmas turkey.

Jerry appeared, holding a dirty apron against the gash on the back of his head.

"Ere chef, it looks like le doggy has le scarpered with le turkey," Jerry said proudly, in his best mock French accent.

The chef just glared at him.

Bevan bolted as fast as she could back across the wasteland, back to the safety of her wooden shed. As she meandered her way through the makeshift dens, dozens of inquisitive noses sniffed at the air.

The normal stale stench of diesel and rotting waste had been displaced by the enticing aroma of the salty, natural juices from the cooked bird. Starving mouths drooled and stomachs rumbled.

With what was left of the bedraggled turkey still firmly grasped in her teeth, Bevan checked behind her to ensure that she was no longer being pursued, or that none of her fellow street dogs were moving in to try and steal her ill-gotten gains.

Over the previous few weeks she had endured several violent scraps, protecting her pups and their ramshackle home; today she would rip the fur off any dog that dared to try and attempt to steal her family's dinner.

Her prized hunt was now looking far less appetising, but nevertheless, this was going to be a culinary feast like none other for her and her family.

The pups' noses started twitching in anticipation. They rose to their paws and looked on in amazement as Bevan carried the still-warm turkey into the shed.

The aroma of the now slovenly bird was divine, and the bouquet of the meat juices filled the air. The pups' mouths drooled; never in their lives had they smelt something so wonderful, the four of them were in doggy heaven.

Bevan dropped the cooked barnyard fowl at their paws.

"Come and join me, and tuck in my lovelies."

They didn't need telling twice, they dived straight in and attacked the glorious greasy bird laying before them.

It didn't take long for the flesh to be completely stripped, right down to the bony carcass. The pups barged each other out of the way as they eagerly lapped at the glistening bare bones.

Happy that not a single piece of meat residue remained, the pups' tongues eagerly darted around their muzzles, then they turned their attention to one another, slurping the remaining greasy residue off each other's furry little faces.

Exhausted after all the exertion of devouring the bird, the pups snuggled up together in a furry, yet greasy little bundle, for a well-earned snooze.

After an hour or so of dozing, the firstborn pup, a robust little fellow, got up, yawned, stretched, walked over to the door and poked his nose out of the shed.

Soft white flakes elegantly fluttered down from above. One landed on his nose, he crossed his eyes and watched as it slowly melted.

He stared in awe at the beautiful transformation of the bleak wasteland that he had come to call home.

A pristine virgin white crystal blanket covered the ground, glistening in the moonlight. Intrigued, he stepped carefully out of the den. More of the strange white flakes that fell from the sky landed on him.

They were cold, but wow, they felt so nice.

He took a few more tentative steps.

His front paws slipped, followed swiftly by his back.

He ended up lying spread-eagled on his belly on the icy cold ground.

He leapt up, slipped again, then barked excitedly to his siblings.

"Wake up, wake up. Quickly come out here."

Woken in a panic, Bevan jumped up and ran outside.

"What the hell have I told you about going out alone?" she growled at him angrily.

"Sorry, mother. But what is this?" he asked inquisitively.

Seeing his joyous excitement, she was unable to remain angry at him. She thought back to how excited she was the first time that she had ever seen snow.

"Snow my dear. One of Mother Nature's most wondrous gifts of winter."

The three other pups were now all standing at the door, intrigued as to what had happened to the usually bleak landscape.

The mysterious shapes of the sastruga that had formed on the wasteland furnished the vista with a ghostly yet alluring glistening white snowscape.

Misty condensation huffs blew from Bevan's nostrils as she sniffed the cold night-time air, carefully checking for any unwelcome scents.

Her eyes, better adapted for night-time vision, meticulously scanned the area for any obvious signs of danger.

Once happy that there were no imminent threats from any of the other dogs residing close by, Bevan smiled and encouraged her three remaining pups to venture outside to join their brother and enjoy this new adventure.

However, before they stepped out of their den, they were each given a firm and stern command not to wander off too far, and to keep well away from the train tracks.

Cautiously, with their mother's command still ringing in their ears, they emerged one by one from the cosy warmth of the shelter. As their faces met the biting cold air, little puffs of steamy condensation gushed excitedly from their mouths. The three eldest pups started chasing each other, slipping, sliding and rolling in the crisp freshly fallen snow.

The smallest puppy, Bevan's special girl, struggled.

Her front legs had a severe pronounced deformity, having developed with a precarious bend from her elbow joint to her carpal joint, and it was painful for her to walk, let alone to run and play.

Her wrists flopped aimlessly around as if unattached from the rest of her leg when she moved. Her hind legs were also starting to bend in an almost scissor action as if they were compensating for her walking in a head-down posture.

Her disability would not allow her to run and play like the others. When she attempted to walk on the snow, her weakened joints gave way, causing her to tumble ungracefully over headfirst. Having bashed her chin on the frozen snow-covered ground several times, she decided it would be far less painful to sit next to her mother and watch the others play.

"Please, my special little one. Have fun, go and join in and play with your brothers and sister."

"Do I have to mother? Can't I just sit here and watch them with you?"

"Please my dear, go and play."

Bevan planted a kiss on the pup's head.

Not wishing to disobey her mother, she reluctantly headed off over to where her siblings were playing. Although she walked tentatively, she still slipped and fell over.

She reached where the now snow-covered little dogs were excitedly having their rough and tumble.

They stopped frolicking and looked over to where she was standing. With their tails wagging in anticipated excitement, they glanced sneakily at one another. They then turned their backs on her.

The little pup sat staring at their bottoms and fluffy wagging tails. She tilted her head to one side, trying to make sense of what was going on.

The three pups looked at each other again. Then the bitch, who was standing between her two brothers, let out the smallest of barks.

"Now!"

Simultaneously, using their hind legs, they began to kick out, the same way that they did when they spread their scent after they had been to the toilet. A barrage of snow flew towards her and covered the little pup.

She spluttered as freezing white crystalline fragments covered her face. She glared in disgust at her brothers and sister, her warm breath formed in an angry misty cloud in front of her.

The elder three pups and Bevan, who was sitting watching, fell about laughing.

"Right, so you want me to join in do you? OK then, I'll show you, standing there with your oh so perfect legs," the snow-covered pup thought to herself.

She turned her back, took a sneaky peek behind her so that she could get her aim just right, and then let rip with all her might, kicking out and shovelling away at the snow with her hind legs. The top layer fluttered up gently, glistening in the moonlight, but it was too delicate to reach its intended targets. The first fallen snow had compacted on the damp ground, this had the most impact, and soon the other three pups stood as covered as she was.

"Gotcha!" she yelled triumphantly.

The biggest of her siblings, a boy who always wanted to be at the forefront of any mischief, ended up copping the most of it.

He blinked to clear the snow from his eyes, then smiled at his little sister.

For the first time in her life, she had joined in with, and enjoyed, frolicking and playing with her brothers and sister, yet more importantly, happy memories were forged at that moment that would last her a lifetime.

The exhausted pups were frozen to their young bones. It was time for them to head back to the warmth of their makeshift home.

As they approached their den, they could see their mother sitting, staring skywards towards the darkness that was only broken by the cloud-covered moon and the millions of glistening diamond-like stars.

Her body was motionless, apart from her ribs, that moved in and out, in perfect rhythm with her breathing. Her warm expelled breath formed fluffy white clouds above her.

Not knowing what to do, they looked at each other. The eldest pup looked down at the ground, thought for a moment, and then glanced at his siblings. His younger brother went to speak.

"Shhh, be quiet," the eldest whispered.

He then nodded at his siblings and sat down. The others took it as a cue to do the same.

Bevan's first tear broke free, followed by the rest; they trickled down her cheeks in an unbroken stream. Yet, all the while her head remained motionless, pointing skywards.

The pups' heads tilted inquisitively from side to side. They didn't want to interrupt their mother's moment of serenity, however they desperately wanted to comfort her. The trouble was, they didn't know how to.

Bevan then spoke in a hushed, gentle voice.

"Dear mother. At that awful moment when your heart stopped beating, mine changed forever. But I now have my own family, and once again my heart is filled with love. Thank you for all that you taught me. Sleep tight, and until we meet again, I love you."

Not once did she take her eyes off the silent celestial firework display, as the words flowed from her mouth.

Intrigued, the pups looked up, trying to fathom out whom she was talking to.

Bevan sniffed, blinked several times to clear her eyes, and then looked over to her pups, who were sitting with their mouths wide open, all staring up at the sky.

"Sometimes a thought trickles from out of my eyes and runs down my cheeks."

The pups had stopped looking upwards, and now sat staring back at her.

Bevan nodded and smiled.

"Good boys and girls. Thank you, my darlings. You're all growing up so fast."

She was so proud of the maturity and sensitivity her pups had shown, in allowing her a moment of peaceful reflection.

"I'm really not making any sense, am I? One day my darlings, when I am no longer with you, you may need comforting, you may be scared, or lonely, in that darkest moment when you need me, look up at the stars. Look for the brightest star, that will be me. Take comfort in the knowledge that I am safe and at peace. I will be waiting for you. I would have crossed the Rainbow Bridge, but I will be constantly watching over you. I will be sat, alongside my own dear mother."

They were too young at present to be taught the legend of the Rainbow Bridge, that would have to wait and be a lesson for another day.

The pups rose to their paws and shook themselves vigorously, from nose to tail, dispelling as much melted snow from their soft, furry coats as they could.

Bevan smiled, then she glanced skywards one last time.

"Come on my darlings. Time to do our wees, then bed."

After relieving themselves, Bevan followed her pups into the warmth of their wooden den.

The puppies snuggled down into one another but were all far too excited to sleep. Unable to hide their happiness, their little tails wagged as they thought about playing in the snow, and the glorious feast of the turkey.

The eldest pup suddenly sat bolt upright and crawled over to where Bevan was lying. His happy thoughts changed, and now he was trying to contemplate the words his mother had spoken to him about the mysterious Rainbow.

"What is the Rainbow Bridge you spoke of tonight, mother? And why won't you be with us?"

"Not tonight, sweetheart. Now come on, please lay down," Bevan whispered.

She gently nudged him back towards the other three. She stretched, yawned and then lay down next to her four cold, damp puppies.

"Good night, my lovelies," she whispered to them, as they snuggled tightly into her before each of them fell asleep.

Even on this bitterly cold evening, she was engulfed by a feeling of warmth as she looked at her beautiful family.

Bevan smiled.

"I wonder if my mother felt like this?" she thought to herself, before closing her eyes and falling into her own peaceful repose.

CHAPTER SEVEN

Spring had arrived early. Even the bleak dust bowl where Bevan and her pups lived, situated smack bang in the centre of the urban sprawl, managed to somehow look beautiful as it metamorphosed into a vibrant flowering meadow.

Mother Nature's planting scheme had no colour coordination, just a free-for-all choreographed by the breeze.

Yellow-centred asters and buttercups, blue cornflowers, red poppies and delicate daisies all grew through the bracken and agricultural grass, a nod to times long ago when the city was fertile, open farmland.

Insects buzzed and male birds tried to attract a mate. They put on a magnificent aerial display as they brazenly showed off. When one of them thought he'd caught the eye of a pretty female, an argument would ensue with any other potential suitor who dared to move in and try to catch her eye. The fluttering of their wings, their chirping and bickering provided a wonderful musical soundscape.

Bevan sat on guard, enjoying the sunshine. She distrusted the prying eyes of the other canine residents on the wasteland. She would growl and show her teeth to any dog who showed too much uninvited interest in her family.

If that didn't work, and one of them was foolish enough to get too close, a swift sharp bite sufficed in fending them off.

She smiled as she watched her pups chasing one another. They barged each other over, growled and fought, playfully torn-off tufts of fur hung from their mouths.

They had now entered their stroppy teenager phase, and this was their daily romp. Burning off excess energy while still trying to sort out the pecking order amongst themselves within their little pack.

Their appearances had changed over the winter months. They now stood their full adult height, they just needed to bulk out. Their cottony puppy coats had shed, each of them now adorned distinguishable German Shepherd colourings, tan with black saddles and masks. They each had a glistening white set of adult teeth, the wooden handles of the discarded tools in the den had been gnawed to shreds during the teething process.

Bevan had also now given each of her pups names.

She named her firstborn Sam. He stood taller than his siblings and was a brave, natural-born leader. Sam reminded Bevan so much of his father, with his strong, muscular body and handsome features.

Tess, a bitch, was the second eldest. She had a kind and gentle nature.

Duque followed her. Somehow, he always managed to grab himself more food than the others. As a result, he had a rotund, portly little belly to show for it.

Finally, there was the adorable little Belle, the runt of the litter. She was much smaller than her siblings, her stature exaggerated by her deformed front legs. But she knew how to stand up for herself – Duque was still nursing a sore bum after he had teased Belle just a little too much and she had bitten him.

Bevan had been born on the streets and had spent her entire life as a nomadic street dog. She had to fight and scavenge for whatever meagre scraps of food she could get, sometimes she went days without eating. Her lack of regular food was exacerbated during her pregnancy by the added strain put on her by the developing foetuses.

Potentially she could have also ingested small amounts of poison-laced food, obviously not enough to kill her, but enough to have affected the growth of the pups within her body.

During her development stage, Belle had got fewer vitamins and nutrients than the other three, and she may have absorbed more of the poisonous toxins.

The deficiency, especially in vitamin D, had caused her to be born with rickets. Her parathyroid glands had not functioned properly and hadn't released enough calcium and phosphorus into her bone structure, which culminated in her deformed, severely bent front legs.

Belle's very special legs.

Bevan had chosen to be a 'lone wolf', having never integrated or become part of a pack. She had spent her life as an ancient Japanese Ronin, roaming the streets in solitude, living a master and lawless vagrant life.

For a brief period, she did have a canine companion, a handsome ex-guard dog named Sun.

Like Bevan, Sun was a German Shepherd. His long coat made him appear much larger than he really was. In another life, his distinct colouring and muscular body would have made him a prized show dog.

One evening, Bevan and Sun were scavenging for food, close to an old derelict school gymnasium.

Without warning, they were suddenly attacked by a pack of crazed wild dogs.

"Run for your life!" Sun barked. "I will fend them off. Don't worry, I will find you."

Bevan, driven by fear, ran for her life, never once looking back.

The ferocious onslaught was by a pack of drugged-up fighting dogs. They had somehow managed to escape from the brutality of their incarceration at the hands of one of the municipality's notorious dog-fighting gangs.

Bevan and Sun had become separated. She spent the following days frantically searching for him.

She spent hours traipsing along filthy pavements, down grimy alleyways, and across rubbish strewn wasteland, which inevitably caused the pads on her paws to become ulcerated. The pain from the bloody sores on her paws was excruciating, but on and on she searched. She sniffed every fresh urine stain on every lamp post, wall and street sign in the areas they had often frequented.

Sadly, her relentless search for Sun proved to be to no avail. She could not pick up on his unique scent, she was never to see him again, or learn of his fate. Several weeks after he vanished from her life, her pups were born.

A few local feral brats had now made the wasteland meadow their playground and had devised a cruel source of entertainment for themselves.

Instead of throwing stones at the passing trains, trying to break the windows, they had taken to chucking their small rocks at the dogs.

Bevan encouraged her pups not to retaliate. She knew full well that they were at the stage where they could inflict severe harm, and potentially draw much-unwanted attention to their secret lair.

"Come back inside," she would command, as the missiles rained down, causing even more damage to the dilapidated structure.

It annoyed her that some of the other dogs on the wasteland would attack the youths, inflicting superficial bites and scratch wounds. The brats would squeal, retreat and then attack again.

Although fully intent on guarding her home, she had to instil into her pups the importance of stealth. Harming one of the rascals too much could result in family members descending on the wasteland, hunting for the canine perpetrator.

Bevan lived in constant worry about the day when her family could be forced to flee their home at a moment's notice. She had lost countless nights' sleep agonising over the likelihood of them becoming separated from one another, precisely like what had happened to her and Sun. The difference was that she and Sun were streetwise, having spent two years honing and perfecting their survival skills.

Bevan couldn't contemplate her beautiful pups having to try and survive on their own, having to fend for themselves, their innocent young bodies adding to the ever-growing population of hated, and if the truth be known, feared feral street dogs.

How would they integrate and live amongst the dogs that roamed the treacherous city? How would they survive the horrors and savagery the other feral street dogs had to endure? Were her pups street savvy enough to be able to avoid capture? Of course they weren't, they hadn't even grasped the mere basics yet.

Bevan had decided that the time was right to teach them a few of life's vital survival skills. She also wanted to try and instil in them the wisdom and prowess they would need if they were to have any chance of surviving as street dogs.

The most important life lessons she would need to teach them were how to scavenge food, evade capture and find a safe place of shelter.

She instinctively knew that the time was rapidly approaching when the next chapter in their lives would unfold. The shed was no longer big enough, nor safe enough, to house the five fully grown dogs. Very soon they would have to move on. Just in case they should get separated, the pups needed to be ready to face their unknown fate, potentially roaming and living on the unforgiving dangerous streets alone.

When she watched her pups hone their gladiatorial skills through play fighting, it did offer her a small sense of comfort, their breed's personality traits made them naturally aggressive when they needed to be.

Bevan beckoned her family to come to her and commanded them to sit.

As if she was about to conduct a sermon, and with immense pride in her voice, she barked at them.

"We are German Shepherds, my lovelies. Be proud of who you are, be proud of your breed, be courageous, be strong, and be loyal to one another."

The pups looked up in awe at their mother.

She knew that what she was about to say was going to cause bewilderment to them in their rapidly developing perception of life

"Many, many years ago, when our ancestors were accepted by and lived side by side with humans, our forefather German Shepherds were valued by them for their tenacity, loyalty and intelligence."

The words she had just spoken to them had really confused the pups. They all looked at one another mystified.

Sam took it upon himself to be the voice for his siblings.

"Our ancestors lived with humans?"

"Yes, my son. We, well our ancestors, became a burden. For reasons unknown they suddenly found themselves being thrown out onto the streets or being taken miles from their homes and abandoned. They were set free and left alone to fend for themselves in the vast forests, or the foothills of mountain ranges. To have any chance of survival they quickly adapted and reverted to their natural canine prey drive instincts, our forebears were predatory and carnivorous."

She knew that her pups were bewildered. Her own mother had taught her of the legend and their ancestral history when she was a pup.

"Search, stalk, chase, bite hold, bite kill, dissect and consume. These essential hunting survival attributes have been passed down to us from our earliest ancestors, thousands of moons ago."

These were the very characteristics that her pups would need to grasp, the violent, but necessary survival skills they would need to perfect and refine if they were to have any chance of existing as street dogs.

"Slowly over time our ancestors began to naturally form into packs. Wolf-like wild packs, with hierarchies, fought for in bloodied fights, sometimes to the death. Once the alpha male was in place the lower pecking orders naturally formed.

Over a period of time, those dogs expelled to the wilderness started to find their way back to civilisation. Their bodies had adapted, and they had managed to survive extremely harsh winters and blistering hot summers. Once they reached the urban areas, they began roaming the streets, fighting with the street dogs who had already established territories of their own."

The pups were bewildered. Each of them had questions they wanted to ask. Before any of them had the chance to speak, Bevan spoke.

"For today the lesson is over. I will explain more another day. For now, please go off and play."

Although completely dumbfounded by what their mother had just said, the pups did as they were commanded.

As Bevan watched them, she noticed that their play fighting had now taken on a more aggressive semblance.

They never intentionally hurt one another, but it seemed to Bevan that her words had instilled a whole new sense of pride, as if the pups now knew their true identity and wanted to honour their breed.

Sam appeared to be vying for the alpha male role. He stood taller, puffed out his chest and raised his hackles and tail as high as he could.

Bevan smiled. "You're definitely your father's son," she thought to herself.

CHAPTER EIGHT

Bevan was returning from one of her daily forays hunting for food in the perilous side streets of the city. Duque was with her, every day a different pup joined their mother, watching and trying to learn her skills.

As they neared their lair Bevan panicked.

Dangerously close to her den, and three other pups, were a group of humans. Bevan dropped the plastic bag of raw chicken she had managed to steal for dinner.

"Stay here and guard our food, Duque."

"Yes mother."

Slowly Bevan moved in closer.

From her vantage point, she could see that the humans had already managed to coax and capture a couple of the dogs who had recently moved onto the wasteland with offerings of fresh food. Luckily Bevan couldn't see Sam, Tess or Belle locked in the cages on the backs of the vans.

Using quick release graspers, a slip noose cable attached to a sturdy pole, three of the larger, aggressive dogs had also been seized.

Bevan moved in a little closer. Most of the maimed, sick dogs had been rounded up and put into steel cages.

If only Bevan had known that the humans were a charity rescue team, trying to help as many of the street dogs as possible, saving them from the horrors that could potentially await them if they remained, and roamed freely within the city.

Kind donations from thousands of people worldwide had enabled the charity to purchase an old derelict dairy farm. The main house was where the volunteers slept and doubled up as the dog food storage area. Two old barns on the site had had their leaking roofs repaired, and along with the ramshackle feed and hay storage buildings, were now full of kennels with small runs attached to them. The milking shed had been converted into a hospital, with a basic operating theatre.

As the donations continued to come in, more of the farm was slowly being renovated, allowing the charity to take in even more street dogs. Once rehabilitated, the dogs would be transported all over Europe to adoptive families.

If only Bevan had known this.

The first gruesome sight the team of four, led by Wilson, a drummer in his spare time for a punk band back in the UK, were met with when they arrived at the wasteland was the decapitated remains of a dog. The carcass had lain not far from Bevan's den since the previous day.

Cruelty to the stray street dogs was considered a rite of passage by some of the younger inhabitants of the city.

A group of feral brats, who had now grown bored of just throwing stones at the strays, had managed to trap one of them.

An elderly Retriever, who had been struck by a car a few days earlier and suffered a broken leg, had tried to escape. The pain of his shattered limb, that dragged behind him, was excruciating and he had been unable to run away from his attackers.

One of the youths grabbed him by the scruff of his neck. The rest quickly piled in, beating him with an array of makeshift weapons, metal bars and lumps of wood, anything the vile brats could lay their hands on.

He tried as best he could to fend them off.

One of the yobs tied a slip knot in a length of blue nylon rope he had found. He lay the noose end on the ground.

As the dog backed away from the barrage of blows, he stepped into the loop. The brat quickly yanked at the rope. The noose tightened around the dog's ankle on his good hind leg.

As he tried to hobble away, the kid pulled hard on the rope.

Another brat jumped in and grabbed the rope. The two of them tugged it until the dog fell to the ground, yelping out in agony as he landed on his broken leg, the force separating the shattered bones even further.

Laying there helpless, he thrashed his head, lashing out at any of the brats who dared to get too close.

He was surrounded, even more heavy blows from their weapons rained down on him from every direction.

A well-directed hit from a short length of scaffold pole knocked him out.

One of the kids used his penknife to cut the rope tied around the dog's leg in half. He tied the new length around the dog's neck.

The senseless dog was nigh-on garrotted as it was dragged by its neck and leg towards the train tracks.

Mercifully, he remained unconscious.

The length of rope around his neck was tied to a metal railroad spike on one side of the tracks. His body was dragged by the rope tied around its leg and pulled across the dirty ballast to the rail on the opposite side.

Its neck remained in place across the steel rail.

A searing pain suddenly roused the dog.

His jaws were being held open by two of the boys; one of the older brats used a brick to hammer a rusty nail he had found through the dog's tongue into the top surface of the oak track sleeper supporting the rails.

He tried to lift his head, but the nail kept it in place; the taste of tar-based creosote from the oak sleeper filled his mouth.

He winced as another nail was hammered through the coccygeal vertebrae in his tail into the oil-soaked sleeper on the opposite side of the tracks.

He was impaled and couldn't move.

Blood dripped from his mouth and tail.

The tracks started vibrating. A gentle metallic rhythmic rumbling sound filled his ears.

Panting heavily, the metallic saltiness of blood that oozed from his tongue combined with the taste of the creosote.

A wind gently blew towards him, slowly it got stronger and stronger.

He could see the train hurtling towards him.

He closed his eyes.

The sound became deafening, the vibrations from the tracks rattled his jawbone.

A loud horn sounded.

Then silence.

The youths cheered as the train severed the dog's head and tail as it hurtled past.

Wilson and one of the volunteers gently lifted the

bedraggled blood and grime-covered torso off the tracks. Thousands of red ants swarmed over the body. Flies had laid their eggs in the holes that had been gouged into the dog's flesh by a murder of crows.

"Can someone see if we have a hammer or something in one of the vans to prise these sodding nails out? I can't bury this poor dog without its head."

Leon, another one of the volunteers, walked over to Wilson with a pair of pliers.

"Best we've got mate," he said as he handed Wilson the rusty old pliers.

"Train approaching!" shouted one of the other volunteers.

Wilson and Leon stepped back. Moments later the sound of an air horn filled the air as a freight train rumbled past.

When the coast was clear, Wilson went back to the severed head that was still impaled to the sleeper. Ants and crows had devoured the dog's once beautiful eyes, eerie black holes were all that remained.

He grasped the nail's head with the pliers and wiggled and pulled at it until it eventually loosened enough for him to pull it out.

He looked over at what was left of the tail. Most of the flesh had earlier been devoured by the crows. Wilson shook his head.

"Nature's circle of life," he mumbled to himself.

Wilson retched as he picked up the dog's head and carried it over to reunite it with its body.

The team gathered around and stood solemnly looking at the mutilated dog in front of them.

Leon made the first move. He dropped to his knees and

began scraping away at the dusty soil with his bare hands. The others joined him, utilising whatever they could as makeshift tools to dig a shallow grave.

They couldn't dig too deep as the dried earth was rock solid and full of builder's rubble.

Wilson picked up the torso and lowered it into the grave.

Leon rubbed his dirt-covered hands over his jeans.

He knelt and closed his eyes. After taking a couple of deep breaths he reached forwards and shuddered as he lifted the severed head, then delicately placed it into the grave, reuniting it with its torso.

The hole was slowly backfilled.

One of the female members of the team picked a bunch of spring wildflowers and placed them on the small mound of dirt.

Through her tears, she broke the daunting, eerie loud silence that had engulfed the group.

"If love could have saved you, you would have lived forever."

The team joined hands and for a few moments stood in solemn reflection.

If only Bevan had known that these humans were there to save the street dogs on the wasteland, and not harm them.

If only Bevan could have trusted them, she would have surrendered herself and her pups into their care.

However, her two years surviving on the streets had taught her to be very wary of humans, they had hurt her in the past, and worse, had killed her mother, so who could blame her? Her violence-filled life had taught her to avoid as best she could any engagement with them.

If only Bevan knew of the dreadful horrors that were to

unfold over the next few days.

Having rounded up as many strays as they could, the team drove off.

Bevan called out to Duque to get their food, then they darted back to their lair.

The pups were cowering in one of the corners.

"I would have fought them mother," Sam said proudly.

"Good boy. No, you and your sisters did the right thing to hide. Remember my son, stealth and cunning. Better to elude the enemy by hiding than getting into an unnecessary fight."

CHAPTER NINE

As if she didn't have enough to contend with protecting her family as it was, there was now a new, even more violent hazard facing Bevan.

There was now an ever-increasing threat of being captured by the expanding number of vigilante dog catchers. Hundreds of stray dogs had already been cruelly culled in the centre of Sofia, and now the thugs were casting their nets farther afield, well outside of the original tourist zone that the mayor's office initially wanted urgently clearing up, so they could carry on earning their meagre ten lev bounty for the capture of a pitiful street dog.

The drunken thugs despised the charity teams operating within the city. They would physically attack the volunteer groups, be they male or female, they encountered operating in the same locations. There was no way that the bully boys were going to be denied their blood money by a bunch of do-gooders.

Those dogs not killed, were rounded up and incarcerated in the infamous 'Isolators', corrupt, state-run dog compounds.

The forsaken inhabitants of these hell on earth death camps, predominantly supplied by the drunken thuggish dog catchers, were given no medical attention, and more often than not, no shelter, food or water.

The incarcerated dogs lived, and died, in misery. Their

corpses left to rot where they dropped.

"Oi, give us two more bottles of Stolichno when you're ready gorgeous," bawled Oz to the barmaid.

Years of overindulgence had severely taken their toll on him.

Oz was the self-proclaimed leader of the dog catchers. He was grossly overweight, his head was adorned by a thin covering of lank, greasy hair, and a scraggly beard, full of the remnants of the day's food, hung from his chin. What little hair he had festooned over his ruddy, battle-scarred complexion. His arms were covered in an array of faded tattoos. Oz was a functioning alcoholic, one drunken stupor merged seamlessly with the next. His fellow hooch hounds gave him a wide berth. The booze ignited his fiery temper, and paired with his dissolute, bellicose personality, often led to fists flying. Although he put on a macho show of bravado, deep down Oz was a gibbering bag of nerves. His face was a pock-marked mass of scabs from where he constantly picked at his skin, his grimy fingernails constantly dug into his flesh. At the age of forty-six, he'd finally found his calling in life, and he relished his role of brutally abusing and ending innocent lives.

Two bottles of beer were slammed down in front of him.

"Would sir like anything else?" the barmaid asked sarcastically.

Oz gave the girls the creeps, the owner of the bar liked him, or more to the point, the vast amount of money that he spent.

Oz winked at the barmaid.

"I'll let you know when I want something else."

"Pervy bloody creep," she muttered under her breath as

she went to serve another customer.

Oz, along with his drinking buddy Hooky, had spent all day toiling in the local slaughterhouse. The dried blood under their fingernails was a constant grim reminder of the merciless suffering they had inflicted. Oz's favourite role in the slaughterhouse was 'sticking'. Using his late father's – who had also been a slaughterman – sharp knife, Oz relished running the blade slowly across the already dead, or stunned, animal's throat, severing the major blood vessels.

The metallic taste of blood mixed with the pungent aroma of death lingered in Hooky and Oz's mouths and nostrils. The cruel demise of the dozens of bovines that they had massacred over the last ten hours remained firmly ingrained in their olfactory and gustatory senses. With any luck, several beers would eradicate the taste of blood and help clear their senses.

"We'll have a few more here each then head off to the side streets off the Boulevard Knyaginya Maria Luiza. The word is that the main goody-two-shoes bleeding charity group is operating in and around the North Park tonight, so we should be OK," slurred Oz.

"What time are we meeting Banks and Cratchit?" Hooky asked.

Oz took a swig from his bottle and glanced over to the 1970's Guinness wall clock hanging next to the toilets in the dimly lit bar.

"About ten. Hopefully, it's gonna be a good earner tonight. I'm bleeding skint."

He could have happily spent all evening in the dingy after-hours joint, but they had a prior arrangement. Hopefully, their prearranged date would earn them some much-needed extra cash. Blood money that they would be able to spend on their beloved liquor. The demon drink that they had now come to rely on to get them through the day.

Still sporting the remnants of a black eye from the previous evening's disagreement with Oz, Hooky was a toothless, wiry-framed, sullen character. His hands permanently, uncontrollably shook. Drink and death were his only true friends, and he relished his time spent in their company.

After half an hour of winding up the barmaids and fellow drinkers, Oz and Hooky finished their drinks and staggered drunkenly out of the bar. They climbed into their beaten-up old van and headed off to find two of their drinking pals, Cratchit and Banks.

Tonight was the night. Bevan had made the gut-wrenching decision that the time had finally come that she and her pups had to move on.

The shed was now on the verge of collapse and a mass of discarded, flea-ridden pelage.

What with five full-grown dogs trying to share the cramped space, tempers often flared. The dogs would snap at each other as boredom set in, torn-off tufts of fur hung on the splintered wooden walls as a reminder of past scraps.

If only she knew the gruesome fate that awaited them, she would have endured the shack for one more night.

She had to teach her pups how to find a safe hiding place to hold up in for short periods of time.

After a quick look around, checking for any signs of imminent danger or approaching trains, Bevan headed off, not once looking back at the den that held so many happy memories. Her four pups followed closely behind.

Once safely across the train tracks, they headed across the wasteland, getting ever closer to the city's dangerous streets.

Bevan led her pups up a bleak, uninviting alleyway. Tall red brick buildings touched one another and loomed menacingly above. The rank smell of urine and decaying food filled the dogs' noses.

For some inexplicable reason, Bevan felt uneasy and walked with her shoulders hunched, continually scouring her surroundings, as best she could under the pitch-black sky. With no streetlights in the grubby alley, the dogs soon found themselves plunged into darkness as they ventured deeper and deeper.

A brief, wry smile engulfed Bevan's face as they passed the restaurant that she had stolen the turkey from just a few months earlier.

Bevan stopped. The street up ahead was still full of revellers, out enjoying the hospitality of the many local bars.

"This is not good," she said to her pups.

Bevan spied some refuse bins for them to hide behind, the same bins the commis chef had hid behind on Christmas Day.

They reeked of rotting waste. The putrid smell, with any luck, would keep any passing humans away from them.

"We'll stop here for a while. When the streets quieten down, we will move on."

The pups squeezed behind the bins and lay down on the damp, cobblestoned road. Maggot-infested, rotting food, the relics of a hundred takeaways, lay strewn all around them. Bevan started sniffing around the bins. Her keen sense of smell soon homed in on the distinct metallic scent of meat.

"Right my lovelies, watch and learn. These things often have food in them," she said as she leapt up onto her hind legs, resting her front paws on the metal rim of the bin and stretching her head out.

She managed to pull out some discarded scraps of meat and fish, covered in a garnish of pig swill. This was going to be their day's only meal, not gourmet cuisine, but nourishment. The pups devoured every foul-smelling, minuscule morsel.

Through the narrow gap of the buildings, Bevan watched as storm clouds blew overhead, and rumbles of thunder echoed far off in the distance.

She curled up tightly with her pups, the same way that she had done every night.

Their peaceful slumber was disturbed by sudden loud shouting and hollering.

"Cratchit look, some stinking strays hiding over there behind that bin."

Banks was a seasoned dog catcher and knew all the tricks that the feral dogs used to elude being captured.

The two men shined their torches in the direction of the large steel industrial bins. Like WW2 bomber searchlights, the blinding flashes of light randomly caught glimpses of Bevan and her pups.

In a state of panic, they leapt up. The two men were moving in, their gruff voices getting closer by the second.

"If there is a big one, get it first. The smaller ones will soon follow," shouted Banks.

Cratchit banged his torch loudly on one of the metal bins.

Confused and scared, the pups looked to their mother.

"Run now. Run as fast as you can back to our old home,"

Bevan barked at them, her voice filled with panic.

Her recurrent nightmares of this horrendous moment, the juncture where her pups would have to scarper for their lives, had now come true.

"Try to stay together and keep away from any humans."

Sam, Duque, Tess, and Belle did as they were commanded. They squeezed out from their hiding place and ran off down the alleyway, back towards the wasteland.

Bevan turned and was now facing the men head-on.

With her lips curled back, and her teeth bared, she growled and barked as loudly as she could, in the hope of giving her pups a good head start.

Sam stopped running and glanced back at his mother. He looked back and could see his siblings were still running towards the safety of their old den.

He had to think fast and decided that he was not going to leave his mother to fight off the men alone.

Although he was still only a pup, Sam had become the man of the family. He knew he had to protect his mother, and no matter what was going to stand and fight off the enemy by her side.

He charged back towards Bevan, barking as loudly as he could.

"Sam, no run. Run and save yourself."

"No mother."

There was no time for arguing.

This was going to be a baptism of fire. None of that fun puppy play fighting he was used to with his siblings. This time he would be fighting for real, for his and his mother's lives.

The two dogs stood side by side, snarling and growling at the men. Adrenaline surged through their bodies, their hackles raised and their tails stood erect.

Sam was no longer a pup; just as his mother had taught him, he was now a loyal defender and protector.

The two men were directly right in front of them. Banks shone his torch at the dogs, and Cratchit banged his into the palm of his hand, trying his best to look as menacing as he possibly could.

Bevan and Sam's sharp canine teeth, illuminated by the torchlight, made for a fearsome sight. The light blurred their vision, they blinked hard, but never averted their gaze.

Although they couldn't get a clear view of their foe, Bevan and Sam continued to bark and snarl.

Drool dripped from their mouths and covered their faces in a slimy mess as their heads thrashed from side to side.

The brave stand-off had given the three other pups a fighting chance of escape.

Fear and curiosity caused them to keep looking back as they ran, catching brief glimpses of their mother and brother.

When Bevan thought her other pups had got enough of a head start, she looked at her son and barked loudly.

"Run my son, run now, I will follow right behind you."

Sam was confused, his natural instincts were controlling him, and fleeing wasn't one of them.

"Sam, do as I say run, run now," she barked at him again. Sam could sense the panic in her voice.

Banks and Cratchit were now trying to snare the dogs with makeshift rope nooses.

Sam glanced over at his mother. How fierce she looked, ferociously snapping and snarling at the humans as they attempted to try and trap her.

Bevan again turned to Sam, but she couldn't hide the look of fear that now filled her eyes.

Sam knew he had to do what she had commanded him. Still barking, he slowly backed away from the humans. When out of harm's way, he turned and ran.

Happy in the knowledge that her son had escaped, Bevan made one final lunge at the two men, then she too turned and fled.

She soon caught up with Sam and slowed her pace to run protectively by his side.

Bevan's keen nose scanned the air as she ran, and she quickly picked up on the scent of her other pups. Luckily, they were heading in the right direction.

They hadn't got far.

Tess was leading, Duque, with his portly little body, was trying his best to keep up with her. Little Belle's deformed legs were not allowing her to run as fast as she needed to.

Her ungainly legs continually caused her to trip and stumble. More than once, she fell face-first onto the slimy, cobbled ground.

Suddenly, more lights appeared in the distance ahead of the pups. Their escape route was blocked.

The blinding bright lights adorned the front of a noisy, fume-pumping old van that had driven into the alley and stopped.

The truck blocked any means of the pups' escape.

Cratchit had called Oz and Hooky to come and help with the capture of Bevan and her pups.

They had been trying to capture a couple of guard dogs that had escaped from a local building site and were only a few streets away.

The two men clambered down from the truck and started to walk up the alleyway.

The dogs could make out two black shadowy forms, their silhouettes illuminated from behind by the van's headlights, eerily, their facial features were obscured by the darkness.

Sam and his mother caught up with Duque, Belle and Tess.

"Mother, what do we do?" cried Tess.

Although Banks and Cratchit were both physically out of shape, they were hot on the dogs' tails, slowly rearing upon them from behind.

The pack found their escape routes blocked in both directions.

"Sam, run forwards and attack," Bevan commanded. "You must protect your family. I will go back and attack the men behind us."

Sam, having watched his mother a few moments earlier, knew exactly what he had to do. He charged toward the men at the front. As he ran, he barked and snarled as menacingly as he could.

He was soon engaged in paw-to-hand combat with Oz and Hooky. The two men frantically lashed out at him. Despite receiving a few kicks to the face, he continued to snap and tear at the men's legs. Somehow, he managed to corral Hooky and Oz to one side of the dilapidated van.

He backed off and quickly glanced behind him.

He knew that the time was right, and he bellowed to his siblings.

"Escape now. Run for your lives."

To the rear, Bevan courageously fought off Banks and Cratchit.

The pups did exactly as ordered and scampered past the van. To give them a fighting chance, Sam lunged at Oz and Hooky again.

When he thought they had gotten safely far enough away, he chased after them.

During all the furore and noisy commotion, he hadn't seen that Belle had tripped and fallen over.

Hooky took his chances and ran over to where she had fallen, pulled out the rope that he had tucked into his belt and slipped the noose around her neck.

In a state of shock, Belle tugged and pulled back to try and break free, but the coarse hemp lariat tightened even more.

She panicked as her siblings ran off, oblivious to her plight.

"Mother!"

Belle had stopped tugging, and momentarily the noose slackened enough for her to splutter the words out.

"Shut up barking, hound," shouted Hooky as he picked Belle up by the scruff of her neck.

Belle snapped ferociously at him. Somehow, Hooky managed to just avoid her attempts at biting him.

"Mother!" she screamed again.

"Stuff you. Shut up," bawled Hooky as he slapped Belle across the nose. He then pulled the rope tighter.

Hearing her squeals of anguish, Bevan turned and saw her little princess being carried away.

Blind terror surged through Bevan's quivering body. The muscles in her stomach clenched as the overpowering fear that overcame her stabbed at her rapidly beating heart.

She had to save Belle.

She left her fight with Banks and Cratchit, turned and ran as fast as she could towards Belle.

"Sod this," Banks grumbled.

"We need weapons, mate," said Cratchit. "Check them bins over there, gotta be something we could use."

Adrenaline surged through Bevan's body. A burning rage hissed within her, pumping through her veins like a deadly poison.

When she knew that she was close enough, she leapt. Her powerful body hurtled through the air towards the thug holding her pup.

All thirty-five kilos of her muscular torso hit Hooky in the stomach, knocking the wind out of him. He doubled up and stumbled backwards, but somehow he miraculously managed to keep his balance. During impact he dropped Belle and let go of the rope that was tied around her neck.

Bevan rebounded off Hooky and she fell to the ground, landing on her side. She rolled over, leapt to her paws and then charged back at the thug.

"Run Belle!" she screamed.

"I'm not leaving you, mother."

"Well keep out of the way then."

Bevan had to avoid accidentally hurting her pup during the brawl.

Two rows of sharp teeth sank into Hooky's scrawny right leg. Bevan shook her head from side to side. She yanked her head back, tearing off a chunk of his jeans. She spat it out, then lunged forwards again.

Hooky let out a high-pitched scream. Blood poured from the agonising, deep bite wounds.

"Get off me, you stinking vermin," he yelled.

"Lads get over here now. This thing is bloody well trying to kill me."

Sensing the panic in his voice, and the fact that it was just the two of them in the fight, Bevan knew that she could save her pup.

She wanted to get an even better grip on another, more fleshy part of his leg.

She quickly repositioned herself at the back, aimed carefully and then sank her teeth deep into his left leg's hamstring muscle.

Hooky dropped to the ground and screamed as Bevan's sharp canine teeth slid deeply into his flesh.

Belle watched on in horror. Never before had she seen her mother like this. Before Belle's eyes, her beautiful ma had metamorphosed into a crazed attack dog.

Bevan let go of Hooky's leg.

"Now Belle, run, I'll be right behind you," she screamed.

Belle turned to run, but sensing her mother in her crazed state was going to keep on fighting, she instead charged forwards and joined in the brawl.

She managed to get a bite in, but Hooky kicked her away, sending her tumbling across the ground.

Seeing her pup kicked over infuriated Bevan even more. Again, she sank her teeth into Hooky's leg, then she started dragging him along the floor. Hooky tried grabbing at slimy cobblestones.

Up until now, Oz had stood well back, in a state of shock, watching the bloody battle and carnage unfold right in front of him.

He relished piling into bar room brawls, but this was one fight he knew he'd be safer keeping well out of.

Belle was just about to attack Hooky again, when Oz ran over and grabbed the rope that was still tied around her neck. At least he'd get his ten lev bounty for the little dog, even if his mate would potentially be ripped to pieces.

He ran back to the sidelines, dragging Belle behind him. As she slid across the ground on her belly, the noose tightened even more around her neck, her eyes bulging as if they were about to burst out of their sockets.

Bevan was just about to let go of Hooky and attack Oz, when suddenly she received a hard kick to her rib cage.

"Gotcha bitch."

Hooky, who was still on his back, had at long last managed to get the boot in, but it enraged Bevan even more than ever.

Belle could see that the two other men were now running at full pelt towards the ensuing melee.

"Mother, be careful, behind you!" screamed Belle.

Bevan didn't hear her.

It was too late, Cratchit and Banks had arrived tooled up with makeshift weapons they had pilfered from one of the wheelie bins, a long piece of two-by-two wood and a short length of old lead gas pipe.

Bevan was still tearing at Hooky's leg, oblivious to the danger behind her, when without mercy, the heavy blows began raining down on her.

Blow after blow hit her head, neck and rib cage.

Belle could only look on as her mother was beaten senseless.

The vile man holding her rope began cheering and egging on his buddies to inflict even more pain.

Bevan slowly got weaker and weaker. Belle tried

everything that she could to block out the disgusting sound of her mother's bones cracking one by one from the force of the frenzied attack on her.

"Mother!" she cried.

Oz tied Belle's noose to a downpipe. Feeling braver now that the frenzied dog had been beaten to within an inch of her life, he strutted back to his van.

As Bevan lay on the cold, damp floor, the men took pleasure in taking it in turns to kick her rib cage. Over and over their steel toe-capped boots slammed into and pulverised her ribs.

Both Cratchit and Banks perversely enjoyed the vile cracking sound as Bevan's bones snapped. Her breathing got steadily shallower and shallower, her lungs filled with blood from her rib bones that had punctured her internal organs.

Bevan managed to glance over at her poor little pup.

Just as with the night Bevan had stared up at the stars, Belle saw a tear emerge from her beloved mother's eye.

Slowly, Bevan's eyes closed.

Oz strutted over to Belle's mother; in his right hand he held a rusty old axe that he had retrieved from the cab of his lorry.

"I'll stop this bloody bitch from running."

Oz raised the axe, and with barbaric precision swung it down onto one of Bevan's hind legs. Even though the blade was blunt, the sheer force of the swing severed the limb just above the femur. The sudden intense pain caused her to regain consciousness momentarily.

Again, Oz rose the axe above his head, and with an almighty blow hacked off her other hind leg. Bevan yelped out in pain, her body writhed in agony. In a vain, last-ditch attempt to try to escape the butchery, she tried to drag herself along the floor by her front paws.

Her rear, bloodied stumps moved as if her legs were still attached to them. Her body was broken and was now being gruesomely dismembered for the disgusting amusement of her attackers.

Belle couldn't begin to comprehend the vile scene unveiling before her eyes; how much more of this sadistic bloodbath could her beautiful mother endure?

Banks moved closer and kicked Bevan in the face, her jaw cracked and several teeth fell out. Luckily the force of the kick knocked her unconscious.

Bevan's head slumped to the ground.

Her body went into shock and shook uncontrollably. Her tongue hung from the side of her mouth and she panted heavily.

Slowly her life was ebbing away, but she needed to know the fate of her pup. Momentarily roused from her unconscious state, she managed to lift her head a little. Although her vision had become hazy, she could just make out the shape of Belle.

"I'm sorry my darling. I can no longer protect you. Be brave my special girl."

Crimson fluid pumped from the stumps of her two severed legs.

Oz looked over at Cratchit.

"Here you go mate, you ain't done a lot. You can have the honour of finishing the bitch off."

Oz threw the axe toward him.

Cratchit just managed to swerve out of the way of the weapon. The blade made a clinking sound as it hit the ground. Cratchit stared at Oz and shook his head.

"Bloody idiot," he said as he bent down and grabbed the hickory handle. Slowly he walked over to Bevan. He looked down at the pathetic sight of the dismembered dog, her body saturated in blood.

He wiped his forehead with the back of his hand, then swung the axe. Although barely alive, just as the blade was about to make contact, Bevan's leg twitched and doubled up. Cratchit missed her shoulder joint, instead, the steel edge hacked off one of her front paws.

He raised the hatchet again but couldn't bring himself to take another swipe.

"Enough is enough." Cratchit's voice quivered as he mumbled the words.

"What's the matter with you? You ain't going bloody soft on me, are you?"

"Shut it Oz, or I'll hack you up."

Cratchit looked down at the pathetic sight laying in front of him and shook his head.

Bevan then gasped her last breath. As the air expelled from her lungs, she made a gurgling sound.

Her body twitched.

She was now at peace.

Her eyes remained open, staring in the direction of Belle.

"Don't run away bitch," laughed Oz, as he looked over at the dismembered, bloodied body strewn on the grimy ground.

Banks and Hooky, through his pain, laughed at the pitiful joke. Cratchit just shook his head.

Banks started to mock Hooky, whose leg was still bleeding from the gaping wounds inflicted on him by the dog that had gallantly tried to protect her pups.

Belle howled out in despair.

"That one is an odd-looking bloody thing. What the hell is going on with its legs?" grunted Banks.

He walked over to Belle, untied the rope from the downpipe, then lifted Belle aloft. The rope leash throttled her even more as the manila hemp fibres tightened around her neck.

The men laughed at her, with her body wriggling, and her legs thrashing about mid-air.

Just for the sheer fun of it, Banks raised his arm as high as he could.

"Here we go, one, two, three."

As he finished counting, he let go of the rope.

Belle hit the ground, hind legs first, with a thud.

She spluttered as she struggled to catch her breath. Disorientated, and in a state of panic, she came to her senses, shook her head, and scrambled up onto her paws. She shook herself down and mentally prepared herself for the next attack.

Her legs were in agony, the cruelty that had been unmercifully inflicted upon her had taken its toll on her deformed body.

"How much more of this can I take?" she wondered to herself.

Belle was in pain. She dragged herself around. Banks still had a firm grasp on the rope and stared down at her.

For reasons that she could not understand, maybe for comfort, maybe just to see her for the very last time, Belle needed to try and look in the direction of the dismembered body of her poor mother.

It was to no avail. Oz, Hooky and Cratchit had moved over to the van to get a packet of cigarettes. From where they were standing in front of the truck, they had obscured its headlights, preventing them from illuminating Bevan's body.

They lit their fags and stood smoking and gloating over their 'brave', as they saw it, attack on Belle and her mother.

Belle never got to see her dear mother again. She strained her eyes as hard as she could but just couldn't make her form as it lay alone, hidden in the shadows on the begrimed, blood-stained cobbles of the alleyway.

Banks, without warning, tugged as hard as he could on the rope secured around Belle's neck.

"Right lads, it's time we made a move. Come on puppy, walkies."

He laughed as he dragged Belle's exhausted little body across the scummy floor towards the rear of the truck.

Belle made futile attempts to pull the rope in the opposite direction, but the cord got ever tighter as it lodged behind her jawbone.

Oz left the other two finishing their fags and strutted around to unlock one of the van's back doors.

"Right, if you're ready I'll open the door."

Oz banged on the metal door loudly with his fist.

"OK mate, open it now," shouted Banks. As soon as the door was opened he picked Belle up and slung her into the back of the old van.

She rolled across the filthy wooden slats that covered the bottom of the dark tomb.

Disorientated and confused, she tried to sit up.

Although the rope was still hung crudely around her neck, it had worked itself loose enough to enable Belle to be able to breathe properly.

The metal door made a terrifying loud bang as it slammed shut.

"Mother!" Belle screamed.

Her cry of anguish for her poor demised mother resonated around the blackened metal tomb that now imprisoned her.

Belle's tranquil puppyhood living with her beautiful mother and Tess, Duque, and Sam had been violently torn away from her. For the first time in her short life, she found herself alone, or was she?

Exhausted, the three other pups stopped running.

"Where's Belle?" Tess's voice was filled with panic.

"She was with us!" exclaimed Duque.

They looked back to where they had run from, straining their eyes to try and focus on any movement they could see in the bleak dimness of the alleyway. But Belle was nowhere to be seen.

"I'll go back and look for her," said Sam. "You two keep running."

"No, we need to stay together. We're coming with you," said Tess.

Poor Duque was too exhausted to say anything.

Knowing that there was no time to argue, Sam reluctantly agreed, and the three of them headed back to frantically search for their sister.

"Keep as quiet as you can," whispered Sam, as he moved as close as he dared to the van.

"You two stay back and hide in the shadows. For us to survive we need to keep away from those two-legged things."

Sam crept around the side of the van, stopped, sniffed

the air and strained his ears.

He could hear faint cries coming from within the van, and he had also picked up on Belle's scent. He moved to the rear of the truck and peered underneath, trying to work out where the men were.

Sam leapt up on his hind legs, resting his front paws on the rear doors.

"Belle, Belle, can you hear me?"

He turned his head and placed his left ear against the locked door.

"Belle!" he called out again.

"Sam, come quickly, I think that our mother is hurt," Tess cried out.

Sam left the van and ran over to where Duque and Tess were hiding.

Tess pointed her nose to where she thought she had spotted their mother lying, her body illuminated by the lights of the van.

"Why isn't she moving? What can we do to help her?" asked Duque.

Sam shook his head. "I don't know. I'll try and get closer to see how she is. I have found Belle, she is in that big box thing over there, but I don't know how to get her out. I was hoping that mother would know, she knows everything."

Just as Sam was going to head over to see what he could do to help his mother, the pups heard human voices approaching. They crept over to the darkened sidewall of the alleyway and crouched down to avoid being seen.

Hooky and Oz walked past and clambered up into the cab of their van.

Banks and Cratchit shouted their goodbyes, then headed

off to continue with their evening's search for stray street dogs, luckily in the opposite direction to where the pups were hiding.

The rickety van's diesel engine refused point blank to start. It sputtered and backfired as Oz repeatedly turned the key.

"Bleeding useless bucket of crap," he shouted before banging the palms of his hands onto the steering wheel.

He turned the key again, this time the air and diesel mixture in the cylinder ignited, and the truck begrudgingly rattled back into life. As soon as it started, it let out a loud bang from its exhaust, a plume of grey smoke engulfed the alley.

The metal tomb that imprisoned Belle filled with the pungent stench of diesel fumes. The acidic smell that resembled a mixture of bleach and vinegar caused Belle's eyes to water, her nostrils assaulted by the noxious chemicals.

The van slowly began to move away, it just narrowly missed hitting Bevan's destroyed, broken body as it passed. Two of the tyres drove through the pool of blood that had accumulated, leaving a sticky crimson trail of what was once her life-giving fluid along the grimy cobbled road surface.

Emerging from their concealment in the shadows, the three pups gave chase after Belle.

Sam was the first to reach the body of their mother.

"Stop running. Don't look!" he shouted.

He was too late. Tess screamed out in horror as her eyes fell upon the gruesome sight.

Although distraught, Sam was now in charge and he knew he couldn't show his emotions to Tess and Duque.

"There's nothing we can do for her. But together we may

just be able to save Belle. Now come on, follow me."

Their attempt at catching up with the van was to no avail, the truck had picked up speed, and was too fast for them.

They stopped running and stood panting heavily as the red tail lights reached the end of the alleyway then turned.

Belle had gone.

Tess looked at Sam

"We need to say goodbye to mother."

"You're right, Tess. Come with us Duque, and don't be ashamed to cry, my brother."

"Nor you, Sam," said Tess.

Together they slowly walked back to where Bevan lay.

With tears streaming down their faces, each of them bowed their heads. Nothing on earth could have prepared them for the violent attack that had been unleashed upon their family.

Silently they stood. Although together, each of them was momentarily alone, reminiscing about the happy times they had shared with their mother, and the beautiful, dignified lady that she once was.

They do not want to leave her, not like this, her dismembered body lying strewn across the bloodied ground in this horrible, undignified state.

Sam took a deep breath and closed his eyes.

He stepped forwards. In a sombre, final act of respect, he placed his nose to the ground and gently nudged his mother's legs closer to her bloodied torso.

He looked over at Tess and Duque, his nose covered in his mother's blood. Tess and Duque stood still, their eyes and mouths wide open, shocked at what Sam had just done.

Sam knew he had to take charge.

He looked over at his siblings.

"One of us had to do it. Right, there is nothing more we can do for her. Our priority now is to stick together and to try and take care of ourselves. We must say our final farewells to our mother and move on."

Thankful that they had Sam to take over their mother's role, Duque and Tess nodded their heads.

Each of them stepped forward, lowered their head, whispered their final farewell to their dear mother, and then licked her beautiful face for one final time.

Solemnly they turned and walked away.

What horrors lay ahead of them? What pain and suffering would they endure?

Three destitute orphaned pups must now try and survive within the wilderness of the vile, violent metropolis.

At the end of the alleyway, they stopped, not one of them having uttered a word. They took one final glance back, then they slowly disappeared into the shadows of the night to face their unknown fate.

CHAPTER TEN

Scared and confused as to what had just happened, Belle found herself being slung across the filthy, damp floor as the blackened tomb that imprisoned her recklessly sped and swerved its way through the back streets of Sofia.

She soon became aware that she wasn't alone. Although she couldn't see them, other incarcerated dogs would yelp out in pain as her body slammed into them.

The van came to an abrupt halt. Belle was thrown forwards and hit the grimy wall that separated the dogs from the drivers cab with a thump. She lay down to steady her shaking body.

She heard one of the men that had captured her suddenly shout, "You sodding idiot, you could have made the lights before they turned red."

Although the engine was still running, through the brief moment of almost silence Belle could now hear the whimpering of the other captured dogs.

Trembling in fear at the ghastly predicament she found herself in, she took a moment's respite in knowing that she wasn't alone, and that other innocent souls were sharing the living hell with her.

Belle joined in with the whimpering. Her thoughts danced between the horrors she had just witnessed and her bewilderment at her siblings' actions.

"Why did they run and leave us? Why didn't Sam save our mother? Why didn't Sam save me?"

Her thoughts were interrupted by more harrowing sounds from within the rancid, metal chamber, full of the putrid stench of death.

Yelps of pain followed by cries of anguish.

"Who's there?" a scared voice cried out from the blackened vault.

"My tail, they cut off my tail," a dog wailed over and over.

"My legs, I can't move my legs." Yet another pitiful cry from the darkness filled the tomb.

Slowly other scared voices started sharing their heart-wrenching stories.

Their stories merged into one as they echoed around the metal tomb, stories of how they were captured, of how they had been hurt, of witnessing their families slaughtered. Stories Belle could both sympathise and empathise with.

She could take no more.

"Shut up, shut up!" she yelled.

She couldn't start to comprehend what had happened to her. She certainly had no compassion for anybody else's piteous tale of woe.

There was a sudden screech as the bald tyres of the van tried to get a grip of the damp tarmac as the vehicle started off again on its journey, to god only knows where.

The captured dogs tried to huddle up together. Each of them trembled in fear, petrified at the awful dilemma they now found themselves in.

As the van meandered its way through the city, Oz made deliberate sharp turns, or would suddenly slam his foot on the brakes, adding to the horrendous predicament – if that were at all possible – that his cargo was enduring. Each of the innocent street dogs were being violently thrown about in the stinking, blackened, metal tomb that incarcerated them.

To Oz, they were a bounty, and he afforded them no compassion. Their lives amounted to nothing more than him being able to spend an evening drinking in one of the city's less salubrious bars. With any luck, there may even be enough left over to pay for the company of one of the city's many working girls. To him, the unsullied passengers' lives were worthless, their innocent ways of existence cut short for the price of an alcoholic binge and a drunken fumble.

The cheap locally brewed grog was the brain-numbing necessity that Oz and his mates relied on to get them through their barbaric days in the slaughterhouse.

Cratchit, Oz, Banks and Hooky all had overrated opinions of themselves. Good citizens, even heroic vigilantes, who gallantly helped the city's residents by putting themselves at risk, capturing the abandoned street dogs that roamed freely and perilously out of control.

The fact of the matter was that they were just four dissipated drunken outcasts, with one thing in common, an inhumane bloodlust. Each of them had been born to kill. Their bloodthirsty desires started when they were kids, pulling the wings off flies or stamping on snails for the sheer fun of it. But they needed more than slime from a slug or snail, they needed blood. In their early teens, they progressed onto snaring and killing vermin, or torturing feral cats. Luckily for them, their murderous fetish culminated in them being hired by a local slaughterhouse when they were in their early twenties. In their minds they had made it, their vision of utopia, their days spent killing, and being paid to do so as well. Their mundane, meaningless lives evolved around booze and blood, in no particular order of preference.

If the in-depth research carried out by the United States FBI was anything to go by, heaven only knows where their sadistic lust for blood lust would eventually culminate.

Oz and Hooky estimated that they had captured enough street dogs to have earned their night's bounty, and they were already making plans on which den of iniquity to spend their ill-gotten blood money in.

"How many vermin did we get tonight?"

"About seven I think."

Oz's mobile phone burst into life. He could see by the caller display that it was Cratchit.

"Hello mate. Is everything OK?"

"Yes Oz. Listen, you should have taken the dead bitch with you. I'm sure we'd have got something for her as well."

Oz strained his ears trying to listen to what Cratchit was saying.

The truck swerved as he struggled to steer the heavy old beast one-handed.

"Useless bloody thing," Oz cursed, as he slung his phone over to Hooky. "Talk to him will you?"

"Who are you calling a useless bloody thing?" came a muffled response from the old handset.

"Shut up and listen will you Cratchit," shouted Hooky. "The signal is bloody terrible. Oz is trying to drive, and I can barely hear a bleeding word that you're saying. And to make things worse, my leg is killing me. Catch up later with you for a beer."

Oz raised his eyebrows.

"Give me strength, pass the bleeding phone back. Hello

mate, Oz again, we needed to head off. I didn't want to run the risk of being stopped and searched by the Zoo Police. How the hell could we have explained a legless dog? Anyway, I need to get this prize prat who managed to get himself bitten back to the Municipal Animal Control Centre. I'm sure we can get his leg bandaged up by the on-duty vet."

He ended the call and threw the handset onto the seat next to him. Oz laughed as he looked over at Hooky, who was still firmly grasping his leg.

Oz reached into the van door's side pocket and pulled out a half-drunk bottle of vodka. He gripped the cap in his teeth, unscrewed it and spat it out.

The van swerved again.

"Here you go mate, have a mouthful of this, it'll help with the pain."

He passed the bottle to Hooky, who didn't waste any time in taking a huge swig.

"Thanks mate, that's better. Thinking about it, that bitch's body would have been worthless. Anyway, the local rats will have a feast and clear up the evidence"

Hooky released the pressure he'd been applying to his leg and looked at his blood-soaked hand.

"That bleeding hurt. I've never gotten bitten like that before. Do you think I will need stitches?"

"Stitches? At the very least. My money is on septicaemia. You know the only way to stop it spreading, don't you?"

"No, what?"

"Amputation, me old son. Otherwise it can lead to sepsis. Read an article on it a few weeks ago. Scary thing that sepsis, a serious complication of septicaemia. Causes inflammation throughout the body, then blood clots. Then you get septic shock, and that is fatal."

Due to the huge quantity of alcohol Hooky had drunk earlier that evening, his blood wasn't coagulating. It didn't take long for the claret-coloured fluid to again pour out of the holes inflicted by Bevans's teeth. Hooky grasped his leg, again trying to stem the flow of blood.

"Bloody dog," he grumbled.

"You'll live. You know what? This could be even worse. What if that dog had rabies?"

Oz was doing his utmost to wind Hooky up and he wasn't going to give up anytime soon.

He glanced over at his mate and tutted.

"Look at the sodding state of you Hooky. You bloody big girl's blouse. You let your guard down, and then that little dog attacked you. You should see your ugly face, sheer blooming terror. Sitting there trembling because you've gotten rabies, or they're gonna chop your leg off. Hang your pathetic head in shame, and don't you dare ever have the audacity to call yourself a dog catcher when I'm around, you bloody wimp."

For the sheer fun of it, and to lighten the mood a little, he slammed his foot on the brake. Unprepared for Oz's actions, Hooky shot forwards, and hit his head on the windscreen.

"Bloody hell Oz, you really are a flipping muppet. Just pack it in, will you? I'm in enough bleeding agony as it is."

"Shut up you tart. I was trying to shake them stinking buggers in the back up."

"Well, you bleeding well shook me up."

The dilapidated van reached its destination.

"Hold on tight Hooky, don't want you to bump your nut again," said Oz as he slammed his foot on the brake, bringing the van to an abrupt halt.

The dogs all slid en masse, hitting the wall that separated them from the drivers' cab with an almighty thud.

"Got the buggers," laughed Oz

"What's happening? Where are we?" came an anxious voice from the darkness.

"I don't know."

Belle was physically in agony. On top of the beating she had endured during her capture, her body had been thrown about in the darkness. Her deformed legs were unable to help her keep her balance during the arduous journey inflicted upon her and her fellow captives by their ruthless captors.

Mentally, her emotions had gone into overdrive; sadness, bewilderment and anger all battled away at once in her mind.

To add to their awful predicament, each of the dogs were covered from nose to tail in blood, urine and faeces. The expelled bodily by-products were not only their own but those from previous inhabitants. The van was also used during the day to deliver bloodied, slaughtered carcasses, and no time had ever been wasted in cleaning out the vile-smelling holding area.

Day after day the unfortunate occupants of the van spilt blood from the wounds barbarically inflicted upon them during their capture. Many defecated themselves through fear. Fear of the unknown, and fear of what was to become of them.

One of the rear doors was slightly pulled open, and moon and torchlight flooded through the gap into the blackened hell holding the prisoners.

The dogs blinked as the bright lights shone into their eyes.

"Bloody dirty hounds. It bleeding stinks in there."

The strays backed off to the rear of the van. They cowered and tried to huddle up against one another for safety.

Oz gagged as he closed the door.

Hooky started banging his fist loudly on the side of the van.

The dogs, again in total darkness, panicked. Tempers flared and they started growling and snapping at each other as they all vied for a place at the back of the huddle, in a vain last-ditch attempt to prolong their freedom, and ultimately avoid whatever horrific fate may await them.

CHAPTER ELEVEN

The rounded-up strays were now 'residents', or prisoners of the Municipal Animal Control Centre.

It was the first dog compound in Sofia and was run by a vile excuse of a man. He had been struck off as a vet several years earlier, because of his drunkenness and the mistreatment of his patients. Somehow, he had managed, with help from the old boys' network, to secure the position of manager of the centre for himself. The saying 'A leopard never changes its spots' proved to be sadly true. Due to reports of the brutal regime of terror inflicted upon the incarcerated dogs, he had once been fired from the position. A generous backhander to the mayor had resulted in the evidence files being misplaced and him being duly reinstated.

Carter, a large fat man, was the night shift security guard, and he had been waiting to meet the van with the latest delivery of street dogs.

"Oi, oi, evening fat boy. Where's the on-duty vet? Need to get me stupid mate stitched up," bawled Oz.

"Where do you think? Sleeping off a hangover in his surgery like usual."

"Cheers mate. You can start getting these buggers off. I've had enough and need to get away toot sweet and hit a bar.

Been one of them bloody nights."

Carter was fuming that he was going to have to unload the cargo alone.

He banged loudly on the back doors with his fist, slightly opened one of the doors, and peered into the back of the van, wafting his hand in front of his nose to try and diffuse the vile stench.

The dogs all remained cowered at the cabin end of the van.

He opened the door fully, then clambered ungracefully into the back of the old truck. He closed the door to stop any of the dogs escaping, allowing just enough moonlight in for him to be able to see a little.

"Stuff these stinking bleeding hounds. I hate them," he shouted out loud.

He swore as he slipped on the faeces and blood, nearly falling face first onto the disgusting soiled floor. The dogs shuffled nervously and regrouped in the other corner. One of them let out a growl, panicked by the sudden sound. Carter was almost right on top of them, and he retaliated by lashing out with his boot.

He randomly grabbed at one of the pieces of rope that had been slipped around the dogs' necks as makeshift leads and pulled at it.

A small white Labrador was dragged away from the group. The Labrador attempted to dig its claws into the floor of the van, but it was no use. Two of his claws were ripped off as they snagged on a joint in the flooring. The dog yelped in pain.

Carter dragged it to the edge of the van, pushed the door open, then jumped down from the truck and pulled at the rope. The rope tightened and then the dog swung through the air. It howled as it hit the floor with a thud. It rolled over, and as it tried to get to its paws, was met by a swift hard kick to its ribcage. It howled out again as the boot cracked two of its ribs.

Carter slammed the door shut.

The Labrador tried to drag itself away from another onslaught as Carter started kicking it, but there was no escape. The rope tied around its neck was secured to a metal chain link fence, which made up part of the smallholding area next to the larger compound.

Carter wiped his grubby hands down his filthy, ill-fitting jeans.

"Vile, stinking filthy beasts."

Two other workers from the compound, Magoo and Rodders, showed up to begrudgingly give him a hand.

"Oz has got the right hump, we'd better get a move on," said Magoo.

"Just ignore the drunken prat. You know full well that silence is the best response to a fool," Carter grumbled as he rolled his eyes. He had well and truly reached the end of his tether.

"Now stuff Oz, shut up, and help me get these wretched stinking things off and tied to the fence. I'm covered in crap and have seriously had enough."

Carter opened the doors, letting Rodders and Magoo take their turn and climb up into the van.

"I'll stop any of them from getting out."

Rodders and Magoo started randomly grabbing at the ropes. Having witnessed what had just happened to their fellow prisoner, the dogs accepted that resistance was futile and could have some very painful consequences.

However, a large dog did take its chances at escaping to freedom. It bravely lunged at Rodders, just as Belle's mother had done in her attempt to save her pup.

Rodders squealed like a piglet as the dog's teeth sank deep into his ankle. Seeing Rodder's predicament, Magoo came charging over to his rescue, slipping and sliding all the way. He kicked the dog squarely in the face, sending it reeling backwards in shock.

He grabbed the rope around the dog's neck, and gave it a swift, sharp pull. The dog cartwheeled, letting out a loud yelp as it landed on its back. Magoo gave the rope another hard tug and dragged the dazed dog towards the edge of the van. In one seamless move, Magoo jumped down, pulling the dog with him. The rope tightened even more around the dog's neck as it flew through the air, before violently hitting the ground. Magoo kicked him in the face, shattering his left cheekbone.

Dazed and in a state of shock, the dog could feel its eyes begin to bulge as the rope garrotted him even more as he was pulled on his belly across the ground.

Rodders jumped out of the van, cursed, and slammed the doors shut. The thunderous noise echoed around the metal tomb.

He hobbled to the cab of the van, and retrieved Oz's crowbar, then headed over to where Magoo had pulled the dog.

"You vile stinking ..."

He was far too out of shape to shout at and beat the dog at the same time. He rained blow after blow onto the dog's body with the heavy iron bar. A direct hit broke the hound's skull, knocking him unconscious.

Carter, who had kept well back and out of harm's way, ran over, grabbed the rope and looped it over the top bar of the metal fencing close to where the Labrador was tethered. Using all his strength, Carter pulled down on the rope. The defenceless dog was yanked skywards, causing the cotton fibres to tighten even more, cutting deeply into his neck.

"Oi Magoo. Hurry up, this thing is bloody heavy. Get over here and tie the rope to the fence!" yelled Carter, holding the cord in both his hands.

With the dog now hanging, Magoo and Carter, although exhausted, yet pleased with their handiwork, swaggered back to continue unloading the rest of the dogs from the van.

The pitiable dog, still dazed from its beating, was unable to bark out in distress, as it was slowly being choked to death. The chain links of the fence started jangling, as in a last-ditch attempt to save itself the dog vainly started thrashing about, trying desperately to get its paws onto the fence's metal links to relieve the pressure of the rope around its throat.

Rodders was still nowhere near finished. He was hell-bent on getting his revenge on the dog that had dared to bite him.

He pulled a switchblade knife from his jacket pocket and pressed the small silver release button. With a swoosh and a click, the razor-sharp blade automatically shot out from the bone handle.

Rodders stared at the pitiful dog hanging in front of him.

Starved of oxygen, the poor beast had slipped into a semi-conscious state.

His heart, which had been beating rapidly, had now slowed in tempo, just barely able to pump blood through the dog's veins.

Its brave, vain attempts at escape had been to no avail. Whatever feeble movements it had been making had now stopped. The hound awaited its imminent death.

"I'll teach you to bite me you bloody stinking vermin," Rodders hissed at the dog through gritted teeth as he moved in closer.

He grabbed one of its ears, and with one swift slash, severed it. The pain momentarily roused the dog; it winced at the brutal amputation.

Although traumatised, in his mind the dog begged his assailant for forgiveness and mercy.

Rodders threw the bloodied gristly organ in the direction of the Labrador.

"There you go, that's your dinner."

He laughed out loud, then slashed the dog across the bridge of its nose. The sight of blood excited Rodders even more, yet his psychopathic desire for brutality was nowhere near satisfied.

Rodders grabbed the dog's other ear and hacked that off as well. He threw it to the floor and spat on it. He wiped his brow with the back of his blood-covered hand, leaving a crimson streak across his forehead. His heart rate had increased. Rodders was in his element; he relished inflicting as much brutality and pain as possible on defenceless creatures.

With his blood lust not yet satisfied, he grasped the dog's tail and started hacking away at it with his knife. It took a few swipes of his blade to get through the small bones, but the furry appendage was soon amputated from the body.

He whooped in frenzied, childlike delight as he swung the severed cauda around in the air, blood splattering all over

Rodder's sweaty red face.

The poor Labrador that was tied to the fence had turned its back on the gruesome scene. Its white fur became speckled in a polka dot pattern as blood sprayed over it from Rodder's antics.

With his hands and face covered in warm sticky blood, Rodder's inhumane cruelty was slowly turning to the point of sexual arousal and now it was time for his climax. He slung the tail at the Labrador.

With his torturous blade still grasped firmly in his crimson-coloured hand, he got closer to the dog. Slowly and systematically he gouged out both the dog's eyes, which, luckily for Rodders, were bulging due to the slow strangulation the dog had endured.

The distressed mutt mustered the strength to let out one final, defiant shrill.

His heart stopped beating. Mercifully he was now out of pain.

"If I had my way, I'd string all these stinking vermin up and hack them to pieces," snarled Rodders.

He coughed, snorted and dragged a mouthful of phlegm from the back of his throat, and as a final act of degradation, spat at the hanging corpse of the slain animal.

"That's two of you who have copped bites tonight," said Magoo, laughing out loud.

"Shut your bloody mouth or I'll slit your throat. No one will ever find you, I'll feed you to the dogs. But you know what? I doubt even these starving mutts would take much pleasure in devouring your stinking foul flesh."

Rodder's pride had been severely dented, he certainly wasn't in a mood for joking.

Sensing that things could quickly turn nasty, Carter, having already pulled another dog from the van, waddled over in an attempt to break the ice. He knew full well that Rodders was an unstable character and could easily carry out his threat and slit Magoo's throat without batting an eyelid.

"Now, now children, play nicely or Uncle Carter won't let you have fun with the doggies."

He looked over at the dismembered corpse of the dog.

"Reminds me of a Stranglers song," he said with a smile on his face.

"What one?" asked Magoo.

"No More Heroes."

Magoo scratched his head.

"I don't get it."

"Bleeding hell, Magoo. It's 'Hanging Around' you prat. My talents really are wasted on you muppets."

The three of them cackled. Carter lashed the dog he had pulled from the van to the fence, and then the three of them headed back to offload the last of the dogs.

Their tough-guy bravado had taken a severe knock after Rodders was attacked, and they behaved more cautiously when handling the dogs. The mutts were terrified, any one of them could suddenly pounce in a last-ditch bid to escape.

Magoo banged his fist on the van's side.

"Back up my darlings," he shouted.

Carter put his ear to the side of the van. He heard the sound of paws scampering on the wooden floor. Gingerly, he pulled the latch, then opened one of the rear doors a little.

"Right mate, take your pick. Don't worry, I've got your back," he said nervously to Magoo.

A little dog suffering from four broken legs was next. It

was dragged from the van, devoid of any compassion, and landed on the ground with a thump. The defenceless dog yelped as it was dragged across the rough stony ground to join the rest of the dogs, unable to put up any resistance. Blood oozed from the wounds that it had already sustained as the scabs that had formed were scraped off by the gravel.

It didn't take long for all of the dogs to be offloaded. They were all purposely tied close to the body of the dismembered dog hanging from the fence, as a warning to not try and escape. Its blood-soaked body moved as the ropes from Belle and her fellow captives pulled at the fencing.

Magoo slammed the van's metal doors shut.

Oz and Hooky returned, a quick sewing job by the vet had managed to stem the flow of blood from the deepest of wounds, and crude bandages had been wrapped tightly around the rest. A few rakias later on would help alleviate and numb any pain he was suffering.

"You took your time, and what happened to her?" grunted Oz, looking over at Rodders.

"Get stuffed."

"You want some?"

"That's enough."

Carter had had enough and handed Oz his bounty money.

"Next time I'll deduct some if I have to unload the van."

"Get stuffed, lard arse," replied Oz, as he and Hooky clambered back into their death wagon.

Oz turned the ignition key, and the engine of the old beast begrudgingly spluttered back into life, it backfired, sending a plume of smoke billowing out of its rusty exhaust pipe. Oz screamed at the old beast as he fought to engage first gear. The cogs of the gearbox crunched noisily together. Oz slammed his foot onto the accelerator pedal and then slowly lifted the clutch. The van juddered as it pulled away.

A cloud of stinking diesel fumes blew over the dogs.

Carter opened the gate.

"Missing you already!" he shouted out sarcastically.

"Up yours, lard arse," replied Oz, sounding his hooter as he drove off to find a bar.

"Prat," Carter thought to himself. He tutted, slammed the gate shut and then headed back to his Portakabin office.

The whimpering dogs tied to the fencing made for a pitiful sight in the moonlight.

"Mother, please help me," cried out Belle.

She hoped that her mother would hear her. However, deep down she knew her plea was in vain, but for the briefest of moments, just saying her name gave her comfort. Tears streamed down her face.

Exposed to the wintry night air, she couldn't stop her body from shaking uncontrollably, a combination of the cold and fear.

Belle had been tied directly beneath the lifeless dog. Its warm, once life-giving crimson fluid dripped onto her, adding to the obnoxious contents from the truck that already covered her.

The blood repulsed Belle, she tried to move away but was prevented from doing so by the rope around her neck.

All Belle could do was sit and await her unknown fate beneath the cold winter's sky.

Having heard the commotion, a pack of dogs from within the compound had moved over towards the fence. They glared menacingly at the new arrivals, sticky drool hung from their jowls, the vapour from their warm breaths billowed out into the cold night air.

In a few hours it would be daybreak, and the new arrivals would be forced into the compound and into the jaws of the ravenous awaiting pack.

Belle looked around, hoping against hope to find a means of escape.

There was no chance.

She had just enough slack rope to enable her to lie down. She raised her eyes towards the velvet dark sky. It seemed so bleak and lonely up there. A few stars shone through the clouds that blew across the heavens, the storm that had been brewing a few hours earlier had come to nothing.

She thought back to the beautiful Christmas evening, just a few months ago.

She scoured the glistening stars, looking for the brightest one.

Belle again barked at the vast expanse of darkness.

"Mother!"

Sadly, her mother still didn't hear Belle's desperate plea for help.

Lying in the small pool of blood, exhausted, petrified and resigned to whatever fate may await her, Belle closed her eyes.

She drifted off, although not into a deep sleep. Her ears remained on guard, twitching at the merest sound, her mind was in survival mode, her body poised, and ready to react to any threats.

The new day's sun had just started to rise in the sky when the dogs were rudely roused by the sound of human voices shouting at them. The dogs leapt up to their paws and prepared themselves for the next savage onslaught.

They were hit by a deluge of freezing cold water. The sudden shock didn't give the dogs time to defend themselves.

Belle was blasted backwards into the chain link fence. She couldn't see or breathe as the water hit her squarely in the face. The noose around her neck prevented her from being able to escape the torrent.

The water was redirected towards the little dog with the broken legs, thrusting him across the ground.

The powerful force of the water caused small stones to pebbledash the dogs. One dog was hit in the eye by a large piece of grit; it winced as the small stone embedded itself into its cornea.

"Alright, alright, turn it off, Carter," hollered Magoo.

The deluge of water stopped as quickly as it had started. Belle struggled up and shook herself down.

"Right, they're all cleaned up. Hurry up, let's get them in. I'm bloody frozen and need a cuppa."

Magoo sloshed through the puddles towards Belle. He untied her and then started dragging her towards the main enclosure gate. She tried as hard as she could to pull back, but he was far too strong. Belle gave up the fight and walked begrudgingly behind him, through the sludge, with her head held low.

Magoo tethered Belle to the gate and then walked back to the dead dog that had hung above her all night. He cut the rope around its neck, and the torso, already harbouring the eggs of blowflies, hit the ground with a thud. Maggots would soon hatch and waste no time in breaking down and devouring the flesh.

Carter walked over with a large black rubble sack. He

laid it on the ground and, as best as he could, stuffed the carcass and severed body parts into it.

The dogs' makeshift leads were all untied from the chain link fencing.

Sodden and shivering, the dogs were corralled towards the larger adjacent enclosure.

Rodders picked up the end of the rope that was tied to the dog with the broken legs, which dragged behind him as he was hauled through the puddles.

When Rodders reached Belle, he untied her.

"I'll take the raspberries," he shouted.

Belle could do no more than stumble alongside the furry little mass of blood.

The little dog had been found lying in agony by the side of a road. For Oz and Hooky, he had been an easy capture, there was no way he could put up a fight.

He had laid there for several days, after being viciously set upon by his master, who, after returning home in a drunken stupor, had launched into an unprovoked attack on his beloved loyal friend. The dog snapped back, in an attempt to defend himself from the barrage of punches. What a mistake, all he had done was fuel the drunkard's rage even more.

He grabbed the cowering dog by the collar before dragging him outside.

"What the hell are you doing? For pity's sake leave him alone will you?" screamed his wife, who had been woken up by the dog's yelps.

"Get stuffed, woman."

With one hand gripping the collar, he turned and punched his wife in the face, breaking her nose.

"Now look what you have made me bloody well do, you useless stinking hound," he snapped at his dog, before kicking it as hard as he could in the rib cage.

He dragged his dog to his pick-up truck. In the cargo bed, he found a nylon tow rope. He forced the dog down and knelt on its throat. After another punch to the face, he pulled the dog's head up and wrapped the cord around its neck several times, then tied it in a knot. He tethered the other end to the battered rear bumper of the truck.

He stumbled to the driver's door, pulled it open and climbed in. The keys were always kept under the sun visor. Full of rage, his hands shook as he put the key in the ignition and started the engine.

He slammed the auto transmission into drive, let off the handbrake, and then put his foot down on the accelerator.

For almost half a mile, he dragged his beloved pet at high speed. The poor dog's legs gave way after a few hundred yards, his body bounced along the dusty, potholed road, fur and flesh flayed from its torso.

Seeing the blue lights from a police car approaching on the opposite side of the road, he slammed on the brakes, turned off the lights and sprawled himself across the passenger seat.

Once the police car had sped past, and the sound of its siren had disappeared into the distance, he clambered out of his driver's seat. He tripped as he staggered to the back of his truck, where he severed the rope with the knife he always carried for protection in the dashboard.

His head started spinning, jets of saliva filled his mouth, and the evening's drink was quickly vomited onto the road. He wiped his mouth and looked over at the bloodied body of his dog lying motionless.

He walked over, grabbed the rope and then dragged the seemingly lifeless body into the gutter.

"Rot in hell, mutt."

After saying his loving farewell, he staggered back to the cab of his truck and pulled an almost empty bottle of homemade rakia from under the driver's seat.

He took a few large swigs, then slung the empty bottle towards his dog. Shards of glass flew everywhere as the bottle shattered on the kerb.

The dog had suffered horrific injuries. All four legs of his legs were broken and his battered body was covered in gaping open wounds. Miraculously, he had not been strangled to death, nor had his neck been broken.

The loyal, distressed mutt lay there whimpering, as he heard his master speed off.

He lay there in agony for three days, desperately trying to cling to life. People took pity on him, offering water and scraps of food, but no one took the time to report his sorry predicament to the relevant authorities, nor take him to the safety of one of the charitable rescue sanctuaries.

As the dogs reached the enclosure, they were either led or lugged in. The now-familiar clanking sound of slamming metal gates filled their ears as Carter secured the paddock, before heading with Magoo back to the warmth of their makeshift office.

The dog that was with Belle lay unconscious. His body began to twitch as he came back to his senses. He opened his eyes and panicked, gasping desperately for air. He tried as hard as he could to shake his little body, in an effort to dispel the water and mud that covered his festering wounds.

The dogs looked around the enclosure they had now been imprisoned in.

Menacing, inquisitive eyes fell upon them from all directions.

The compound consisted of the holding area, where Belle and the other dogs had been kept the previous evening. Not far from that there was a Portakabin that the staff used as their office and restroom, and a fenced-off block of cleaner-looking pens, situated close to a single-storey, grey-bricked building where the manager had his office and the vet his surgery.

Then there stood an eerie-looking red-brick building, with imposing steel bars on one side. The loud barking that came from within caused Belle to shudder.

Now came the main compound, where Belle and her fellow captives had now been moved to, a two-acre site that consisted of makeshift ramshackle shelters randomly strewn all over the place.

Next to the main gates was the waste dumping area. Foul-smelling bins and sacks didn't exactly offer the most pleasing of welcomes to visitors.

Belle carefully scanned the bleak compound exposing itself in front of her.

Midges performed aerobatics as they darted overhead, occasionally dipping into the stagnant, foul-smelling puddles.

Over to her left, a swarm of blowflies buzzed around a heap of black plastic sacks, waiting to be moved to the waste area.

Even though the sacks were several metres from where Belle was, a rancid scent of dogs' bodily waste, rotting flesh and decay filled the air.

Blowflies can smell dead human or animal matter from up to a mile away. No need for them to rely on their sense of smell in this hell on earth, death lay all around, the perfect place for these little spreaders of multiple diseases to lay their eggs.

For some strange reason Belle found herself fixated by the heap of black sacks.

She closed her eyes to momentarily block out the vision of the death camp.

Over and over the continual sounds of barking and wailing resonated around in her head.

She utilised the eighteen-plus muscles that controlled her pinna, allowing her to finely tune the position of her ear canal to home in on a hauntingly distinctive sound coming from the pile of rubbish bags, and block out the agonising cries of the inmates from within the compound.

Wave after wave of flies emerged from holes in the black sacks. Thousands of tiny wings beating together as the insects took flight. Their little bodies filled the air like a swarm of black confetti thrown at a wedding, randomly scattered by the breeze.

With her eyes still closed, Belle turned her head towards the mound of black sacks.

The putrid aroma of death oozed out of them.

A strange taste filled Belle's mouth. A vile disgusting taste. A taste she had sadly become acquainted with over the last day or so. The repulsive taste of death.

Hesitantly she opened her eyes.

Belle's senses were being bombarded by the frightening little mound of sacks.

They looked, sounded, smelt and tasted of death.

Something in the distance caught her eye.

A pack of dogs were moving in.

Like a pride of lions stalking their prey on a hunt, with their scrawny bodies crouched low to the ground. They moved slowly and rhythmically, their lips pulled back, exposing bared teeth in anticipation. Each of them had a look of hatred in their eyes. Their sinister deep growls were steadily getting louder.

As the pack reached the terrified new arrivals, they began encircling them.

Belle and the others found themselves being corralled into an ever-tighter group.

Not once did Belle take her eyes off them.

In a well-practised and honed manoeuvre, they were looking for a weakness, where they could strike most effectively and claim their first victim.

Belle and her pack huddled closely together. Bunched up, facing outwards, waiting for any chance they may get to escape from the dogs.

The poor little crippled dog could do no more than lie and watch. He was, for the moment at least, protected in the centre of the huddle.

He was in agony, he could take no more pain, yet he knew it was coming, he knew that he would be the first victim.

He closed his eyes and waited for the imminent attack.

"Survival."

The words kept echoing round and round in Belle's mind, the word regularly instilled in her by her mother.

Luckily, a small gap appeared in the pack surrounding them.

Belle drew on all her strength and ran. As she did, the

wrists on her deformed front legs flopped awkwardly, and the calluses that had formed on her carpals cumbersomely pounded across the ground.

She was followed by the four other surviving dogs that were able to run.

The dogs that had trapped them didn't bother giving chase.

They turned their intentions to the little crippled dog lying trembling on the floor. He could offer no resistance; the pickings would be easy.

The attack was swift and ferocious. The pack worked as one as they tore at the defenceless dog.

The sounds of their snarling, as they ripped him apart, drowned out his yelps of pain and pitiful pleas for help.

His demise was painful but mercifully quick.

A gruesome puddle of blood and fur covered the filthy ground. Silence descended over the vile scene of carnage as the pack moved back. A large dog, its hardened face scarred from a lifetime of fighting, stepped forwards and looked at the pathetic feast lying there before him. He took his first bite of the warm, fresh meat, tearing through the skin and muscle to get to the internal organs.

The rest of the pack stood waiting patiently, drooling in anticipation of what pitiful scraps would remain for them. After a few bites, he looked over at his pack.

"What are you standing here for? There's enough meat for all of us, and you idiots are letting it run away."

Belle was now stumbling behind the four other dogs, tripping and falling. Together they ran, aimlessly trying to find a place to hide.

From behind her, Belle could now hear the sound of

heavy panting and dozens of paws thumping on the muddy soil as the pack that had been set free by their leader closed in on them.

Fuelled by hunger and their eagerly anticipated meal, their pursuit turned into a hate-filled frenzied charge.

In her state of panic, and with the added problem of her deformed legs, Belle tripped and somersaulted. She couldn't maintain her balance and landed headfirst on the ground.

She tried to leap up, but it was too late. The pack had caught up with her and she now found herself surrounded.

She was exhausted and closed her eyes, resigning herself to the fact she was finished, ready to bravely face whatever gruesome fate awaited her.

As the dogs slowly moved in for the kill, stinking, sticky drool slobbered from their jowls.

At least she would now be reunited with her dear mother.

"Leave her alone!" a booming, gruff commanding bark filled the air. "Leave her, I command you."

Belle's body trembled uncontrollably.

Her eyes remained shut, her teeth gritted. Yet strangely, she felt no pain from the expected savage attack.

She could hear the sound of paws plodding on the sodden ground, however, for some inexplicable reason, they seemed to be moving away from her.

Belle tentatively opened one eye.

She was shocked, and relieved, to see that the pack was retreating. They glanced back and snarled at her in contempt. Nevertheless, although disgruntled, they were leaving.

Belle struggled up onto her paws and shook herself down.

She looked around and saw a large Bullmastiff heading

toward her.

"Starving dogs soon revert to the barbaric instincts of their ancestors. Don't take it too personally, little one," the brute of a dog said in a gruff voice. "Allow me to introduce myself, my name is Hamish. What do they call you, small fry?"

Belle tilted her head from side to side as she stared him up and down. He certainly was a formidable-looking beast. She couldn't help but notice that his imposing body was badly battle-scarred.

Belle tried as best she could to try and comprehend what had just happened. Why had this stranger, unlike Sam, Tess and Duque, saved her life?

"What do you mean 'small fry'? My mother named me Belle, I was her special little girl," she replied.

"Oh, I bet you were. No offence meant."

Hamish raised his eyes as he replied, an air of sarcasm filled his voice.

"None taken."

Hamish couldn't help but stare, intrigued by the small, yet beautiful little dog standing in front of him.

A combination of still being soaked through after the drenching of the hose, fear and adrenaline caused Belle to shake. Hamish looked down at her legs. He couldn't help but notice how deformed they were, bending outwards and then back inwards, making her walk face down.

"Bit small for a Land Shark, aren't we? And how on earth do you run with those bloody things?"

"What bloody things?"

Belle was confused by his question.

"Your legs, they look all, well shall we say, erm, wonky."

"Wonky? What do you mean wonky? My mother told me that these are my special legs."

Belle had known no different and had had to adapt to living life in her misshapen little body.

"You're a little bit young to be out on your own, aren't you? But there again, humans always chuck out the runt of the litter, don't they?"

Hamish's questions and perceptions of life were blunt and forthright.

"What's a runt?"

"You know."

"No I don't. Could you explain to me please."

"Well to put it bluntly, the smallest, weakest, or in your case, a combination of both, plus disabled for good measure. I bet the rest of the litter weren't like you."

"I'm not a runt, I'm an orphan. My brothers and sister are lovely, just like me. My mother was proud of all of us. And you know what? Those vile two-legged street dwellers killed my mother."

Belle's eyes filled with tears. She looked away; she didn't want to let Hamish see her cry.

She then glared back.

"I may have tears on my face, but they are through sadness. Please don't think that they mean I am helpless. I don't need your pity, nor your help, do you understand?"

"Well, after what I have just saved you from, I beg to differ."

Hamish was shocked at Belle's maturity and bravery at standing up to him. Knowing full well that his abruptness had upset her, he moved closer, raised his paw and gently placed it on her head.

This time as Hamish spoke, it was in a soft, gentle voice.

"One thing that my senior years have taught me, little one, is that grief is the ultimate pain we pay for love. Follow me, Belle."

As Belle followed Hamish through the compound, she saw dogs everywhere. In the distance, she could see the survivors of the pack she had arrived with. Yet again they were being taunted by the dogs that had killed their crippled friend.

Hamish let out another almighty bark.

"Leave them alone, they have suffered enough."

Again, only now joined by their leader, the hunting pack scowled at Hamish, yet nevertheless, they did exactly as he had commanded.

"They have also had a bad time of it as well," Hamish said, looking over at the pack who had wanted to kill Belle.

"They were dumped here a couple of months ago. Don't be fooled by their bravado. Just like you, they cried and were petrified when they first arrived. That macho machismo is all a front. From what the ugly brute who is their self-proclaimed leader has told me they were rescued from a remote farm. Do you know what their sole purpose in life was? Bait dogs."

"Bait dogs, what are they?" asked Belle.

"Fresh meat, cannon fodder for dogs being trained to kill another dog for the pleasure of humans. You'll meet the fighting dogs one day; they're kept locked up over there."

Hamish pointed his snout nose towards a brick building. The sound of the ferocious barking that emanated from within the red-brick block sent a shudder down Belle's spine.

"They can sense that that lot is close by. Given half a chance they'd tear them, and to be honest, any other living creature to pieces."

"So why did the scared dogs attack us?" Belle asked.

"Sadly, those that were once abused have now become the abusers. You must understand that through no fault of their own they have been badly hurt in the past. They're an ugly bunch, every one of them is physically disfigured in one way or another. Some have their ears or tails missing. However, they all have one thing in common, each of them had been mentally traumatised by the cruel existence that they had once led."

"Are you the mother?" Belle asked.

Hamish guffawed out loud.

"There is a hell of a lot about life you have to learn, my little friend."

He continued to laugh as he looked around at the little dog trotting alongside, trying as best as she could to keep up with him.

"Mother indeed."

Hamish shook his head at the very thought.

Eventually, the two of them arrived at a small makeshift kennel. Pallets had been crudely nailed together, and they had plastic sheeting thrown over them to make the den semi weatherproof.

Hamish barked, not his usual loud, gruff bark, but nevertheless, it was still a booming sound. A nose popped out of the bleak shelter, twitching and sniffing the air. The inquisitive nose was followed by a small, elderly female dog. She looked up at Hamish, and then down at the small dog by his side. The elderly dog moved towards Belle and sniffed her all over. As the wet nose snuffled through her fur, Belle closed her eyes. For the briefest of moments, she was back with her mother.

"She needs taking care of, her name is Belle."

The elderly dog nodded.

"This is Artemis, she will be your mother now. Be a good girl for her, you hear?"

"Come in little one, make yourself at home and join my special little family."

Artemis spoke in a gentle, kindly voice. She had a matriarchal role within the compound.

As she tentatively stepped into the kennel, Belle could see two other pups, neither of them bore any breed resemblance to Artemis.

"I'm given all the waifs and strays," Artemis said.

There was a natural, kind maternal compassion about her voice, and at last for the first time in a day, Belle felt safe.

"There are some scraps of food over there in the corner. You look hungry, my little one, please help yourself."

Belle didn't need telling twice. She was hungry. Slowly she moved to the corner and helped herself to some of the meagre offerings of discarded food that the dogs had been given.

"Hamish said your name is Belle."

"Yes, Belle was the name that my mother gave me."

"When your belly is full, and you are ready, come join your new family, Charlie, Mason and me for a cuddle."

Artemis spoke softly as she lied down and rolled over onto her side.

Although it was still only morning time, Artemis knew that the poor new addition to her family had been to hell and back over the last few hours. The chance for Belle to rest with her and the two other fostered pups would do her the world of good.

Mason and Charlie had already snuggled into Artemis. Belle couldn't resist the opportunity to feel that once again she was a part of a family, but more importantly, the chance to experience the wonderful feeling of snuggling into her beloved mother. She walked over and nestled tightly into Artemis, lying cosily between Mason and Charlie.

As she lay there recollecting the horrific events that had forgone over the last twenty-four hours, Belle's emotions got the better of her. Unable to withhold her tears, she began to sob uncontrollably, and whimpered her poor little heart out until she eventually fell asleep.

CHAPTER TWELVE

Over the coming weeks, Belle would slowly come to accept her fate. Yet deep down she reluctantly relished the time she spent with Artemis, Mason and Charlie. She knew that she would never see her mother again, but every night, before she settled down to sleep, she popped out of their makeshift kennel and glanced up at the shimmering stars way above her. For a few moments, she sat alone in deep reflection, before walking, with her head bowed, back into the den.

Belle's last prayer every night, before she fell into a peaceful slumber snuggled up safely with her new family, was that Sam, Tess and Duque were living their lives in safety, frolicking and playing happily in some far-off flower-covered meadow.

Hamish now had a newfound purpose to pass his time, a break from his up-until-now humdrum, mundane routine of living his incarcerated existence within the shelter.

Daily he would chaperone Belle as she wandered around the compound; the gruff old dog had taken to his new surrogate paternal role like a duck to water. During their walks, Belle told him all about the way her mother had begun to teach her the important life skills she would need to survive as a street dog. Hamish took over with the lessons, and he took immense pride in sharing his wisdom and knowledge with his young protégé, continuing her vital education to help her gain the skills she would need to survive. Belle was still a street dog, albeit for the foreseeable future, an imprisoned one.

During one of their walkabouts, Belle pointed her nose towards the brick building close to the guard's cabin that Hamish had pointed out on their first meeting. As they walked past it, Belle could see the heavy iron bars of one of the securely locked cages that housed the loud and extremely ferocious dogs.

The imprisoned dog spotted that Belle had the audacity to glance over at him. He instantly lunged at the steel bars of his cage and clamped his powerful jaws around one of the rusting, horizontal metal bracing bars. Three of his teeth cracked and shattered, and a jagged edge on the bar cut deeply into the flesh at the back of his jaw. But the pain did not deter him, he was hell-bent on ripping the little dog, who had dared to disrespect him, to pieces. His front legs thrashed about aimlessly, he continuously barked and snarled, and blood and drool splashed in a slobbery mess all over his scarred face.

"Why are they so angry?" asked Belle.

Hamish sighed out loud. "Them? Those poor dogs are crazy. All they want to do is kill everything and anything that they see. It's really not their fault, they have been used by humans to fulfil their crazy sadistic bloodlust. Humans take immense pleasure in killing, or ordering something else to kill for them, any innocent living being they can for their perverse pleasure."

Hamish could not stand there with Belle any longer.

"Belle, let us get away before that poor dog kills itself. Now you make sure that you never, ever, get too close to those cages. Do you hear me?"

Hamish barked his command at Belle with both a sense of urgency and fear. He had seen what those dogs were capable of. Even he, the big, brave Hamish, was wary, if not afraid of them, and he didn't want the innocent young pup anywhere close to them.

Hamish looked down at Belle.

"I didn't want to alarm you, but they, just like us, are broken. I could always see hope in a fellow dog's eyes before I arrived here. No matter what they had been through, or were going through, there was always that glimmer. This place destroys your soul, all I see now is fear. But those poor dogs, their eyes are black, there is nothing, no compassion, hope, fear or remorse."

The savage dogs locked securely in the cells had been delivered to the shelter several months before Belle had arrived. The newly formed Zoo Police had infiltrated a notorious dogfight gang and had arranged a carefully coordinated raid at a disused school gymnasium that had been set up as a fight venue, with a specially constructed ring, encased within old iron railings, welded together to protect the hordes who gathered to bet on the outcomes of the vile blood sports carried out there every Saturday night.

The raucous crowd, which included local dignitaries and police officers, all fuelled up by a cocktail of cheap booze and drugs, waved leva notes in the air as they placed bets on the dog they were going to back.

The dogs were led into the ring, muzzled and straining wildly at their chains, their eyes fixed intently on their equally maddened and frightened opponent.

As the muzzles were released, and the maddened dogs were freed from their chains, the trainers quickly ran out of the ring and shut the metal gates. They knew full well that the starved dogs were ready to attack and kill the first dog, or thing, that they encountered.

The dogs spent a mere matter of seconds on their warning snarls and growls before they lunged at each other, going straight for the muzzle or throat, knowing instinctively that they had to kill or be killed. The blood-filled fights often lasted for just a matter of a few minutes, and the sad, brutal outcome was always that one dog ended up dead or seriously injured, and often the victor would also be severely maimed.

To prepare a dog to fight, the gangs had subjected the hound to both physical and mental trauma, this was to encourage and exaggerate their violent streaks. The dogs' existence was one of being chained up and beaten ruthlessly within sight of the other dogs, to increase fear and create extreme territorial responses. The dogs were regularly injected with gunpowder, the outcome of which corroded the brain and the stomach, causing internal ulcers, making the dog even more ferocious. The dogs were also fed a daily cocktail of multivitamins, hormones and psychosis-inducing amphetamines. On the day of a planned fight, this concoction was sometimes, if available, mixed with heroin. This was to both numb the inevitable pain that would ensue during the fight and increase stamina. In theory, the dog was now more likely to fight to the death.

Some dogfighters sharpened their dogs' teeth without using anaesthetic and would also often barbarically hack off the dogs' ears to prevent another hound from latching on. It was not uncommon for them to add very small quantities of rat poison to the dogs' food in the run-up to a fight so that their fur and flesh would taste vile to its gladiatorial competitor.

Another means of increasing the dogs' armour was for razor blades to be sewn under the skin. The sole reason was for the blades to cut, and slash open their opponent's paws during the fights.

The dogs were systematically starved, but their bulk was maintained through steroids. When the dogs reached the point of extreme hunger, the trainers would throw them a live animal, which the dogs tore to pieces in a starvation-induced frenzy. This ensured they were rid of any empathy towards any other living being and learnt that blood and killing resulted in a reward of much-needed food.

These poor dogs lived and would eventually die in extreme agony.

On the evening of the raid, things didn't quite pan out as planned. Several arrests were made, but the main gang leaders escaped during the confusion and furore. Many of the fighting dogs, the evidence the police would need for successful prosecutions, were released by their trainers and unleashed hell within the confines of the gymnasium. Five of the dogs had to be shot dead by the Zoo Police. Several dogs ran and wreaked havoc in the neighbouring areas for weeks, killing street dogs and any other unfortunate animal they should happen to come across.

A task force was hurriedly set up by the city's mayor to hunt down as many of the fighting dogs that had escaped during the botched raid as possible. The Zoo Police enlisted a team of dog handlers and vets to assist them. Strengthened cages were placed on the back of a flatbed lorry to transport any captured dogs to the Municipal Animal Control Centre. Tranquilisers had been loaded into dart guns and issued to a team of police marksmen. The darts were loaded with a dose of a fast-acting paralytic solution, which once injected would temporarily impair the dog's physical function to a level that would allow it to be safely approached and moved to the awaiting cages.

Seven dogs were eventually captured and taken to the compound. Each of them was locked up in their own secure cage upon arrival.

There was no cure available to heal the irreparable damage to the fighting dogs' internal organs caused by the concoction of chemicals that had been administered to them. Sadly, or mercifully, their life expectancy was only a matter of months.

CHAPTER THIRTEEN

Conditions within the barbarous compound changed with the seasons. The dogs had to endure blistering hot summers and bitterly cold winters. Mother Nature's climatic changes helped control the ever-growing population. Sadly, many young, elderly and infirm dogs succumbed to the savage natural elements thrown at them.

Spring had arrived, and against the odds, Belle had managed to survive her first winter.

Over the previous months, she had integrated into the pack community she had been forced to live amongst. In general, most of the dogs were kind to her, how could they not be? Many bore the scars from injuries they had received while living on the streets. Some of the younger ones mocked the way that she walked, but she had learnt how to take care of herself. A swift bark followed by a stern glare usually sufficed in warning them off.

She had still not grown much in stature, she should have been nearing full size, yet she was still not much bigger than an adolescent. Her deformed front legs forced her head to face downwards; this, in turn, made her back legs uncomfortable, and to try and compensate from the strange angle that she walked in, they too now had a distinct bend in them, making her appear even smaller.

The pack of ex-bait dogs she ran from on her first day now ignored her. If nothing else, even they did have a small element of respect for the pack they lived amongst, but they chose to keep themselves to themselves. For their amusement, they did mock and tease the older, weaker and more timid dogs, barking insults and stealing food from them. They took their chances when new arrivals were delivered by the vigilante dog hunters, and occasionally managed to cannibalise an injured, lame new arrival. As barbaric as it was, to them it was a feast of fresh meat. It disgusted the others in the compound, and although he was the alpha male and the savagery repulsed him, even Hamish did not always stop them; he knew that it would at least be one less hungry mouth to feed.

The cages that had housed the fighting dogs were slowly becoming devoid of their occupants, only four out of the original seven were still alive. The three corpses had been taken to the Zoo Police's HQ for post-mortems to be performed to ascertain their exact cause of death.

The compound's manager had been given strict orders to not dispose of the bodies as they were an integral part of the investigation and prosecution case being compiled relating to extreme animal cruelty, against those arrested during the raid on the dogfight.

The Zoo Police wanted those who had been arrested to be made an example of and were going to pin as many charges on them as possible. The police were banking on the non-documented promises they had made for reduced sentences or fines, as an incentive for some of those arrested to grass up the ringleaders.

Belle had seen many new dogs arrive during her time in the compound, but more strangely, she had also seen some dogs leave. These dogs had been kept away from the rest, in the special block, where they were given clean water, fresh food and fresh warm bedding. Why were they so special?

They had not had to fight, they had not been almost starved to death, none of their lifeless bodies had been hauled out across the soiled filthy ground, and their perished emaciated carcasses had not been carted off in a wheelbarrow because illness had taken its toll on their frail bodies.

No, these dogs left in the company of humans, and more to the point, kind humans. These strange humans didn't mercilessly drag the dogs with ropes tied tightly around their necks. These humans didn't kick or beat the dogs with sticks. No, these odd humans came to the compound and picked a dog, a pretty dog, a dog without scars, a dog with two eyes, a dog with four legs, four nice straight legs.

Belle had never been to the nice clean kennels, she had never been looked at by the kind humans, and sadly she never would be chosen.

She would never know the luxury of living in the special block. She would never experience what it would be like to hear a gentle, kind voice. She would never know how it felt to have hands reach down to her and lift her off her paws. Belle was condemned to spend the rest of her life, however long or short that may be, in the horrors of the compound.

"Where do they go?" Belle asked Hamish.

"Who?" Hamish replied, knowing full well who Belle was referring to.

"Those dogs from the special kennels over there."

Hamish shook his head and looked down at her.

He was about to broach a subject that he normally chose to ignore.

There was huge uncertainty about the future of any dog incarcerated at the compound. Usually, he never asked dogs about their pasts, nor would he divulge his own. But deep down inside he knew he had to tell Belle the truth.

He admired her intellect and her resilience, the way that she coped with life and all the disgusting horrors it chucked at her.

"Consider yourself a very privileged little lady. I'm going to make an exception and answer your question."

Hamish coughed, composed himself then looked up at the sky.

"You grew up wild, a feral dog on the streets, didn't you?"

"Yes, I told you when I first arrived, with my mother, two brothers and my sister," replied Belle.

Hamish took a deep breath, looked down at Belle, then continued with his story.

"I was one of the lucky ones, I lived with humans. Although they kept me outside, in all weathers, chained up in their yard for their protection. If you look closely, you can see I still bear the scar around my neck from the heavy chain that I wore for years. But they fed me and gave me all that I needed."

Hamish could see that Belle was bewildered by what he was saying. Her head tilted to one side inquisitively as she tried to comprehend the wise old dog's words. Her mind had been made up the night her dear mother was hacked to death, that humans were nothing more than barbaric, nefarious entities.

She thought back to the words that her mother had

spoken to her and her siblings just before that fateful night about their ancestors living with humans many generations ago, before they were discarded into the forests and mountain ranges. Yet now, here was Hamish, her surrogate mentor telling her that he had actually lived with humans.

Belle, although confused, told Hamish of her mother's teachings.

"Humans? The savage two-legged things that beat us at every chance they get, the vile remorseless creatures that destroyed my beautiful mother? I do remember though, before she was cruelly taken from me, one night she did talk of dogs living with humans, but she also told us of how they were thrown out, to fight and fend for themselves."

Hamish nodded.

He felt a sense of embarrassment telling Belle the tale of his past life, of relative luxury, living with a human family.

Hamish looked down at Belle and continued with his tale.

"Then one day, for reasons only known to them, they brought us to this hell on earth."

"Us?" Belle was confused.

"Yes, there were originally two of us. Me and a spoilt brat lap dog. He lived indoors with them. The little sod would taunt me every day through the window, sitting there living his life of grandeur. In the end though, they abandoned the pair of us here, just as your dear mother spoke of. They chained us to the compound gates and never once looked back at us. I barked and called to them, but they just walked away. My so-called beloved two-legged family."

His gruff voice quietened. For the briefest of moments Hamish was in deep, sad reflection.

"What happened to your little companion?"

Hamish shook his head.

"He got killed the day we arrived. We were separated, I heard him scream for me, but I was too late to save him. To be honest, I was in the middle of my first fight. An arrogant Rottweiler took liberties with me, the fool. I tore him to ribbons. Took me ages to spit all of his fur out."

Hamish laughed.

Belle glared at him, shaking her head in disgust.

"I'm sorry, I shouldn't make light of what I did. My inappropriate dark humour helps me with the guilt of not being able to save the little brat."

Hamish had been kept as a guard dog, his sole purpose in life was to protect the family that fed him and to guard their property. They lived a few miles from the notorious Lyulin district slum, but when it was demolished in 2012, Hamish became an expensive luxury. His master had read in the Bulgarian Presa Daily:

'The demolition was completed Friday, and all trailers and run-down houses have been removed. The blot on the landscape slum, on Europa Boulevard, that for the last 14 years had "greeted" visitors to Sofia arriving from Western Europe via Serbia was no more.'

"I know I shouldn't complain, well not to you anyway, not after your having to survive on the streets and all that. I was blessed to have experienced that life, but us dogs became an expensive luxury. Yes, I was at the end of a chain, that heavy, rusty chain was still secured around my neck when I was abandoned here, but I had been part of a family. I didn't have to survive alone, living in constant fear of being hunted down, scavenging for paltry scraps of food. But sadly, we have now all ended up in the same boat. We are family now, we may be vagabonds, waifs and strays, but we are alive, and we all have to share this horrendous predicament. So, in answer to your question, those dogs that leave here with humans go on to live their lives in their homes with them, just as my spoilt brat buddy once had."

He paused momentarily and took a deep breath.

"Look, as I've already said, I'm sorry. I shouldn't have made light of my ripping that Rotty apart, but you need to understand that if I, and now even yourself, don't try to make light of our past horrors, the guilt, hatred and resentment will make us go mad. I know for sure I would have done so ages ago. Honestly? No, I'm not proud of some of the things that I have had to do, it really is a dog-eat-dog existence in this hell we live in. As I have already told you, I was fighting when my little mate got killed. We were separated by those vile two-legged guards. I was taken one way, my little buddy the other. For pity's sake, we'd only been here fifteen minutes and he was dead."

Hamish was getting angry, but he needed to finish his tale.

"To survive I had to fight daily. I fought for food, a place to sleep, I fought just to bloody survive. Eventually, there were no dogs prepared to fight me anymore. At last, I had gained respect. The dogs in here looked up to me, in fact, they started to listen to me. Just look at me, my body and face still bear the deep scars from the fighting. Luckily for me, there is no more fighting, the pack obeys me, even them."

His stubby snout nose pointed towards the pack of ex bait dogs.

"I have never had to fight," Belle replied. "My mother

always took care of us. Until that awful night."

Her voice trailed off as her thoughts drifted back to the horrific night of her capture, the disgusting night when she bore witness to the barbaric slaughter of her dear mother.

"You won't ever have to fight in here, I'll always be around to protect you. Please, Belle, don't torment yourself little one, remember the good times and bury the bad. We are dogs, we live for the present, don't dwell and torment yourself with the past, that's part of our lives for us to learn from, and not live in, it's long gone. Just squat and pee on it, metaphorically speaking."

Hamish looked down at the little dog sitting next to him.

"Belle my dear, one more bit of advice. Please be very, very careful of who you trust. The harsh reality is that we, well those of us who lived with humans, looked at our two-legged family members as our providers and saviours. I trusted my family with my life. They gave me shelter and food, and in return, as I have already told you, I protected them."

Belle sat in silence, looking up at Hamish.

"But I foolishly placed my trust in them. Just think about how a sheep places its trust in the shepherd and hounds who protect it."

Belle's head tilted to one side.

"Belle, your ancestors were shepherd dogs, right? Bred to herd and protect flocks of sheep. They worked faithfully alongside the shepherd. He also helped in protecting the sheep from the wolves and other predators. He cared for his flock, but in the end, it was he who betrayed them. He raised them and then sent them for slaughter. My human family raised me, they didn't send me to my death, well maybe they have, but they, the people I trusted and loved abandoned me.

As I said, please be careful who you trust my little friend, the world is full of shepherds. But we are not all bad, remember anyone can love you when the sun is shining. In the storms is when you learn who truly cares for you."

To reassure Belle, and to hopefully give her a fighting chance of survival, Hamish gave her one last piece of advice on the subject.

"Belle, I know that at this present time this will sound ridiculous, but please try not to hate all humans. One day, and believe me, I know that the day will come, you will have a two-legged family to call your own, away from this hell. I know it's hard for you to believe, but all dogs actually know how to love a human, sadly, the same can't be said for them, not all humans know how to love a dog."

Belle was even more confused than ever.

She went to speak.

"No more, little one. That's more than enough for you to try and take in for one day."

The day's teachings were over. Belle and Hamish parted company and headed back to their respective shelters.

Before she retired for the night, Belle sat staring up at the bleak night sky. Little clouds of condensation surrounded her as her warm breath mixed with the cold night air.

"Mother, it seems like forever since I last saw you. I hope your body was laid to rest with the respect you deserved. I pray that you have crossed the strange bridge that you spoke of and are at peace. But I am not, my sadness comes in waves, it washes over me, grief engulfs me. Often I am blinded by the tears that fill my eyes."

She inhaled, raised her head, opened her mouth, and tried to expel her grief with one almighty howl. It never left her. The damp night air had filled her lungs, and her howl? Well that mockingly came out as a cough and splutter.

"I can't do a bloody thing right," Belle huffed to herself, as she stomped back to her den.

CHAPTER FOURTEEN

Several weeks passed, and Hamish was paying one of his regular visits to Artemis.

He had noticed that she had kept Belle in her den a few months back, for Belle, it had proven to be three weeks of sheer boredom.

However, Artemis had explained to her the reasons why, and how her body had changed. Most importantly, she told Belle why she had to be kept away from the male dogs, many of whom Artemis had to fend off daily.

At first, Belle had panicked at the sight of blood. The only time that she had ever seen the gruesome claret fluid in her life, it had always been closely followed by death.

The very sight of blood seeping from her adolescent body had terrified her.

Surviving in the compound had made her a very wise and mature juvenile, and

now that her cycle was about to return, Belle would have to be on her guard, even more so than the first time.

"When is the, erm, you know, the next time?"

Hamish shuffled uneasily and couldn't look at Artemis as he asked the awkward question.

He was far too embarrassed to broach such a delicate

subject outright. Artemis laughed, there he was, the big brave alpha male, looking all shy and sheepish at trying to ask her such a question.

"Very soon," Artemis replied. "She is nearly one two-legged street-dweller year old now."

"OK, just let me know when, without going into too much detail please, and I'll keep an extra vigilant eye on her. We don't want any accidents, there is barely enough food being thrown in here for us, and we certainly can't handle too many more mouths to feed."

Little did they know of the horrors that lay ahead for Belle.

Autumn arrived, the days were getting shorter and colder, and the leaves on the trees that were once green, exploded into beautiful hues of gold, red and orange.

Yet again, the tears of red liquid reappeared, only this time, Belle wasn't frightened by the sight of the blood that seeped from her body.

To try and keep Belle occupied in the kennel, Artemis had been whiling away as much time as possible trying to explain to her the riveting subject of lunar cycles.

The barrage of information had all proved very confusing for Belle. Although she knew that she needed to grasp the basics, important information that she may need to one day pass on to her own daughter.

"Right dear, I'll go over it one last time," Artemis said in her best teacher's voice. "So, you are now coming up to the end of your first street-dweller year, or thirteen lunar cycles. We as dogs mature far more than street dwellers do, well if they ever do mature, bloody inhumane things that they are. Sorry I digressed, so in fact, in their years you are now fifteen."

Belle's head was already spinning, yet there was still the complex bit to come.

"But by the end of next year, or a total of twenty-six lunar cycles, you will be the equivalent of twenty-four street-dweller years. But, now this is where it may get confusing, from then on, at thirty-nine lunar cycles, you will only age five dog years for every one street-dweller year, and when broken down over our lifetime, one street-dweller year will work out to seven dog years, do you understand me my dear?"

Belle was bewildered, her head tilted from side to side as she tried to comprehend the sheer complexity of the lesson.

Artemis was so proud of her explanation, although Belle's head was spinning.

To save herself from another barrage of numbers, she nodded that she had fully understood the day's lesson.

"Right, I'm off to try and find some food," Belle said to Artemis, backing quickly out of the kennel.

"Belle, please, just stay in for a few more days."

"I really do need to get some fresh air."

Artemis sighed. She felt uneasy at contemplating letting Belle wander off alone, but she knew that she couldn't keep her incarcerated in their little shelter for the entirety of her being in season.

She gave Belle her best surrogate mother advice.

"OK then, but please listen to me. Be very careful my dear, make sure you keep your wits about you and be on your guard at all times. You are a very pretty dog and stand out like a beautiful flower in a meadow of ugly weeds. We don't want any untoward attention paid towards you during your special time. Please let me get Charlie and Mason to go with you"

"Stop fussing, Artemis, I'll be fine."

Belle had developed into a natural-born survivor, even a fighter, so she deludedly thought.

She was heading to the other side of the compound to see if any food had been thrown into the food troughs.

On her way, something strange occurred to her. Normally she had to run the gauntlet, enduring vile comments such as Flipper Legs or Wonky Legs, hurled at her by the adolescent male dogs.

But not today. Strangely, and unnervingly, they stared at her differently. Peculiar, almost loving glances.

Belle was naively oblivious to the fact that even before the male dogs had clapped eyes on her, the pheromones that her body was exuding were driving them crazy.

Just as she had expected, when she arrived at the feeding area, the troughs were empty. Thousands of wriggling maggots with their endless appetites devoured the decaying scraps that covered the bottom.

Belle inhaled.

The stench of the rancid remains reminded her of how the wasteland next to the train tracks sometimes smelt. Momentarily catapulted back to her puppyhood, she could hear her siblings frolicking and her mother barking at them.

She smiled to herself as she reminisced about far happier times.

Belle had become reliant on her sensory organs to bring back happy memories.

Loving, fun times that would only come back to her random flashbacks.

She shook her head, huffed to herself, turned and started to walk back to her kennel.

All the while, Belle kept a watchful eye out for any unsuspecting birds that may happen to land in the compound. Hopefully, she'd be able to catch one, the only problem was choking on the flea-ridden feathers, before reaching the meagre morsel of flesh.

As she walked, again she noticed the adoring glances from the male dogs.

"This really does make a pleasant change," she innocently thought to herself.

The compound was enjoying a glorious, sunny autumnal day. Dogs lay snoozing all around, enjoying the sun's warming glow on their backs and bellies.

On days like these, Belle didn't feel quite so resentful, somehow the sun helped her to accept life.

Still on the quest to source some food, she raised her head and sniffed the air, hoping to home in on scents within the compound that may provide some scraps to take back to Artemis.

Engrossed in her mission, she foolishly wasn't taking notice of her surroundings, and inadvertently Belle found that she had wandered into the part of the compound the rest of the incarcerated dogs tended to avoid.

This was the domain of the pack of ex-bait dogs who had attacked her on her first day, a place the other dogs knew full well that they entered at their own peril.

"Well, well, well, look what we have here then? We don't get many visitors, and when we do, they are never as pretty as you."

Belle, startled as to where the voice had come from, looked up. Her eyes met those of the self-proclaimed leader of the small pack of ex-bait dogs, ogling her.

She was confused, why was he being so uncharacteristically nice?

The rest of his pack sat grouped behind him.

Belle felt uncomfortable, not only at being confronted by the pack, but by the way that they all leered at her. In fact, it felt more worrying to her, them being kind, rather than their usual boisterous, tormentous behaviour.

"Why are they not taunting me?" she thought to herself.

"To be honest I really am not as bad as they say," he continued, trying as hard as he could to be pleasant, the total opposite of his usual vile, aggressive nature.

"In fact, I really would like us to become friends. I'm sorry, how very rude of me, we haven't even been properly introduced have we? Well, my name is Sykes. Look, Belle, your name is Belle, isn't it? Here's a peace offering."

A wry smirk engulfed Syke's disfigured, scarred face.

"They are so foolish. The weak and innocent, who give their enemy the means of destroying them," he thought to himself.

Belle felt repulsed as she stared at his battle-scarred body.

Matted, dirty white fur covered most of his body, except that is for the left side of his torso, which was covered in exposed areas of gnarled, greyish, pink skin, permanent reminders from his days as a bait dog. A scar ran from his forehead, then across his right eye. He only had half his tail left, two of his canine teeth were cracked, he was missing several front claws, and his left ear had been bitten off. He constantly had to sit and scratch himself. As if Sykes didn't have enough personal problems, for some strange reason he was riddled with more fleas than any other dog in the compound.

He turned his mutilated body around and picked up

something from behind him.

As he turned back, in his mouth he held the biggest beef knuckle bone in his mouth that Belle had ever seen.

Bloodied sinewy flesh hung from it. The one good thing to come from the abattoir was the bones. However, Hamish usually always got first pickings, whatever bones that were left were fought over by the other dogs.

Why on earth was Sykes offering Belle a huge, prized bone that he had potentially had to fight for?

"What a feast this will be for us. It will be just like the warm bird my mother once placed in front of us in our wooden home," Belle thought to herself.

Drool dripped from her mouth at the thought of lapping the fresh marrowbone from the giant knuckle.

Sykes dropped the bone in front of him and lowered his head, in a begrudged mark of respect.

In an almost trance-like state, Belle moved towards the gleaming white bone lying at Sykes's paws.

As she got closer, the aroma of the marrowbone filled her nostrils. The sweet smell excited her taste buds. Mesmerised, Belle found herself drawn ever closer and closer to the unexpected gift, and dangerously closer to the grotesque Sykes.

Sykes's vile smell brought Belle back to her senses. She shook her head.

Worryingly, Sykes's pack had now surrounded her, just as they had done on the day she arrived at the compound.

This time Belle was alone. She probed the pack, hoping to find a gap to enable her to make her escape.

Sykes drooled, and he shook his bulbous scarred head, his one ear flapped and slimy slobber flew over his ugly jowls.

Belle was in a state of panic. Terror seemed to suck the very last breath from her mouth.

She paced round in a circle, again looking for a means of escape.

Every time she turned and attempted to make a run for it, one of Sykes's henchmen snapped at her, forcing her back into the centre of the pack.

The dogs moved in closer. As they did, they nipped at her body, their fangs just barely cutting into her flesh.

Belle yelped at every bite, she could do no more than stand her ground and snap back at them.

Although the pack's bites drew blood, they were not going in for the kill.

"You're all mine!"

Two of his henchmen parted, and Sykes entered the circle of dogs and moved in on Belle. Grotesque-smelling slobber hung like frothy white ropes from his filthy mouth.

There was no chance of her escaping.

Belle resigned herself to whatever horrific fate may await her.

CHAPTER FIFTEEN

Artemis was lazing about outside the kennel, enjoying the warm sunshine with her other two adopted pups, who playfully fought one another, gently nipping and biting at each other's bodies.

Their idyllic lazy sunny afternoon was suddenly disturbed by a pitiful loud howling in the distance.

Artemis recognised the owner of the woeful sound.

"Belle!" Artemis barked at the top of her voice.

She looked up to see her little Belle, running back to the safety of her family.

Artemis ran over to her to meet her, closely followed by the other two pups.

Belle stopped running and hung her head low in shame at what had just happened to her.

Bright red blood dripped from the bite marks that covered her body, and she was in searing pain from where Sykes had forced himself upon her.

Artemis instinctively knew what had happened; she didn't need to ask Belle.

"There, there, my dear. Follow me, poppet"

Artemis's years of worldly wisdom had taught her not to say 'I told you not to get too close to other dogs'. Belle needed consoling, all Artemis could do for now was to be there for the innocent little pup, to listen without judgement, and offer her a shoulder to cry on. Artemis's main worry was how on earth could she help Belle ever come to terms with the vile, traumatic experience she had endured?

Belle was gently ushered into the den by Artemis.

Mason and Charlie didn't understand what had happened to Belle. Artemis's teachings had taught them that in such a scenario, just say nothing.

"Stay out there, boys," commanded Artemis.

Through her tears of pain and embarrassment, Belle told Artemis of the disgusting, unsolicited attack inflicted upon her by Sykes.

Artemis, with tears streaming down her face, sat in silence, listening to every grotesque detail.

When she could speak no more, Belle crept into a corner and turned her back on the world.

"Oh my poor baby. You are not to blame, he had no right to do that awful thing to you. Please my dear, feel safe again, we will protect you."

Belle sat shaking yet said nothing. Then she started sobbing again.

Artemis went outside.

"Go get Hamish now. Hurry up, be as fast as you can."

Charlie and Mason did as they were told and ran off, barking Hamish's name as loudly as they could.

Hamish was out of puff when he arrived at the den.

"Go play elsewhere," Artemis commanded Charlie and Mason.

"What's happened? The boys said Belle had been hurt but they didn't elaborate," Hamish asked.

He was ushered out of Belle's earshot; Artemis didn't want to upset the traumatised pup even more.

Hamish was told what had happened, of how Belle had been violated by Sykes.

He could hear the poor little dog whimpering from within the makeshift shelter.

Uncontrollable rage surged through his huge, powerful body.

He raised his large brown and tan head skywards and let out a blood-curdling howl.

The sound startled Belle, and she started to shake uncontrollably. Even in the sanctuary of her den she no longer felt safe.

Hamish clawed at the ground, paced in a circle and then howled again.

"He's a dead dog walking."

Sykes was the perpetrator of the violation of Hamish's beautiful, innocent little dog. The dog he had grown to look upon as his surrogate daughter. The little dog who had brought out a kindness in his character that he never knew existed, well a kindness that did once exist when he was a family pet, a kindness that was discarded at the gates all those years ago when he was abandoned at the dog shelter.

Sykes was lying nonchalantly licking the marrowbone out of the knuckle he had enticed Belle with.

His pack of bodyguards were close by. A couple circled him, congratulating him on his brave conquest. A few of the younger dogs fought playfully, and three of the older dogs lazed on their backs, enjoying the warm autumnal sun on their bellies.

As of yet, none had picked up on Hamish's unmistakable

scent as he made his furtive approach.

He could hear them barking vile, graphic recollections and despicable mocking jokes about the savage assault on Belle. Those disgusting words enraged him even more.

The pack were oblivious of the formidable figure of the large Bullmastiff that had descended upon their lair.

Hamish was aware that he was heavily outnumbered, this added to the adrenaline that surged through his body even more. The rage had grown and was ready to spew from him as violently as any mythical dragon had ever flamed.

He could feel his heart rate speeding up. His pupils dilated, his breathing gradually got deeper and faster.

With his years of wisdom, Hamish used stealth and cunning to manoeuvre himself downwind, with the odds stacked against him he needed the advantage of surprise. The words of his late father resonated in his mind 'Silence is not a weakness. Smart dogs don't plan big moves out loud'.

The intended deliverance of revenge for the attack on Belle was going to be swift and brutal.

Hamish knew that he was an old, out-of-shape dog whose joints were riddled with arthritis.

Sykes on the other hand was younger, stronger and far more agile. Strangely, he had not yet vied for the role of alpha male against Hamish.

Hamish knew that if Sykes had ever turned on him, it would have been a long, brutal fight, a bloody, final gladiatorial scrap, with the death of one of them inevitable.

What was about to unfold was for the honour of Belle. Hamish was under no illusion that this battle would be to the demise of one of them.

He had no intention of becoming the vanquished, his

mind was intent on justice, and there would be no mercy.

Deep within his body, natural changes were taking place in preparation for what was to follow. The increased blood flow had caused his muscles to tense. His blood pressure was dangerously high. Most worryingly for him though was his state of his mind. The wise old dog had mentally lost all impulse or control.

Sykes on the other hand, had had no time for his body to prepare.

He lay, imperturbably engrossed with his bone, oblivious to the immense danger that approached him from behind.

With no barks or growls of warning, Hamish charged at full speed towards Sykes. He grabbed him by the back of the neck. Sykes's body was lifted and dragged forwards by the momentum of his aggressor's speed and power.

Sykes could feel his neck bone being crushed by Hamish's immensely powerful, vice-like jaws.

Hamish's mouth filled with the metallic taste of blood as his teeth pierced deeply into Sykes's neck.

Still pushing forwards, Hamish changed tact, and forced Sykes's head downwards, pushing his nose into the dirt.

Sykes struggled to see and breathe, as his nostrils and eyes filled with dust.

He attempted to try and break free, roll over and get up. His efforts were to no avail. He had been overpowered by a formidable adversary.

Sykes could feel his body weakening, the searing pain had turned into an ice-like numbness. There was no way he could escape the immense strength of the grip that held him, his vision became blurred and then darkness engulfed him.

Blinded, all he could rely on was scent and sound, yet

the only sound he could hear was that of his own heartbeat.

In one swift movement, Hamish yanked his head backwards, shaking it from side to side. The soft fleshy tissue gripped between his teeth ripped from Sykes's body.

Hamish's mouth was full of flesh and blood.

The sudden painful shock brought Sykes back to his senses. Blood poured from the gaping hole in the back of his neck, his brachiocephalic muscle was severely damaged. He was paralysed, unable to run or defend himself. Searing agony engulfed his body, as he lay writhing on the blood-soaked dust, at the paws and mercy of Hamish.

Hamish showed no compassion to his defeated opponent. He chewed and swallowed the warm flesh that filled his mouth.

As he let out a rousing howl, Sykes's blood gurgled in his throat.

Hamish glared down in contempt at the pathetic dog in front of him.

With a sudden ferocity that he had never exuded before, he lunged his head downwards and tore at the pitiful dog.

Hamish slowly shredded Sykes's body to pieces. His bones were crushed and flesh ripped from his woeful torso.

Sykes had been unable to defend himself from the onset of the attack due to the initial wound Hamish inflicted with devastating precision.

He made a pitiful, pathetic sight lying bloodied and torn in the crimson-coloured dirt, making a distressing gurgling sound as the ichor filled his throat. His breathing was ragged, he could only take shallow breaths as blood slowly filled his lungs.

Mercifully for him, the end was close, his fate lay in the

teeth of his conqueror.

Hamish still wasn't content.

Sykes's body started quivering involuntarily as Hamish's powerful jaws grasped at his ribcage. The feeble bones crunched and splintered as Hamish's teeth made light work of penetrating straight through them.

Hamish thrust his head backwards.

Sykes's body went into shock as a gaping hole appeared in his side.

Hamish spat out the bloodied flesh and splinters of bone, then plunged his face into the cavernous gape.

In one swift move, he ripped out Sykes's heart.

Hamish drew back his lips and devoured Sykes's warm, pulsating internal organ.

To add to the humiliation of the body of his perished foe, and in a final act of degradation to his conquest, Hamish cocked his leg and urinated over the exterminated carcass.

The ferocious onslaught had happened so quickly, that Sykes's pack could only look on in shock and horror.

They had never seen anything like what they had just witnessed. This was not a dog-on-dog fight, this was slaughter.

Their revered pack leader, the fearless beta male of the compound, was destroyed without even the chance to bear his ferocious teeth.

They stood, petrified and quivering, facing Hamish. The disembowelled body lay bleeding and motionless at his paws.

They lowered their heads, hoping that their grovelling act of respect would be construed as a plea of mercy, enough for Hamish to spare their pathetic lives.

Hamish's face and body were covered in warm, sticky blood. He was an old dog and the fight had left him exhausted.

He looked up at the autumnal sky.

His body shook and he panted heavily. Drool and gore dripped from his mouth.

He drew a breath and let out a gurgling, blood-curdling howl of victory, as loudly as he could muster.

He had deployed his own severe form of justice.

With hatred and bloodlust in his eyes, he stared with contempt towards the pack who stood quivering in fear. Their heads remained lowered, and none of them dared make eye contact.

One of the pack uncontrollably urinated. Fearful to make any form of sudden movement, he didn't dare cock his leg. Urine ran down his scrawny leg, forming a smelly yellow puddle in the dust under his paw.

Thoughts of tearing each of them to pieces reverberated around Hamish's mind.

He wanted to slowly kill each of them in turn, in the same ruthless manner he had just inflicted on Sykes.

His mind was in turmoil, he involuntarily growled. His breaths were getting heavier by the second. His lips quivered, and his sharp canine teeth were exposed. His snout nose twitched, picking up on the metallic scent of the crimson fluid that trickled from the lifeless corpse behind him.

He closed his eyes, and then howled at the pack.

"Get out of my sight, you vile worthless scum."

Anger and contempt filled his words.

With no need to be commanded twice, they fled for their pathetic lives, with their tails firmly between their legs.

His role as judge, jury and executioner had been fulfilled.

His body ached, and strangely, as he regained his senses, he felt ashamed of the terror he had unleashed.

However, justice had to be served on the perpetrator of the cowardly, vile attack on his beloved little dog.

Hamish had killed for the honour of the innocent little Belle, his little Belle.

He turned and left the scene of the carnage that he had inflicted.

As the dismembered body of his nemesis lay slain in the warm sun, a swarm of flies were attracted to the carcass, they didn't waste any time in laying their eggs in the bloodied fresh meat.

Within twenty-four hours the freshly hatched maggots would start devouring the carcass.

With his head lowered, Hamish slowly trudged back to the small shelter where Belle was.

Dogs throughout the compound turned their heads as he walked past them.

Others cowered in fear.

There was no sound, for once an eerie silence engulfed the usually raucous compound. All the captive inhabitants had heard the slaughter of Sykes.

Artemis was lying at the entrance of her shelter. Her nose twitched; she could smell the fresh metallic scent of death that lingered on Hamish's body getting closer.

The plaintive sound of Belle's uncontrollable whimpering could be heard from within.

Hamish stood and stared at Artemis, although he had served justice, he felt both embarrassed and ashamed of the way he had executed the punishment.

He plunged his head into the rusty old bucket that was kept close to Belle's shelter and gulped down mouthfuls of the warm water.

In his mind, he could still taste the bitter, saltiness of blood. His throat tickled from a few scraggly strands of Sykes's fur.

He stood up and stared down into the bucket. The water and slobber that dripped from his jowls distorted his reflection. Slowly the water settled. Hamish blinked and shook his head; the taste of blood was now cleared from his mouth.

Happy that all remnants of the fight were now cleared from his appearance, he looked over at Artemis.

"How is she?"

"She is very confused. Life has not been good for that poor little one."

Artemis had helped many bitches within the compound come through the trauma of such an attack. Her mind was already worrying about the fact that

Belle could now potentially become a mother herself.

"He can't hurt her now. Justice had been served."

Artemis said nothing, and just nodded at him. She, along with the rest of the compound, had heard his victory howl.

An embarrassing silence ensued. Hamish turned and headed back to his shelter.

He needed to rest his aching body and contemplate the events that had foregone.

One of the workers at the shelter discovered the dismembered carcass of Sykes. Just in case there was an unexpected inspection of the compound by the authorities, he decided it best to remove the gruesome mess.

He retched as he stuffed the cadaver into a thick black rubble sack. The body filled the bag up, and the worker couldn't tie the end up. It was also too heavy for him to carry. To avoid spilling blood throughout the compound, he retrieved a squeaky old wheelbarrow and wheeled Sykes to his final resting place, the stinking pile of death that Belle hated so much. At least good would come of his demise, he'd be fresh meat for the rats to feast on.

Oz would pop over and collect the sacks later. The decaying rotting flesh within them would be driven out of the city's boundary and dumped.

A few weeks later, Oz's actions sparked the beginning of an investigation by the Zoo Police when they received reports of mass dog killings.

A farmworker had discovered over fifty plastic bags, crammed full of bloodied dog corpses, dumped next to a slurry pit. The Zoo Police attended and subsequently found another twenty bodies of poisoned dogs that had been thrown into a ditch leading off the pit. Luckily, during the investigation that followed, one of the corpses had an identification tattoo on one of its hind legs. The tattooed number was cross-referenced, and it was found to match a logged number that was part of the investigation into illegal dog-fighting gangs. The police knew where it had been taken for safety during the court case and were now looking at launching a covert operation at the compound where Belle was incarcerated.

The municipal-run shelters, the 'Isolators', were nothing more than dog-concentration camps, a disgusting hell on earth, where dogs very seldom left, alive anyway. Once a dog, especially a young pup, had entered one of these vile hell holes they stood a very slim chance of survival. It literally was a dog-eat-dog existence, where only the strongest had any chance of living. The shelter was always filled with malnourished dogs surrounded by stinking, disease-ridden faeces, dead bodies lay strewn everywhere. To survive, some of the incarcerated dogs soon had to become cannibalistic, picking off the weak and elderly as a vital source of sustenance.

CHAPTER SIXTEEN

Belle was traumatised, her body had gone into shock. She lay panting heavily, and her body quivered uncontrollably.

Artemis entered the bleak den. She knew that there was nothing that she could do to help the distraught little pup, except to sit silently next to her.

"Why me? Why am I cursed? Why was I ever put on this damned planet? I have never caused another dog any harm. My mother once told me that I am a German Shepherd. She told me of my ancestors, and the legacy that I have to live up to, and to carry the name of my breed with pride. But look at me, a crippled waste of space, destined to live my pathetic life as a victim, a plaything to be abused by other dogs, and them disgusting two-legged street dwellers. Please believe me, I don't want pity, but just for once in my life I want to be shown mercy."

"He will never be able to hurt you again, poppet."

"He won't, but I know there will be others. How many more years do I have to live? What have I done to deserve this? How much more pain can I take? Death is all around me, I see it, I hear it, I smell it, I taste it, I even dream about it, I dream of my death. I yearn to cross the bridge, to once again be with my beloved mother. She would have protected me from him, unlike the others, who let me down. One thing that I know for sure, things would have been much better if I'd never been born at all. In protecting me, my mother lost her life."

Belle stared angrily at Artemis as the words spouted like venom from her mouth. She needed to vent her anger, and as her words flowed, it was almost as if she blamed Artemis for what had happened.

Artemis shook her head, then she slowly backed out of the den. For once, she didn't have the words to comfort a pup in distress.

As night fell, Belle slowly drifted off. Her body twitched and made involuntary running motions as she dreamt, her beautiful recurrent dream of running free, side by side with her mother.

As she fell into a deeper sleep, slumber-induced nightmares caused her to cry out, followed by little whimpering sounds. Artemis, who had crept back in to watch over Belle, could do nothing more than to sit and watch. She had no idea what awful thoughts were running through the little pup's once innocent mind, but if Belle should abruptly awake, she would at least be there to comfort her.

Belle opened her eyes as the sun rose and the birds began their musical dawn chorus. For the briefest of moments, she lay taking in the wondrous sounds and beauty of the new day.

She yawned, then stretched.

The pain of Sykes's attack caused her to yelp, then the vile horrors of the previous day suddenly came flooding back to her. In an attempt to release her pent-up anger, she howled out loud.

Startled by the sudden noise, Artemis, who had

momentarily dozed off, leapt up onto her paws.

She tried to speak, yet a random blurb of words spluttered out.

"Erm, morning darling. Poor Charlie and Mason, bless them, they ended up sleeping outside of Hamish's shelter."

Artemis closed her eyes, waiting for Belle's backlash.

"And that's my fault as well, is it?"

Belle glared at Artemis and shook her head as she walked out of the den.

Her neck was sore, still weeping blood from where Sykes had forcefully restrained her, and his sharp teeth had sunk deep into her flesh.

The early morning sky was the colour of blood, adorned with golden clouds that reflected the new day's sun as it slowly climbed high up into the sky. For now, the world was silent, as if all life had ended during the night.

Belle's deformed front legs left their own unique prints in the cool morning dew, as she walked to her usual spot. Tentatively she squatted and urinated, her rear end was still sore from the previous day's horrific attack.

She turned and glared at the steam rising from the small pool of liquid. In an act of defiance, she angrily kicked her hind legs. Her paws scraped her urine, spreading the faint ammonia scent as far away from her as she possibly could.

The compound never usually reeked at this time of the day. It was as if the vile aromas mysteriously vanished into the night sky. Sadly, it wouldn't last for too long, in a few short hours the usual vulgar stench of death and decay would have returned.

For the briefest of moments, Belle wanted to immerse herself into the peaceful serenity of daybreak. She looked down at the glistening droplets of dew on the grass. She closed her eyes and lowered her head and wiped her face on the cool moist grass.

Her resilient nature would hopefully get her through the traumas of the previous day. She had suffered far worse, and Belle would try not to allow Sykes to destroy her life. If anything, his vile actions would have made her even stronger. But, the little pup's innocent life had been disgustingly torn away from her. Long term, what consequences would Sykes's moment of forced pleasure have on her, mentally would she ever be able to recover?

Unbeknown to her, the seeds of new life had been implanted in her body, and Belle, who was still merely a pup herself, was soon going to become a mother.

Belle walked slowly through the silent compound. She stopped and stared at some pitiful, older sick dogs who had been evicted from the little ramshackle shelters they had once made their homes. Some of them had already awoken, and misty vapour blew from their mouths as they gasped frantically for air.

Fencing wire had been wound tightly around their necks, the opposite end staked into the ground.

The wire had been purposely cut short, to prevent the dogs from gaining shelter from the treacherous weather.

Sadly, they had no chance of scurrying back into the safety of the dens they had once occupied. Other, healthier dogs had seized the opportunity and had already moved in. There was nothing the bound dogs could do, mentally tormented by the predicament they found themselves in. To make matters even worse for them, they could no longer access food or water, the wire slowly cut deeper into the infected wounds around their necks. The steel cable prevented them from being able to defend themselves from attack. Slowly, and painfully, they were reduced to skin and bone. Death was going to be a very long, drawn-out process for these poor defenceless souls.

Belle knew that there was nothing she could do to help them, but there again, why should she help them? Who had ever helped her in her moments of anguish?

She carried on walking through the compound. A sudden sound startled her, she spun around and glanced back to where the noise had originated from. Her heart raced as she scanned the area. She breathed a sigh of relief when she saw that it was nothing to be afraid of, it was merely another chained-up dog awakening. It had yelped out loudly in pain as the rusty chain around its neck reopened the infected wounds on its neck. A flesh flow of blood and infected pus oozed from the open sores on its nape.

She soon found herself at the food trough, hoping in vain that there would be just a few paltry scraps of meat that may have been left over from the previous day.

The sound of a bee buzzing nearby caught her attention. To while away her time, Belle had found herself a new hobby, although it had its consequences. Wasps and bees were her new playthings. She lowered her head, homed in on the sound, and moved in for the kill. In one swift move, as the bee flew past her, Belle lunged at it. With her lips pulled back, to avoid being stung, she grabbed the insect mid-flight. Sounding like a set of pretend false teeth from a joke shop, she crashed her teeth together, crushing the bee and swallowing it. On rare occasions, if they had not been crushed to death, they tickled her throat and belly as their wings flapped as the insect travelled through her body. Hopefully, the natural acids in Belle's body would kill it before they entered her gut, if not, in a last defiant act the insect would sting her innards. This inevitably caused her to be sick as the sting reacted with the lining of her stomach. Oh well, at least she could eat her vomit; to her, it was a meal.

Belle's ears suddenly pricked up. Her head tilted as she stared inquisitively in the direction of the strange noise. A noise that for some strange reason aggravated her, a noise that sent a shiver down her spine.

Her mind went into overdrive. The rackety, deep rattling sound was getting closer. Belle started to tremble. She was confused. Her initial reaction was fear, but her emotions went deeper than that, the sound repulsed her.

For reasons she couldn't understand, her body went into fight mode, and her hackles and tail stood erect. She stared intently through the thin veil of ground mist as a dilapidated and battered white van slowly came into view. It juddered as it pulled into the compound, its diesel engine rattled and its exhaust randomly backfired. Then it dawned on her, the rusty white heap of metal was the van that had delivered her to the hell on earth she now found herself trying to survive in, the hell on earth that was causing her so much pain.

She glared, her eyes full of hatred, as the driver alighted from the cab of the truck. She closed her eyes and lifted her head, her nose twitched as she tried to pick up on his unique odour, above the rancid aromas of the compound that had slowly developed around her.

Belle gagged. The man reeked, the gentle morning breeze that wafted over her from his direction, was laden with the repulsive stench of death.

An instant flashback overcame her. Smells can do that, a certain perfume, type of flower, or a cake baking, can catapult someone back to a long-forgotten happy memory, bringing back happy thoughts. Although, for Belle, the memories that were evoked were awful.

Oz was delivering a couple of bovine corpses that had sat on his van overnight. He'd also been tipped off in the bar the previous evening about a few dogs he could capture en route, easy pickings, and a bit of blood money towards the coming evening's drinks.

The compound's slovenly security guard strutted over.

"Morning petal. Got a couple of new lodgers for you," Oz shouted as he opened the van's rear doors. He clambered up into the grimy cavern.

"Bloody hell, look at the state of me hands," he moaned, wiping his palms down the front of his jeans to clean off the blood.

Belle recognised the voice, the same despicable voice that had mocked her mother when he had helped mercilessly murder her on that horrific night. The despicable voice that had mocked Belle as he had thrown her to the ground.

That vile thing on the other side of the gate was the human who had destroyed her life. She stood poised, ready to attack, if the moment should arise. An angry growl resonated from deep within her. If the gate should open, revenge would be hers, she was prepared to forsake her life to get her revenge.

However, her mind battled mixed emotions.

Strangely her heart raced in excited anticipation. What if the van contained Sam, Tess or Duque? Just to see them once again filled her with joy, although she hated the thought of any of them having to endure the life that she now led, and just maybe, they would be the ones able to protect her.

Belle looked on as a bloodied dog was thrown from the van. Straight away Belle could see that it wasn't one of her siblings. The poor thing was in a terrible state and required urgent medical attention. Oz had found him tied to a lamp post, silver gaffer tape had been used to bind his hind and front legs. Some lowlife had decided to put a lit firecracker into the little dog's mouth. After putting a cable tie around its jaw, and getting out of harm's way, the firework exploded, blowing the dog's face to bits. His jaw was shattered, his tongue split in half and his eyes were badly damaged, but miraculously he was alive.

The next dog slung out of the van was also in a distressed state. It had been found hiding under a dumped burnt-out car. The poor dog had been shot, beaten and had part of its skull smashed in by several heavy hammer blows.

Two dismembered bloodied bovine carcasses were pushed out next. These would become the rancid meat that the dogs in the compound would fight over. The disgusting putrid meat that the corpses contained would eventually cause the deaths of some of the more frail, vulnerable dogs, their bodies unable to fight off the problems the inevitable chronic diarrhoea would cause.

Belle looked on as yet another wounded hound was slung from the van. The clanking sound of heavy chain links followed the dog, hitting it hard in the face.

It yelped out in agony as it hit the heap of revolting, rotten raw meat lying on the ground. The rancid-smelling flesh had already attracted a swarm of flies.

The dog looked like Hamish, only it was much smaller. A large rusty metal butcher's hook was protruding from the scruff of his neck. The hook's eyelet had been crudely welded to a thirty-pound tow chain.

The hook had been ruthlessly skewered through his flesh, and the chain had been secured to the fence of the home he had loyally guarded.

The wound caused by the hook had become infected, the metabolic processes of anaerobic bacteria were causing rapid tissue degradation, and the resulting foul putrid stench of the pus weeping from the wound could be smelt from ten feet away.

The swarm of flies that descended had a field day. Some gorged on the rancid carcasses, others homed in like vampires on the feast of blood and pus oozing from the dog's infected wounds.

The gates were opened by the security guard, and the newly captured wounded dogs were kicked and forced into the muddy, rat-infested compound of death. The chain attached to the dog's neck was lugged along the ground by the guard and slung in behind him. The poor dog winced as the hook through his neck twisted slightly. A fresh stream of blood poured from the reopened wound.

Belle lowered her body into a stalking position and slowly started to move forwards. She was fully ready to kill, she was also prepared to potentially be killed.

Sadly, on this occasion she didn't get her chance of revenge, the gates were quickly slammed shut. Belle knew that the bastard would return and that her time would come. Retribution would be hers, hopefully very soon.

Belle watched as the ex-bait dogs, minus their leader Sykes, moved in on the compound's new arrivals, just as they had the night she had arrived. Before they had reached their new prey, they looked over and scowled at Belle. She wasn't scared, instead, she bared her teeth and snarled back at them. One of the compound workers ran over and turned a high-powered hose on them, and they quickly fled.

He got the rusty meat cleaver from the Portakabin and began hacking the bovine corpses in chunks. He loaded as much of the meat as he could into his wheelbarrow and wheeled the first lot of rotting cow carcass over to the feeding trough.

Belle took her chances and moved in on the delivery of food. She tore at the rancid flesh and gagged. She quickly chewed and swallowed a few mouthfuls of the foul disgusting meat. Even though she was starving, she could eat no more of the festering flesh.

She couldn't stand there any longer, the stench of rancid meat repulsed her.

She was just about to tear some off for Artemis and the other two pups.

"Would they get any for me? No, I doubt it. Stuff them, they can fight for their own."

Belle turned and was about to head back to the den, when she spotted the dog with the rusty chain skewered to its neck lying whimpering close to the gate.

Belle walked over to it. She was anxious to know if by any chance the dog may have seen Tess, Duque and Sam on his travels, and that they were safe.

"I know you are in pain, but I need to know, have you seen my siblings? Two boys and a girl. Like me but bigger, and they don't have wonky legs."

"I'm lying here dying in agony, and you ask me of your brother and sisters? No offer of help?" the dog yelped as it looked up at Belle.

She didn't care about his distress, for her, she was now alone in her dog-eat-dog existence.

"Answer me, have you seen them?" Belle barked at him angrily.

The dog closed its eyes. Flies had already started landing on the open, infected wound on its neck.

"Stuff you. Die for all I care, at least that way you'll do some good and reduce the surplus population," Belle snapped. She turned and started to walk back through the grounds.

Dogs were emerging from their dens. Some of them stared at her, only now she stared back at them. Some barked at her, she retaliated, deep down it felt good.

One dog approached her, mocking her about the vicious attack she had endured. Belle didn't waste any time, she bit him straight on the nose, he yelped and backed off.

Belle had made up her mind, no dog would ever hurt or humiliate her ever again. From now on, any dog who dared to get too close to her would feel the wrath of her teeth.

Sadly, she gained a strange sense of self-satisfaction from causing that dog pain. Sykes's disgusting actions had changed Belle, she had lost her innocence, and she was hell-bent on never allowing another dog to violate her in that heinous way ever again.

Charlie and Mason were waiting outside the den for Belle. As she walked toward them, they both lowered their heads, but they couldn't hide their excitement as their tails began to wag. Although eager to see her, neither of them knew what to do, or how she would react towards them.

Belle walked up to them.

"What are you looking at?"

"Belle, please, we don't know what to say to you, or how to make your pain go away," said Charlie.

"There wouldn't be anything to say, or pain to take away if you'd been there to help me, would there?"

Mason and Charlie looked at each other and shuffled uneasily.

Belle stared at them. She knew it wasn't their fault, they were only pups themselves. Without saying a word, she moved closer and gently licked each of their ears. They both responded likewise, then together, the three of them scurried into the safety of the den.

Artemis was curled up in a corner, catching up on some much-needed sleep. She had spent the previous night watching over Belle. The dogs entering the den startled her. Artemis leapt up and barked.

Without thinking, Belle snapped and barked back at her.

Her teeth were exposed and she was poised and ready to lunge forwards and attack.

Mason and Charlie dropped down and cowered on the floor in fear. Artemis was too old and feeble to fight back, she closed her eyes. For the briefest of moments, she expected the young dog to attack her.

Belle, although she at present hated the world, was ashamed of herself. The fact that she had bared her teeth in anger, at the kind, loving dog who had cared for her for so long. She turned and ran out of the den.

Through the compound, she aimlessly scampered as fast as her legs would allow her.

Confused at what had happened, Mason ran off to try and find Hamish.

Hamish ran as quickly as he could to Artemis's den.

"She did what? Why the hell did she do it?" asked Hamish.

"Fear. I'm scared Hamish, I know that we have lost her. You know as well as I do that there is no going back for the little one. Sykes has destroyed her," replied Artemis.

She bore no malice towards the little dog she had taken care of. She knew full well that Sykes's vile actions had both physical and mental effects upon her. The physical trauma would hopefully sort itself out in due course. The mental? That would probably haunt her and stay with her for the rest of her life.

"I'll go and try to find her."

"Be careful Hamish. She may well attack you."

"I don't think so. Anyway, if she should try, I am afraid that I will have to give her a swift, sharp lesson in respect. But I promise that I will not hurt her."

Hamish entered the den and sniffed the tatty, soiled blanket that Belle slept on, trying to pick up on her scent. Once he had gathered all the information he required, he went back outside and pointed his snout nose skywards. Using the millions of olfactory receptors within his nose, he air scented, trying to ascertain the direction that Belle had fled in.

Like all canines, Hamish's brain had a section devoted to analysing smells, many dozens of times greater than humans.

He sniffed and snorted, then put his snout nose back to the ground.

It didn't take long for him to pick up on her, she had only left a few minutes earlier. Hamish headed off, face down sniffing the muddy ground in the direction that Belle had run off in.

His olfactory receptors were allowing him to ignore the other distinct vile aromas of the compound. All the while he exhaled through the slits on the sides of his nose. This breathing process allowed him to continually take in Belle's unique scent while expelling the old ones of no use to him. He knew that he had to find Belle as soon as possible before she potentially got herself into a lot of trouble.

In the distance, he could hear a brawl. It didn't sound like a full-blown fight to the death, but it was a scuffle nevertheless. Hamish knew that it involved Belle, he heard her yelp a few times.

He followed the sounds and arrived at the scene of the brawl. Belle had somehow managed to pin a young Rottweiler to the floor by his throat. She was snarling and shaking her head from side to side, her teeth firmly embedded in her foe's neck.

Hamish charged over, lowered his head, and bulldozed into Belle. The force of Hamish bowling into her caused her to lose her grip. Belle was knocked off balance and rolled across the ground. The small Rottweiler yelped as Belle's canine teeth tore his flesh from the force of Hamish's barge. He was in a state of shock, he rolled over, leapt up onto his paws, shook his head and ran. Belle was panting, she glared angrily at Hamish, strands of black and tan fur hung from her mouth.

"What the hell are you playing at, young lady?"

"What do you care?"

"I don't. But I tell you this, I'm not going to stand by and allow you to attack every poor sodding inmate in this place we have to call home."

However, Hamish did care, he was more worried that

Belle would pick on the wrong dog and get herself badly injured, rather than the superficial flesh wounds that she would inflict. Belle was not a natural-born fighter, she was merely releasing her pent-up anger.

"Do you know what, old man? I enjoyed hurting that dog. I could see the fear in his eyes, and you know what? I felt powerful, it made me feel good. He feared me, just as I feared Sykes. And where were you when I needed you? You weren't there to protect me, were you? So, leave me alone, from now on I will fight my own battles. Do I make myself clear?"

Belle laughed as she turned to walk away.

Hamish glared at her.

"You stand fast. Old man? You dare call me old man? I could tear you to pieces in the blink of an eye. I'm warning you, be very careful young lady, and just you remember who took care of you."

"You took care of me? Ha, what a joke, you never once took care of me."

The two dogs stood glaring at each other, neither wanting to make the first aggressive move nor back down.

After what seemed an eternity, Belle relented. She turned her back on Hamish and walked away, not once looking back.

Sykes's disgusting attack had changed Belle. It had made her stronger, but sadly it had also blackened her heart.

She had made her mind up to follow in her mother's paw steps and be a lone wolf, never to be a lowly member of a pack. From this day forward, Belle wouldn't rely on another dog to protect her or fight her battles for her ever again. Or so she naively thought.

It didn't take Belle long to find a home of her own. Some old corrugated galvanised steel roof sheets had been propped up against a couple of oil-soaked railway sleepers. She sniffed around, luckily the den appeared to be vacant. She wiggled in, scraped the top layer of dusty soil away and laid down.

The distinct smell of the oak sleepers instantly brought happy memories of the hut she had grown up in close to the railway tracks flooding back to her.

Belle smiled.

"At last, my very own home sweet home."

CHAPTER SEVENTEEN

Mid-December and the seasonal, bitterly cold weather had arrived with a vengeance.

Belle had been living in her own shelter for seven weeks. To protect herself from the elements she needed to try and find some rags, just like her mother had done, to keep herself warm. She knew only too well how unforgiving and harsh the weather conditions could become.

Belle set off on her search. She hadn't been looking for long when she came across what she thought was a pile of rags lying on the floor. Excited at the prospect of some luxury in her den, she bounded over to investigate.

As she got closer, she shuddered. The rags turned out to be the body of a dog.

Its eyes were wide open, lifelessly staring towards the sky.

Tentatively Belle moved in closer, all the while sniffing the air.

She lowered her head and gently nudged the dog. It didn't move. Belle stepped back, again she shuddered. She tilted her head trying to comprehend what had happened. The dog's body was in a strange, contorted position. The grotesque expression on its face, frozen in time, scared Belle.

She had seen death inflicted on dogs in many vile forms, instinctively, she knew that this poor soul lying in front of her had died in agony.

She walked around the corpse. Strangely it seemed familiar, Belle was sure it was one of the dogs who had arrived in the van on that horrific night with her. She looked at where his tail should have been, yes it was him. She had affectionately named him Stumpy, due to his not having a tail, the result of it being ruthlessly hacked off when he was captured.

She closed her eyes and moved closer to her little friend.

"Poor Stumpy," she thought to herself.

She recoiled, her nose had accidentally touched Stumpy's side. The poor lifeless hound's body was frozen solid.

The previous evening Stumpy had inadvertently wandered too close to the Portakabin offices and as a result had succumbed to a drenching of freezing cold water.

Carter, just before he had left to go home for the evening, had been washing away the day's blood and grime from the area closest to the reception block.

He spotted the dog searching desperately for food. For the sheer, sadistic fun of it, he directed the high-powered hose he was using at the dog.

The powerful deluge of icy cold water bowled Stumpy over.

Laughing to himself, Carter continued directing the water at the dog. A sloshing sound filled the air as Stumpy took the full power of the torrent of water, a huge puddle of freezing Adam's ale and mud accumulated. Only in that compound could an implement originally designed in 1673 as an aid to fight fires and save lives, be used as a torture device.

In an attempt to save himself, Stumpy rolled over, got up and tried to run out of reach of the water. When he thought he was far enough away, he vigorously shook his body from his head to tail as hard as he could, to displace as much of the cold water as possible.

But to no avail, the sheer force of the water, and the few seconds that he had lain in the resulting puddle, had enabled the water to penetrate through his three layers of fur and had soaked his skin.

The evening's temperature rapidly dropped to well below zero, and the water soon started to turn to ice on Stumpy's body. It didn't take long for his fur to clump together into a frozen matted mess.

His natural bodily defences caused his blood capillaries to constrict, which in turn increased the blood flow to his vital organs. He started to shiver as his body tried to generate additional heat by rapidly contracting his muscles.

He became delirious, his mind played tricks with him as he began to hallucinate.

For Stumpy, death and his journey over the Rainbow Bridge was imminent.

There was nothing more that he or his body could do to save his life.

Within a matter of minutes, he was unable to control his bladder, urine flowed uncontrollably from him, adding to the freezing cold water gathered in the puddle he had fallen into.

Stumpy became unable to move. He lay, slowly freezing to death.

Like all the dogs within the compound, his body was skin and bone. The lack of body fat had enabled the cold to penetrate deeply into his muscles, very quickly.

Hypothermia set in. His heart and respiratory rate slowed down, as his core body temperature dropped.

One by one, his vital organs failed.

Stumpy fell peacefully into his eternal sleep.

There was nothing that Belle could do for him, but more annoyingly for her, she still had not been able to find any rags to take back to her den. She huffed to herself, turned and returned to her lair.

Belle's body had changed rapidly since she had been violently assaulted by Sykes. Walking was even more difficult than normal, as she had piled on a few extra kilogrammes. She had been putting the sporadic strange feelings of bubbles and movements in her abdomen down to hunger, just like her mother had done.

Christmas Day.

It was exactly a year ago since Belle and her siblings had gorged on the glorious turkey that their mother had stolen for them. Sadly, there would be no family feast today.

Due to the seasonal festivities, no staff would be attending the compound today, why would they? They had their families to spend the joyous day with, and none of them would sacrifice that for the benefit of the vermin stray dogs.

The ground was frozen solid, and the buckets of stagnant green drinking water scattered around the compound were all iced over. If the freezing cold didn't eradicate a few dogs, dehydration certainly would.

Belle decided not to head off too far in the bitingly cold wind. A quick wee, then back to her snuggly shelter.

She licked at the condensation that had formed on the metal roof. It didn't quench her thirst but it at least moistened her mouth a little.

Unbeknown to her, as she lay on the dirty old woollen jumper she had found next to the fencing at the Portakabins, today she was to become a mother.

Midday, and the bright winter's sun had taken its rightful place, centre stage high up in the sky.

"Right, I think it's time for a stroll," she thought to herself as she ventured out of her den.

The ground still had a light covering of ice. Belle closed her eyes and pointed her face skywards. The apricity stroked her face and washed over her body. For a few moments, Belle stood dazed under the glorious winter sky.

She marvelled at how her breath rose as a neat and pure vapour, floating in misty rhythmic patterns up towards the heavens.

For once the compound seemed eerily quiet. The peaceful silence was only broken by a peal of bells ringing in the distance from one of the local churches, and the involuntary gurgling sounds coming from her belly.

She yawned and stretched and pushed her front legs as far out in front of her as they would go.

A sudden stabbing pain in her abdomen caused her to double up, and then she involuntarily retched. To try and get some relief from the discomfort, she sat down.

The pain disappeared as quickly as it had arrived.

Belle sat still for a few moments, panting heavily, before heading slowly back to the safety of her den.

She had just walked through the door when yet another bout of pain hit her; again she began to pant heavily.

Her body began to shake and again she retched. Although she went through the motions of vomiting, her stomach had no food to expel, only a small dribble of bile trickled down her chin.

She shuffled about, trying to find herself a more comfortable position.

After taking a few deep breaths she lay down. The pain subsided, but strangely, the jumper she was laying on felt damp. She turned her head and sniffed.

"That's odd," she thought to herself, as she watched a straw-coloured liquid seep from her rear end.

The pain returned, even more violently than before.

"Artemis help me!" she howled out as loudly as she could.

Belle was overcome by the urge to push. Over and over, she squeezed her stomach muscles. The searing pain caused her to bite into the sodden jumper.

Gripped tightly in her teeth, she pulled with all her might on one of the threadbare arms.

Belle lay there panting. Only now she wasn't alone. She turned her head and looked at the little sac lying behind her. Carefully she bit through the thin membrane, exposing a bundle of damp fur.

She shuffled her body around a little more to allow her to gently lick her firstborn pup.

After a few seconds, the little pup gasped, before taking its first gulps of air.

Belle bit through the cord attached to its belly, then carefully picked it up by the scruff of its neck and snuggled it into the warmth of her stomach.

She couldn't help but wonder how something so beautiful could have come from within her.

Little did she know that the beautiful little puppy was

the result of the heinous, disgusting attack inflicted upon her by Sykes.

A cool breeze filled Belle's den. The sky began to turn black. Far in the distance, a drum roll of thunder drowned out the bells that were still ringing. A bright flash of lightning followed.

Belle looked out of the door. Debris swirled aimlessly all around the compound, caught up in the wind that was getting stronger by the second.

A storm was on its way.

Today was eerily reminiscent of the day when Belle had been born. Glorious sunshine that soon turned to rain. Belle and her siblings had also been born during a violent tempest, her pup's introduction to the world would be the same.

Black clouds gathered and reared up, like a cobra getting ready to strike. The giant snake let out booming hisses of thunder, and then spat burning bolts of lightning towards the city.

The wind screamed, and a few seconds later, heavy raindrops pelted down on the metal roof like a barrage of stones.

She manoeuvred herself and her pup to a draught-free part of her shelter.

Belle lay there listening to the soft grunts made by her little pup, every now and then she gave it a gentle lick.

She drifted off for the briefest of moments but was awoken when the pain in her abdomen returned.

She shuffled away from her pup.

After going through the same motions, soon a little sac lay motionless behind her.

Belle frantically tore at the membrane and began to

nuzzle at the lifeless pup as vigorously as she could.

Over again she tried to force her pup to take a breath and spring into life.

Belle was panicking, alternating between gently pushing the pup's stomach with her nose, and then firmly licking it.

After what seemed an eternity, Belle had to sadly come to terms with the fact that her efforts were all to no avail.

Tears rolled down her face as she nudged the tiny, lifeless body away from her.

She looked back at her firstborn.

"Sorry my darling, I have failed you," she said quietly to the sleeping pup lying behind her.

Within the hour, Belle gave birth to a second lifeless body. She howled out in anguish.

"Why? Why do you continue to punish me? What the hell have I ever done wrong?"

Tears streamed down her face as she gently pushed the little cold body to lie next to her other still-born pup.

"Keep each other safe, my darlings," she said to them as she lay sobbing.

Suddenly the pain abruptly returned.

Belle's fourth puppy, a boy, was a little fighter. It took her a few nerve-biting moments to get him breathing, but as soon as his body sprung into life there was no stopping him.

The rain was still lashing down, echoes of thunder rumbled high in the sky.

A large puddle had formed outside of Belle's den. She dragged her exhausted body out of the door and began lapping at the cool water.

Having quenched her thirst, Belle went back into her den, shook herself down, and went over to where her pups were lying.

She nuzzled them both, and then gently pulled them in towards the warmth of her stomach.

They both found a teat and began drinking from Belle's body.

The three of them lay there, just as Belle had done as a newborn puppy with her dear late mother.

How could her life have changed so much? How could she now be a mother herself?

Her pups' bodies were nestled closely into hers, moving in rhythm with her breathing. The gentle soothing motion caused them to drift off.

Exhausted, Belle also fell asleep.

Her happy dream of running through a flower-covered meadow with her mother and siblings was abruptly interrupted.

"Well, well. What do we have here then?"

Belle leapt to her paws. Dazed, not yet fully awake, she shook her head to try and focus her eyes.

She stood glaring at the three unwelcome guests standing in the doorway.

Spike, Sykes's second in command, with just one ear and a scar running from his left eye to the tip of his nose, stood at the front. He was a repulsive mixed breed, with a repugnant flatulence problem.

Behind him was Victor the one-eyed Lurcher, and Aldo, an ex-racing Greyhound.

Aldo had found himself abandoned in Bulgaria after a short career as a racing dog in Ireland. His tissue-paper-thin skin bore several deep scars, from when he had gotten too close to one of his competitors leaving the traps or taking the tight bends tearing around the racetracks.

It was like a scene from a horror film. Darkness had fallen, and the rain was still pelting down. A crack of thunder erupted far off in the distance, followed by a streak of forked lightning, that illuminated the grotesque hounds and the bleak grey sky.

The pungent musty smell of their dank fur filled Belle's den, even one of Spike's spontaneous eye-watering farts couldn't defuse the mouldy aroma of sodden fur.

"What do you want?" barked Belle nervously.

"Just being friendly," replied Spike.

"I remember all too well the last time one of you lot were friendly," Belle snapped back.

"No need to pour fuel on the fire, my dear. That is all in the past now. Anyway, our brave leader's honourable memory lives on in the little bundles of joy lying next to you. Well, for now anyway. I'm sure our dear departed Sykes would give his blessing in us rejuvenating our malnourished bodies with the fruits of his labour."

"What do you mean, honourable memory? And why just for now?"

Belle was growing worried.

"I hope Sykes never made it to the bridge. Well, what was left of him after Hamish tore him to pieces," she retorted.

"Ah, Hamish. And where is your fairy godfather now when you need him?"

"Why would I need him? Anyway, I take care of myself, and I'll take care of my puppies."

"Brave words my dear. Very brave. But do you honestly believe the worthless words that you hiss with such venom? Do you honestly think that you, a crippled dog, can back up the bravado that you spout?"

Belle was becoming ever more concerned as to where all this was leading. She moved back and stood guard over her two pups, who were still asleep, oblivious to the events unfolding in front of their innocent bodies.

Spike and his henchmen edged further into Belle's den.

"Get out. Get away from my pups!" she screamed.

Terrified, not knowing what to do, Belle found herself frozen to the spot.

A menacing, unexplainable aura emanated from Spike that grasped her in an ever-tightening grip of subconscious submission.

She shook her head, snapping herself out of the trance she momentarily found herself in.

Belle glared at the dogs looming in front of her, she bared her teeth and started snarling.

It didn't faze them, they laughed as they mockingly growled back.

Belle barked, then snapped at them.

She knew she couldn't beat them and was becoming all the more anxious.

The sudden sounds caused Belle's pups to stir. They made little high-pitched squeals as they restlessly moved.

Spike looked down at the two pups, a wry smile engulfed his face.

Drool dripped from the filthy bedraggled fur that covered his muzzle.

He lunged forwards.

Belle retaliated and leapt towards him. They met mid-air, Belle managed to bite Spike's neck, and he yelped as she tore a lump of flesh off.

They landed, Belle spun around and lunged at Spike, who ran towards her, this time she caught him on his tail.

Although outnumbered, and exhausted, she was prepared to fight to the death to save her newborn puppies.

Adrenalin surged through her body. She was terrified and had to swallow hard, trying to cool the fury she had digested as a fire seed. Her face tightened and her eyes bulged.

She charged again.

Spike and his cronies were hell-bent on a feast of fresh meat, and they weren't going to let Belle stop them.

Spike charged back at Belle. He got the first bite in, and grabbed her by her throat, he spun her over, forced her down, then pinned her to the floor.

Blood from the open wound on his neck dripped onto Belle's face.

Victor ran forwards and grabbed Belle's firstborn pup. The innocent little dog squealed as it was crushed to death.

Victor dropped the corpse on the floor and then turned his attention toward the sole surviving pup.

Just as his teeth were about to sink into its flesh, Belle broke free from Spike's hold. She leapt up and attacked Victor, sinking her teeth into his face.

Spike snuck away from the fight between Belle and Victor and grabbed the little pup. With it hanging from his mouth he ran out of the den. Its soft sinewy bones easily succumbed to his powerful jaws.

Aldo, who up until now had kept well out of harm's way, grabbed one of the still-born bodies.

"Leave my babies alone!" screamed Belle.

She broke away from Victor and leapt on top of Aldo. She was in a frenzy; in one swift move she bit one of his ears off.

Victor joined in the brawl, focusing his one good eye on his target, then grabbed one of Belle's front legs.

She screamed in pain.

The den was covered in blood and fur. The frantic snarls and yelps from the fight echoed under the tin roof.

Spike, who had devoured the pup he had taken outside, re-emerged, waiting for the right moment when he could pounce.

As luck would have it, Hamish was on his way to make his secret daily visit to Belle's den. Every day he kept a watchful, ever paternal eye over her. He always kept his distance, staying downwind so she wouldn't pick up on his scent and know that he was there. After their argument, he couldn't lose face and admit just how much he cared about her.

Hearing the ferocious onslaught, he darted as fast as his ageing body would allow, through the thunder and lightning, towards Belle's shelter. His paws slipped as they pounded through the muddy puddles.

He charged straight in, hitting Aldo in his ribcage with his sledgehammer head. Aldo bowled over, yelped and tried to leap back up onto his paws.

Hamish had shattered three of Aldo's ribs. The powerful blow had also winded him. Aldo gasped for air and limped out of the way to catch his breath.

Hamish ran out of the den to try and entice the dogs out and move the fight away from Belle.

Spike, with blood and fur hanging from his chin, charged out after him.

Hamish, still running, turned, but slipped, falling over

into a puddle. His heavy body hit the ground with a splash. Spike had caught up with him and lunged, managing to grab one of his hind legs.

Hamish winced, he tried to roll over to attack Spike.

He wasn't an agile young dog anymore. He was riddled with arthritis, making matters even worse. Spike had managed to get a firm grip. His teeth were deeply embedded in Hamish's leg.

Spike shook his head from side to side, trying to snap Hamish's hock.

Victor piled out of the den and ran over to the fight.

Hamish was still on his back when Victor reached them. He grabbed Hamish by the throat and pushed the back of his head downwards into the muddy puddle.

Aldo, who had now got his breath back, ran over to join in, tearing ferociously at Hamish's stomach.

Although exhausted after giving birth, Belle ran over to help her beloved Hamish. She couldn't see properly, her eyes burnt through the salty tears she had shed over the demise of her beautiful puppies.

She grabbed Victor by one of his hind legs. He yelped, then kicked out, causing Belle to lose her grip.

Victor let go of Hamish, spun around and faced Belle head on.

She pounced forwards, grabbing one of Victor's ears. With her teeth piercing the fur-covered cartilage, she yanked her head back. Victor howled out in pain as most of his right ear was torn off. With the blood-covered gristle in her mouth, Belle lunged again.

Victor ran off, turned and then at full pelt shoulder-barged Belle, sending her flying backwards. Her head smashed onto a rock as she hit the ground.

With Belle out of the way, he turned his attention back towards Hamish, who had managed to break free and was now up on all fours, scrapping with Aldo and Spike.

A melee of snarls, barks and yelps echoed around the compound as the ferocious fight ensued.

Hell-bent on destroying each other, flesh, blood and fur was torn off as the dogs ripped each other apart.

As quickly as it had started, the fight finished.

A deathly silence replaced the gruesome racket of battle, broken only by the soothing sound of rain hitting puddles, and the pitiful whimpers and desperate gasps for breath.

Spike, foaming at the mouth, with bloodied sinews of flesh hanging from his teeth, looked up at the moon. The rain pelted down on his face as he let out a loud piercing howl.

Aldo and Victor joined in.

"Owooooo, Owooooo!"

Over and over, their rousing, victory chorus echoed around the compound for all to hear.

Steam rose from Hamish's once powerful body. He now lay ripped to pieces, and gasped desperately for air, as blood pulsed from his gaping wounds.

He yelped as he tried to lift his bloodied head off the gore-saturated mud that he lay on to look for Belle.

She had been knocked unconscious when she hit her head and had missed the final gruesome, bloody throes of the fight.

Belle staggered to her paws and slowly limped towards Hamish, her cumbersome front legs slopped heavily through the blood-soaked puddles.

She looked down at her Hamish, the loving old dog who

had protected her. The loving old dog she had disowned in her fit of anger.

There was nothing she could do for him.

"I'm so sorry," she sobbed, as she lowered her head and started licking his wounds. The steady flow of blood that seeped from the lacerations found itself turned a muted red by the pounding rain that beat down on his body.

Hamish winced as her tongue gently lapped at the blood streaming from a gash on his side.

He looked up at her and took a deep breath.

"Belle, please believe me, I have spent my life in this hell struggling, just as you have. The care I gave you was because I loved you, not because I wanted to help you. Take care of yourself, my beautiful little one. Until we meet again."

His words trailed off, he gasped and then Hamish stopped breathing.

Belle wailed out in despair.

Spike, Aldo and Victor had sat watching as Hamish took his last breath.

"Now that he's finally dead, I'm the alpha male of the compound. Do you understand me, cripple?" grunted Spike.

The three of them let out one final howl and then strutted off.

Belle sat silently next to the body of Hamish.

The rain had stopped, and by now the temperature had dropped rapidly. Belle had sat silently with Hamish for what seemed like an eternity.

A soft white snowflake fluttered down and landed on Belle's nose. Memories of that happy day, exactly one year ago, when her dear ma had encouraged her to play with Tess, Duque and Sam came flooding back.

In the span of just a few hours, she had become a mother, witnessed her pups massacred, and her dear patriarch Hamish slaughtered right in front of her. Just how much crueller could life get?

Slowly the snow began to fall heavier.

Belle knew that there was nothing more that she could do for Hamish, and that she had to take shelter, or potentially face the same fate as Stumpy. She dragged her saturated body back to her bleak den and stumbled through the doorway. Belle stopped, closed her eyes and inhaled. Initially, all she could smell was the vile salty, metallic scent of blood. She breathed in deeper, and slowly she picked up on the beautiful aroma of her demised pups.

She dropped to the ground and began to sob.

"Maybe I should just go and lie outside and let the cold night air kill me. At least then I will cross the bridge and be reunited with all those I have loved and lost."

Suddenly, a kindly voice disturbed Belle's anguish.

"Belle, are you alright dear?"

Belle lifted her head.

Artemis was standing next to her.

"They killed my puppies and Hamish."

Belle struggled to splutter the words out.

"I know poppet. I am so sorry. Come home with me darling, we all miss you so much."

"What about Hamish? We can't leave him lying there all alone like that."

"Belle, we all loved him so much, but there is nothing that we can do for him now."

"I'm not coming back with you and leaving him there in that state."

"OK dear, wait here and I'll go and get Charlie and Mason."

Artemis scurried out of Belle's den and scampered through the snow to find the other two pups.

Belle got up and walked out into the dark cold night air. The snow was now falling heavier.

She headed back to where Hamish's body lay. He looked so peaceful tucked up in one of nature's soft white blankets. How ironic, snow is generally considered a good omen, symbolising peace, purity and rebirth, yet here it was, covering Hamish's body that had been brutally slaughtered.

She sat staring, reminiscing about the lovely walks they had shared together, the lessons about life he had taught her, reminiscing about just being with him, her beautiful Hamish.

Her happy thoughts were disturbed by the sound of Artemis returning with Mason and Charlie. Their paws slipped on the fresh layer of snow and slopped through the muddy puddles as they scuttled towards her.

Charlie and Mason could do no more than stare at Hamish. Tears streamed down Charlie's cheeks, falling to the ground, melting two little pools of snow.

He turned away; he didn't want anyone to see him sob. He tried squeezing his eyes shut as tightly shut as he could, hoping to stop the tears from flowing.

"Artemis, what can we do for him?" asked Belle.

Artemis couldn't answer.

Mason spoke up, his voice quivering.

"There is nothing we can do. But we must try and bury his body."

The four of them stood silently in the moonlight. Their cold breaths combined and formed into a soft baby cloud.

None of them wanted to be the first to make a move.

Mason looked over at the other three, took a deep breath, and then stepped forwards. He got as close to Hamish's body as he dared, turned to face away from the carcass, looked back over his shoulder, and then he began kicking at the snow-covered, sodden earth with his hind paws.

Belle thought back to that happy day when her siblings had done the same thing to her, covering her with snow, and the fun she had doing it back to them.

For the first time in hours, she smiled, only briefly, but a smile nonetheless.

At first splashes of dirty water, mixed with snow, splattered over Hamish's back. As Mason's paws dug deeper into the soil, lumps of clay started hitting the body of his demised friend. Artemis looked over at Charlie, she didn't need to say anything. He moved over next to Mason and joined in.

"We'll do this side, Belle," Artemis said.

They moved towards Hamish's belly, then started digging at the mud. The clammy soil stuck between their claws.

"Be careful of his face," uttered Belle. "I want him to look his best for his journey over the Rainbow Bridge."

Clumps of sodden mud slowly started sticking together on Hamish's body, displacing the snow. Slowly his bloodied tan fur began to disappear under a blanket of sludge.

"How he starts his journey is of no consequence," panted Artemis. "When he arrives, his body will be restored to the handsome, healthy young beast that he once was."

After what seemed an eternity, Hamish's body was concealed under a ceremonial mound of dirt.

"It's the best that we can do for him," wheezed Charlie.

"We have done him proud. For the next few days, we will take it in turns to guard him. We don't want any of them vile rat things attacking him," replied Mason.

Artemis looked over.

"There is no need. Hamish has already left this hell that he once called home. As we stand here mourning him, he is already bounding through the clouds on his way to the bridge. When he arrives, he will rest for a short while, preparing himself for the final part of his journey. The carcass that lies here in front of us is no longer our dear Hamish, it's flesh and bone. Let the rats have them, it's all a part of nature's ongoing circle of life. Hamish will live on forever in our hearts and souls. One day we will all be reunited."

The four of them stared at the pile of earth. Already it had started to turn a ghostly white under a fresh veil of freshly fallen snow.

"Whisper your goodbyes, then we must head back to our home. Remember, seven days from now to look out for his sign. He will let us know that he has arrived, and is at last at peace," said Artemis.

"How will he let us know?" asked Belle.

Artemis looked over at her.

"He will drop a single white feather."

"Did my mother let me know?"

"Yes, my dear, she would have sent you the sign."

"I didn't see it. Why didn't you or Hamish tell me to look out for it? At least I would have gained some comfort knowing she was there."

"Belle my dear, I'm sorry, I should have told you what to look out for. You didn't know about it, so you weren't looking. You have had the worst day of your life, I know that you are angry, but please, come home and sleep. I promise you my darling, you will feel better in the morning."

Belle turned, and slowly she started to walk back to her old home, the home Hamish had taken her to all those months ago. Artemis smiled, then nodded at Charlie and Mason.

"She's coming home with us, where she belongs."

Belle couldn't sleep. She tossed and turned, her mind recollecting every horrendous, graphic detail of what had happened that day.

Something that Spike had said bothered her, she needed to know the truth.

"Artemis, are you awake?"

"Yes dear. Are you OK?"

"What did that disgusting Spike mean when he said 'Honourable memory lives on in the little bundles of joy lying next to you'?"

Artemis sighed, this was the very question that she had prayed Belle would never ask her.

"Belle, please put what has happened behind you. There are things that you are too young to understand."

"What do you mean, too young to understand? I have been through more horrors in one year than most dogs will experience in a lifetime. Now you tell me, what did he mean?"

Artemis knew that Belle wasn't going to give up.

"On that awful day when Sykes attacked you, he …"

She shook her head.

"Sorry, I can't carry on."

"He what? Go on tell me."

"Belle please, I'm begging you, not tonight."

Belle could hear in Artemis's voice how her questions

were upsetting her.

"You will tell me one day, won't you?"

"Yes dear, I promise."

Belle rolled over. Eventually, through both the mental and physical traumas of the day, and after what seemed an eternity, she dropped off.

The horrific nightmare she was enduring was suddenly interrupted by a beautiful dream.

There was Hamish, floating on a soft white cloud looking down at her, then his voice echoed as he spoke to her.

"Instead of being ashamed of what you have been through Belle, be proud of what you have overcome my darling."

Belle sat bolt upright and called out his name. She closed her eyes and sighed, then the vile atrocities of the previous day came flooding back to her.

She was startled by the distinct cock-a-doodle-do from the cockerel that lived in the adjoining smallholding.

"Oh well, time to get up then."

She shook her head, and huffed as she rose to her paws, stretched and yawned.

More recollections of the previous day came back to her.

Tears welled up in her eyes as she thought of her newborn puppies. Her teats hung low and felt painful, full of the life-giving milk that her beloved pups never got the chance to sup from her body.

Artemis had lied, Belle did not feel one little bit better, in fact, she felt a whole damn worse.

Her thoughts turned to Hamish, her dear beloved patriarch who had guided and protected her when she was first incarcerated within this hell on earth.

Belle was met by a muddy quagmire as she walked out of Artemis's den. The snow had stopped falling in the early hours and had already melted into an icy, muddy sludge, adding to the puddles from the deluge of rain the previous day.

Winter comes from an old Germanic word that means 'time of water', today it certainly lived up to its name.

Strangely, although a picturesquely beautiful season, a winter's morning can look so gloomy, the light somehow plays games, making everything look hazy.

She headed over to where they had buried Hamish's body.

As she approached, she could hear human voices.

Although it was Boxing Day, Oz had been told by his manager to make a brief visit to the compound, along with one of the other workers, a surly little character called Butler. The two men were looking at the mound of earth that had mysteriously appeared.

Belle glared at Oz.

Her nostrils flared and her eyes hardened into narrow slits as she watched his exhaled breath turn into vapour as it hit the biting cold air.

"Every vile breath you take is a breath you took from my mother," she thought to herself.

Her rage grew.

"You are going to pay for all you inflicted upon my mother. Whatever happens to me happens. Maybe I will be reunited with all those cruelly taken from me sooner than I expected."

She charged forwards, hurtling as fast as she could through the puddles.

Although in pain, her little legs sped towards the vile human that she had waited so long to kill.

Revenge would be hers.

Her pent-up anger made her want to scream and bark, yet she remained silent.

Words Hamish had once spoken to her echoed through her mind – 'The axe forgets, but the tree remembers.'

She reached her target, and her teeth sank into Oz's calf. He squealed out in agony.

Belle ripped her head backwards, but lost her grip, so just as she had watched her mother do, she lunged forwards again.

Oz, in a state of shock, turned around to see what had attacked him. As he did, his right kneecap ended up in Belle's mouth.

He slipped backwards, landing with an almighty splash in a puddle.

"Get this stinking thing off me," he screamed at Butler, all the while, the little dog continued tearing ferociously at his flesh.

Butler, himself now in a state of panic, frantically looked around for any form of makeshift weapon.

Belle let go of Oz's knee, looked him in the eyes then thrust her face towards his head.

Her teeth met with the soft flesh covering his cheekbone. She yanked her head back, tearing a strip of clammy flesh from his face.

Belle felt revenge was now within her reach as her mouth filled with the salty metallic taste of Oz's blood.

Oz screamed. He lashed out, aimlessly hitting his assailant anywhere he could. Blows rained down on Belle's torso, but she kept on tearing away at him.

Butler had managed to find a short length of hosepipe. He ran over and started whipping the frenzied dog attacking Oz.

Belle was out of control. The fists that pummelled into her body hurt, and the continual whipping from the rubber hose stung, but nothing was going to stop her.

Butler raised his arm to take a swipe. He brought the rubber hose down with all his might but was caught off balance and slipped over.

The length of hose flew out of his hand as he hit the ground, landing just out of his arm's reach.

Belle turned her intentions towards him. Butler started randomly kicking out, hoping to fend off the dog now intent on ripping him to shreds.

Half buried in a puddle close to where he had landed was a lump of timber. Butler grabbed at it with one of his hands but couldn't get a firm grip.

"Come on you useless piece of crap!" he shouted as he readjusted his grip and pulled at it again.

Luckily for Butler, the wood moved. It squelched as it begrudgingly slid out of the mud.

Belle had by now grabbed his left boot with her teeth. Butler took an almighty swing, and brought the lump of wood down, hitting Belle's head with a thump.

Dazed, Belle fell to the ground.

Butler scrambled up as fast as he could, ran over to Oz, slid his hands under his armpits then dragged him out of harm's way.

With blood dripping from his face, arms and legs, Oz grabbed at Butler's clothes and pulled himself up onto his feet.

He threw his left arm across Butler's shoulder.

"Get me the hell out of here."

Belle stumbled back up onto her paws. She looked around, although her vision was blurred, she could just make out the two figures she had attacked, hobbling to safety through the security gate.

"I've waited for you for almost a year. Another day, week, month or year won't make any difference. I vow that I will kill you. I've proven that I can hurt you, you stinking vile two-legged things. Revenge will be mine."

Butler helped Oz into the Portakabin office.

He wiped his muddy hands down the front of his jeans and went over to the cabinet where their stash of girly mags, cigarettes and bottles of cheap local vodka and raki were stored. He found the tatty old shoebox that doubled up as their first aid kit.

"Hopefully there's some stuff in here I can use to patch you up," Butler mumbled as he rummaged through the random selection of emergency medical kit.

"Right, we've got a few dried-up plasters, safety pins, some out-of-date eye wash, a rusty pair of scissors, a syringe thingy which I don't know what it's for, and a couple of bandages, which both looked as if they have been used before."

"Shut your bleeding mouth and get a sodding move on will you Butler? I'm in bloody agony. Sling me that bottle of vodka."

Oz swigged at the bottle of vodka, as Butler improvised with a bit of first aid.

He cleaned the cuts with the eyewash, he did contemplate

using vodka but decided that it would be a waste of good alcohol. He used some superglue he found in the stationery drawer to stick a couple of the dried-out plasters onto Oz's face, having decided not to try and hold the cut together with safety pins.

"I'm not touching your legs, Oz. You'll have to wrap the bandages around them yourself."

Butler soon had Oz patched up as best he could, with a mass of bandages and a couple of glued-on plasters strewn across his face and legs.

"I'll get that damned hound tomorrow, mark my words. But right now I need a drink, you coming with me Florence Nightingale?"

"No thanks mate, under strict orders to get home. Got the bleeding outlaws round for nibbles and drinks."

Oz locked the compound, hobbled to his car, then drove to his favourite local bar. Boxing Day getting drunk with his pals would be the best that this Christmas could get for this lonely pariah.

"Three, no four of them attacked me. The biggest, most ferocious dogs I have ever seen in my life. Like bleeding wolves, they were. Killed every single one of them with my bare hands I did."

As the night progressed, and the drink flowed freely, Oz's tale got more dramatic every time he told it. The number of dogs, or wolves as he now referred to them, in the pack that attacked him multiplied, and his methods of disposing of them with his bare hands got ever more heroic and gruesome.

A few of his fellow hooch hounds hung adoringly onto his every word, none of them brave enough to question his ever-exaggerated tale.

After a late-night punch-up, Oz staggered back to his car and somehow drove home.

He awoke early the next morning. His mouth felt as dry as the Sahara Desert, and a thumping headache pounded away with no mercy.

Daylight mockingly thrust itself through the torn curtains.

"Bloody hell this is the granddaddy of all hangovers," he mumbled to himself whilst massaging his temples.

He sat up, rubbed his eyes, and scratched his chin, taking off a layer of freshly formed scabs. He reached over and groped about on the small bedside table, where he found his packet of cigarettes and lighter. Oz took out a fag, lit it, took a huge drag, and then coughed. Sitting on the table was also an opened bottle of now flat Zagorka beer.

He picked it up and took a sip, blinked a few times, and then took another drag on his cigarette.

The plasters covering the bite wounds on his face were still miraculously glued to his cheekbone. The bandages had ended up wrapped around his ankles.

His vision was still blurred. He rubbed his eyes with the palms of his hands and slowly they came into focus.

He looked to his side and shuddered.

Laying there sprawled out on the bed next to him, snoring away like a congested rhino, was an elderly, rather large lady. Her make-up was smeared all over her face, and her purple-dyed hair, which was showing its grey roots, hung in ruffled greasy clumps.

To add to the image of beauty, her top set of dentures lay on the pillow next to her, and a dried dribble stain lay tangled in the wispy facial hair on her chin.

"Definitely had me beer goggles on last night."

Oz shook his head in disgust, dropped his fag end in the beer bottle, and then carefully climbed off his bed.

Just as he did, the lady let out an almighty trump.

"Bloody hell, I seriously need to give up the booze," he thought to himself as he grabbed his fags, picked up his clothes that were strewn across the floor, then crept out of the bedroom, not wanting to awaken the sleeping beauty in his bed. He got dressed on the landing, avoiding the squeaky floorboards, before heading downstairs.

He picked up his car keys and then headed out to the brick shed in the backyard.

Although he was hell-bent on revenge, he wouldn't admit to anyone that he was also fearful of the little dog that had attacked him.

In his shed, laying on a battered wheelbarrow was a canvas holdall. Oz unzipped it and pulled out his rusty old Baikal 12-gauge, side-by-side, double-barrelled shotgun. He reached up onto the top shelf and grabbed a dented Gama biscuit tin. He opened it and stuffed a handful of No. 5 shot cartridges into his jacket pocket.

As he walked to his car, he lit another cigarette.

It only took him twenty minutes to reach the compound. It was still the Christmas holidays and the roads were nice and quiet.

"I'm gonna blow that stinking bloody hound's head off!" he yelled as he stomped into the compound.

Butler came running out of the Portakabin.

"For crying out loud Oz, not again. Just leave it will you? We gave her a bloody good beating yesterday."

"Shut your mouth wimp, or I'll blow your sodding head

off as well."

Butler stepped back, Oz's breath reeked of stale beer.

Due to the vast quantity of alcohol he had consumed the night before, his hands shook as he struggled to load two live cartridges into his antiquated gun.

"Out of my way, tosser!" he shouted at Butler as he marched towards the main compound gate. The gun's break-action was hinged open, the weapon was loaded and hung over his left forearm.

Oz closed the gate behind him, but to be on the safe side, just in case he needed to make a quick escape, didn't lock the padlock.

He snapped the barrels shut, and then let off a warning shot into the air. Dogs, frightened by the sudden loud bang, scarpered for cover in all directions.

Oz strutted through the compound, all the while his eyes darted from side to side looking for the distinct little dog that had attacked him.

He kicked over pallets, his gun poised and ready to shoot.

"Don't feed these vermin or give them any water until I have killed that bitch!" he shouted as he knocked every rusty bucket of stagnant water over. He had lost the plot and hoped that the dogs in the compound would understand his words and reveal Belle's hiding place to him.

"I'll bloody well flush it out, one way or another."

A crow took flight from behind a shed, startling Oz. He fired off the second barrel and a mass of black feathers filled the air.

He broke open the barrel and loaded two new cartridges. Hearing the loud bang from the shotgun, Belle left

Artemis's den and headed toward the source of the noise.

In the distance, she could see Oz.

She watched as he raised the gun to his shoulder.

Crack, Crack!

The two loud bangs were followed by the sound of a dog yelping in agony.

"Sod it, wrong bloody dog!" shouted Oz.

Twenty yards from where he stood a dog writhed on the ground, its hindquarters peppered with lead shot.

Oz loaded two more cartridges, walked over to the dog, pulled the first trigger and then blasted it at point-blank range in the head.

Belle moved in closer. She could smell Oz, his normal repulsive bodily odour was today combined with the stench of stagnant beer that hung on his breath.

Her movement caught his eye, he raised his gun and fired. Shards and splinters of wood from the pallet shelter Belle was hiding next to flew into the air like wedding confetti.

Belle knew nothing of the loud object that Oz was holding. She didn't know that he had spent the two cartridges in the chamber and that the gun was empty. She didn't care, all that she knew was that she wanted to kill him.

As she had done yesterday, she hurtled towards him like a whirlwind, barking as loudly as she could. Oz raised his gun, aimed it at Belle and pulled the first trigger. Click, then nothing. He panicked, quickly squeezing his finger on the second barrel's trigger. Again, there was a click, yet still, the gun didn't fire.

"Sod it."

He panicked, the little dog that hurt him yesterday was getting closer.

He lowered the gun and broke the barrel open. His hands shook, fear had now combined with the alcohol. He rummaged through his pocket for two live cartridges, all the while watching the dog.

He pulled out two cartridges but was too late. Belle was already on him.

She soon got another taste of his putrid flesh as her teeth sank back into his scrawny leg, reopening the wounds she had already inflicted.

Oz screamed. With one mighty blow he brought the wooden stock of the gun down on Belle's head.

He quickly slid the gun down through his hands, grabbed the barrels, raised his hands, and took a side swipe, hitting Belle on the side of her face with the butt of the rifle.

Belle shook her head, then thrust herself towards the vile human in front of her.

"Bloody hell, this thing is bloody indestructible," Oz thought to himself.

Panicking, he thrashed about with the rifle. His grubby hands were clammy, the weapon slipped from his grasp and flew off into the distance.

"Butler, Butler, get your fat arse over here now!" yelled Oz.

Butler had remained in the Portakabin office. He knew Oz was on a mission with his shotgun to kill the little dog that had bitten him and knew that it would be far safer for him to stay well out of harm's way.

Hearing Oz's screams, Butler grabbed a rope and ran out of the office.

In the distance, he could see the little dog, who was by now tugging at Oz's green combat trousers.

"Flipping hell, here we go again," he thought as he ran towards the fight.

Belle was tearing at Oz, who in turn was trying to pull his leg away.

Oz fell to the ground.

"Get off of me you stinking hound."

Undeterred, Belle carried on biting at his legs.

Butler reached the scrap.

Belle caught a glimpse of him out of the corner of her eye, yet she ignored the threat. She was adamant this was going to be her final revenge, and that she wasn't going to let the man who had killed her mother get away this time.

"Throw that bloody rope around its neck and pull it off of me!" shrieked Oz.

Butler moved in as close as he dared.

"Sod this."

Butler backed away from the scrap.

"Stuff you, bloody well do it now!" Oz screamed.

"You and your bloody vendettas," hollered Butler as he moved forwards, attempting to try and slide the noose around Belle's neck.

Her grip on Oz's leg prevented the rope from reaching her throat.

Butler pulled the rope as hard as he could. It had caught just under Belle's nostrils and was lodged on her top gum, just above her sharp canine teeth.

The manila hemp twine cut into her gingiva.

Her eyes watered as Butler applied more pressure. With her head pulled backwards, she was forced to let go.

Oz clambered across the muddy ground on all fours, grabbed the noose and then pulled it over Belle's head.

"Pull the bloody rope as hard as you can. Strangle that bloody thing to death," bellowed Oz, as he scrambled to his feet and started kicking Belle.

She tried to pull away, but just as with the night she was captured, the rope was garrotting her.

While Oz carried on kicking, Butler dragged Belle towards the brick-built block that housed the last of the ex-fighting dogs. As her body was pulled through the puddles, sharp stones that were embedded in the mud cut into her flesh.

Belle tried to bark, in the hope of attracting attention. Just maybe, with a bit of luck, she would get some help from some of the other dogs wanting their own piece of revenge. It was to no avail, her barks came out as stifled, spluttered grunts.

They reached the kennel block.

"Oi, cop this!" yelled Butler as he threw the rope to Oz.

Butler yanked open the wooden door. As he entered the dank building he walked into a cobweb. He let out a high-pitched squeal, before quickly wiping the silk thread from his face. Cratchit had been winding him up for weeks about tales of poisonous false widow spiders that had been found in the area.

Oz, with Belle literally in tow, was right behind him.

"Open that bloody cage. I'll throw her in with that dog and let him tear her to pieces!" he shouted as he limped into the darkened building.

Belle was trying to fight him off, although she was exhausted and on the verge of unconsciousness.

Butler ran over and hauled at the door of one of the unoccupied cages. The door creaked, its rusted hinges fighting back at Butler's feeble attempts.

"Not that one you idiot. The cage next to it."

"Shut up and get her in here. I'm not risking opening the devil dog's cage."

When he had managed to pull the door open a fraction, he shoulder-barged it, giving Oz enough room to get the dog in.

The dog locked in the adjacent cage became animated at the thought of getting a cellmate. It ferociously lunged at the bars.

Butler kicked the bars.

"Back off and shut up."

The dog took no notice, snarled and pounced again.

Oz squeezed through the small opening, pulling Belle in behind him. He grasped the rope with both hands, and with all his might, spun her around, across the sodden straw. Belle slammed into the brick wall at the rear of the cell.

Not wanting to hang around and get into another scrap, Oz dropped the rope and hobbled to the door.

The crazed dog in the next cage went berserk. It spun around and around in circles, barking as loudly as it could. Oz picked up a can of stagnant water and chucked it over the dog.

"I need to get out of here. Lock that sodding cage, and never bloody well open it again. That beast can bleeding well rot to death."

Butler kicked the door; it creaked as it begrudgingly slammed back into its metal framework.

Hanging from one of the horizontal strengthening bars was a rusty, unlocked padlock. Butler unhooked it and slid the shackle through the retaining clasp. He squeezed the padlock between the palms of his hands. His face turned bright red, as the lock put up a fight, but in the end, it gave up and clicked shut.

Oz, who was doubled up, hands on hips gasping for air, looked at Butler.

"Stuff that for a game of soldiers. Let's get out of here. I have got a bottle of Balkan in the cabin. I think we've earned a drink."

Butler checked for any spiders before running through the doorway, slamming the door behind him.

Belle lay in the darkness of the damp, stinking cage.

The barking from the dog in the next cage brought her back to her senses.

She winced as she clambered up onto her paws. Her neck was sore, her ribs hurt from the kicks, and her belly stung from the cuts she had received from where she'd been dragged across the ground.

Her eyes slowly became accustomed to the darkness.

She looked around at her new surroundings.

The sides were thick gauge steel, and the wall at the back was covered in dried blood. The floor was a mass of urine-soaked straw. Teeth and ripped-out claws lay strewn all around. A rat lay dead in one corner, its body pulsating as hundreds of maggots devoured its flesh.

To try and loosen the rope that still hung around her neck, Belle shook her head. The rope wouldn't slacken. Out of frustration, she started clawing at the rope with her left paw. One of her claws caught the slip knot of the noose loop, it loosened a little. After several more attempts, she managed to slacken it enough to put both her front paws on it and pull her head out. In an act of defiance, she squatted over the rope and urinated on it.

She glared over at the dog in the cell, who had stopped barking, and was now watching her. Their eyes fixed firmly on each other. Belle curled her lips back and then barked. He didn't retaliate, the stand-off lasted a minute or so before he turned his back, walked away, and then slumped down in the corner.

"That's right wimp, walk away. You know what's best for you," Belle laughed.

She had another look around her cell and spied what looked like a small area of dry straw. She wandered over, ruffled the thick brown strands with her front paws, circled her freshly made bed a few times to flatten it, and then laid down.

As she lay there a strange thought came to her. For the first time in her life, she found herself in an awful predicament, yet she shed no tears. Why? Had she become accustomed to, and now accepted being continually dealt life's cruel hands of fate?

She thought lovingly back to the happy times with her beloved mother and the grotesque way that she had been mercilessly murdered. Despite the harrowing memories, Belle didn't cry. She shuddered as she thought about the vile way her pups had been conceived, then brutally murdered in front of her, yet still the tears didn't flow. She remembered the happy times with Hamish, and how he had been slaughtered. Again, no tears.

Belle had changed. She was now battle-scarred and hardened to life's atrocities. The once happy-go-lucky little dog had become a warrior. But more importantly, she was a survivor, she could take on anyone and anything that life could throw at her, and no longer would she wallow in self-pity and live her life as a victim.

Deep down, she knew in her heart of hearts that she would one day escape from the hell on earth that she had been incarcerated in. She may have spent most of her life in Satan's dark abyss, but retribution against the perpetrators would one day, somehow be hers.

CHAPTER EIGHTEEN

January 2015, and Susan was working as a volunteer for one of the new street dog rescue charities that had recently started operating in Belle's home city. The harsh winters in Sofia were no place for any living being to try and survive on the streets, where the daytime temperatures regularly dropped to below -10°C.

She had flown out to East Europe at the end of November to assist with the charity's mission: To round up as many homeless dogs as possible and get them to a place of safety at one of the new charity-run shelters.

Elizabeth, a retired UK vet, was the lead coordinator for the UK-based street-dog charity working in Bulgaria.

She had been trying to negotiate with the mayor's office to allow some volunteers to carry out a fact-finding mission at the main Municipal Animal Control Centre. Although not part of the original brief, covert reports that Elizabeth had received highlighted the grotesque way the state-run shelter was operating.

Permission was eventually begrudgingly granted, although Elizabeth had to agree to one caveat: the mayor would read all reports before they were published.

Elizabeth had paired Susan with the newest member of

the team, Syd.

If the truth was known, Syd's main purpose was to provide Susan with a bit of backup muscle, if the need should arise. He had only been in Bulgaria for a few days, and this was going to be his first visit to a compound.

Elizabeth called Syd just as he was heading down for a coffee in the hostel that he and Susan were staying at.

"Morning darling. A cab is on its way and should be with you in about ten minutes. Now Syd, listen to me, please will you be a good boy for Susan. She's very experienced in the ways of this country. I know you've been reading up on the atrocities the poor dogs suffer. Susan will give you a full, X-rated history lesson in the cab en route."

"Yes boss, you know that you can trust me."

Elizabeth laughed. Through the grapevine she'd heard plenty of gruesome tales about Syd's reputation.

At just after eight the cab pulled up. The driver sounded the horn.

After waiting a couple of minutes, his fare still hadn't shown up. He tutted, then pressed the palm of his hand onto the horn again, leaving it there for a few seconds.

"Alright, alright, keep your bleeding hair on, dickhead," yelled Syd as he walked towards the cab.

"You'll have to wait for a mo, the young lady is just getting her bits together."

Again, the driver tutted.

"Is that a problem?" asked Syd.

"No boss, no problem at all."

"Good."

The driver pulled a crumpled packet of cigarettes from the top pocket of his shirt, took one out and put it between his lips. He was just about to light it when Syd yanked open the driver's door, reached in and then snapped the cigarette in half. The driver crossed his eyes and looked down at the broken fag hanging from his mouth.

Syd wagged his finger at him.

"Nasty habit that."

Syd moved to the rear door and opened it.

"Bloody hell, what a tip. Couldn't you of at least bleeding well hoovered it?"

The back seat was a combination of pot-marked fag burns, a variety of food remnants from every local takeaway and spilt drink stains. The footwells were covered in a layer of ash as thick as the winter's first snow.

Susan walked out of the main door. As she looked over at Syd, she raised her eyes, shook her head and then pointed to her mobile phone that was pressed tightly against her ear.

"OK Liz. Look, I've got to love you and leave you, Syd's waiting next to the cab. I'll give you a call later to update you."

She nodded and smiled at Syd.

"Morning mate. Sorry I've kept you waiting, a couple of last-minute orders from her ladyship."

"No worries, darling."

Syd and Susan had met a couple of times in the hostel. So far they had exchanged some polite small talk, shared some banter and spoken briefly of their pasts and reasons for being in Bulgaria.

They climbed into the back of the cab. Susan slid off her rucksack, pulled a piece of paper from one of the side pockets and handed it to the driver.

"Could you take us here please?"

The cab's stench of stagnant cigarettes was soon replaced

by the fresh floral aroma of Susan's body spray.

An awkward silence ensued for the first few minutes of the journey before Syd broke the ice.

"Elizabeth seems like a nice old bird. Have you known her for long?"

Susan raised her eyebrows and smiled.

"Nice old bird? She'd rip you to shreds. In answer to your question, I've known of her for a year or so. I followed her animal rescue work via social media before I flew out here. I'm only just getting to know her personally now. One thing I have learned is that she's a very complex character, a bit like an onion."

"An onion? What, she stinks and makes your eyes water?"

Susan put her face in her hands and laughed.

"No silly, there are many layers to her persona."

"Oh, I get it. One thing I have noticed in my couple of meetings with her is she does ramble on a bit. If you want to know how a watch works, ask Liz the time."

Susan tutted, then glanced out of the cab window trying to spot any injured stray dogs by the side of the road as the cab slowly meandered its way through the rush hour traffic.

After a couple of minutes of silence, Syd sparked up again.

"Liz said you'd bring me up to speed regarding the street dog politics of this city."

Susan looked over at Syd.

"In a nutshell mate, the local government officials really couldn't care less about the dogs. It's all about lining their pockets with blood money. One example is instead of using surgical thread to suture the wounds, the compound's so called vets use unsterilised household string. Bitches' stitches often burst open, allowing their insides to spew out from the incision wound after spaying."

The cab driver suddenly slammed on his brakes and began shouting out of his window at another driver.

"Oi, drive carefully, will you? Bloody muppet!" Syd yelled.

The driver shrugged his shoulders and mumbled something under his breath. Syd slapped him on his head. The driver glanced at him in the rear-view mirror, and Syd waved an index finger at him.

"Sorry about that, carry on Susan."

Susan smiled and continued telling Syd what she had ascertained for herself over the past few weeks.

"The rounded-up street dogs, and especially those who pose any form of threat to the city's inhabitants, remain at the compound we are heading to, in a nutshell, it's nothing more than a death camp. I'm dreading what we are going to see today, I really can't begin to imagine. From what I can gather, where we are heading is a corruptly run compound that somehow, up until now, has managed to slip through the net, and has so far avoided having to comply with local government guidelines."

Susan paused, took a deep breath, then continued.

"Some of the non-aggressive, healthy dogs are returned to the locations where they were initially caught, only to be caught again. I really don't get how things work out here, but in theory all that this never-ending circle of abuse does is line the pockets of the dog catchers, and the staff of the concentration camp. A very small percentage of the captured dogs do get rehomed, but they really are very few and far between. Any dog that looks like a pedigree will be sold by the manager, although to the mayor's office it appears to be a successful adoption, in reality it's just another bit of corruption. Our problem doesn't stop with the abuse inflicted on the dogs by the staff, we are also going to have to try and deal with the everyday welfare problems, such as starvation, illness and injuries sustained after an attack by another dog, or the results of them already having been maimed in an accident before they arrived at the compound. Sadly Sofia's street dogs also find themselves exposed to the daily risk of sporadic, violent abuse, being barbarically mutilated, shot, run over, poisoned, burnt, or even raped by humans are all commonplace."

Susan glanced over at Syd. He was looking out of the window, shaking his head.

He looked back at Susan.

"Sorry, did I hear you right? Did you say 'raped'?"

"Yup, you heard right. There are some very sick individuals."

"How on earth could they?"

"Listen Syd, things are not all bad, and are at long last slowly moving in the right direction. The Municipality of Sofia has begrudgingly joined forces with ours, and several other voluntary groups operating in and around the city. The joint effort is spearheaded by compassion and care from us, the volunteers. The paltry finances provided by the government are, at long last, helping with some of the strays' issues. New 'Open Shelters', with individual kennels and runs, are being opened. New vans, with trained staff, are being sent out onto the streets to capture dogs. A multitude of charity-run veterinary clinics have opened, all with fully trained surgeons and nursing staff available to treat any sick or injured dogs brought in. The strict legislations are well and truly in force now for the protection and welfare of any captured strays."

"Bloody hell," mumbled Syd.

"As I said, things are slowly moving in the right direction."

"Well, they couldn't get any sodding worse, could they?"

"Other of the city's municipal-run shelters have already adhered to the guidelines and now have programmes in place where stray dogs receive urgent medical attention. Neutering, decontamination, vaccination and permanent identification markings to help keep a track of them, usually in the form of a blue plastic ear tag. Luckily these decent-run sanctuaries are preventing dumps like the one we are going to from getting their greedy paws on any of the allocated cash."

Susan smiled at Syd.

She had been forewarned that he could be a volatile character and didn't want him going off half-cocked at the staff when they arrived at the shelter.

"Syd, most of the rescue centres we deal with over here are slowly coming around to our way of thinking. In my opinion, their intentions are good."

"The road to hell is littered with good intentions," Syd replied sarcastically.

The atmosphere in the cab was getting frosty. Susan was relieved when a few minutes later they pulled up outside the grim-looking compound.

They got out of the cab, Susan grabbed her rucksack, took out her purse and paid the driver.

"He should have given us that ride for free. That was the most traumatic twenty-minute cab journey ever," Syd grumbled.

He banged his fist on the roof of the car.

"Clear off, muppet," he shouted as the car drove off.

"Feel better for that?" asked Susan.

"Yup," replied Syd.

They walked over to the small wire mesh gate, slid the bolt across and walked into the compound, looking all around at the grim surroundings.

"What a bloody dump."

Syd couldn't believe the sight that met his eyes.

"Please, behave yourself. At least let us introduce ourselves and get to see the dogs before you kick off."

Susan spotted a sign hanging over the door of a small Portakabin – 'офис'

"I think that means office."

Susan knocked on the door.

"*Vŭvedete*"

Came the reply, in a gruff Bulgarian accent.

Susan looked at Syd. She took a deep breath and then opened the door.

The Portakabin doubled up as the main reception area. Behind the desk, smoking a strong Victory cigarette, was a middle-aged, overweight man, who grinned a toothless smile at Susan.

Sitting at the other end of the cabin, on a stained two-seater couch was the compound's security guard. He took a sip of his espresso coffee, laced with a nip of rakia, and leered at the pretty lady standing in their office. A thin stream of dribble trickled from the corner of his mouth.

Syd glared at him. He gritted his teeth, and thoughts of ripping the guard's throat out ran through his mind. Syd coughed and the guard looked over.

Still scowling, Syd mouthed "*Perverznik*" to the guard.

He got the hint, averted his eyes and quickly swallowed a mouthful of his drink.

Syd stood staring at the guard, who, to try and avoid any further eye contact, picked the previous day's copy of the Sofia *Globe* off the floor and pretended to read it.

Syd managed to remain silent, while Susan did the best that she could to overcome the language barrier and explain the reason for and the official permissions and formalities for their visit.

Once she had covered everything in detail, she thanked the two men for their time.

Susan beckoned Syd, and the pair of them headed out of the office to begin checking on the welfare of the incarcerated dogs.

"What did you say to that leering creep in the office?"

"I didn't think you heard me."

"Well, I did."

"I called him a pervert."

"How on earth would you know the Bulgarian for pervert?"

"Read it on the wall in the bog at the bar I was drinking in last night. In great big letters, it said 'Susan is a *perverznik*'. I asked the barman what it meant, and he translated it for me."

They burst out laughing, then Susan slapped him.

"Enough of the silly stuff. Let's get on with what we are here to do."

Through covertly gathered intelligence reports, they knew that both the shelter's manager, and the so-called on-duty veterinarian, turned a blind eye to the violence and inhumane cruelty inflicted upon the dogs. The manager had already been fired once from his role due to the disgusting violence the compound's residents endured, this time, if enough evidence could be gathered, he had no chance of being reinstated, in fact, he could even face a lengthy spell in prison.

Susan and Syd were appalled at the gruesome sight that met their eyes as they slowly walked through the compound. Decaying bodies, skeletal dogs fighting over rotting food, old tin cans containing stagnant water, dogs chained to posts with no protection from the harsh elements, the list of atrocities just went on and on.

"Well the reports seem to be true. Where the bloody hell do we begin?" asked Syd.

"They have the sodding audacity to call this dump a 'sanctuary'? This is far worse than I could ever have imagined. But, you know what really worries me? They knew that we were coming, so is this the cleaned-up, ready for inspection version." Susan's lower lip quivered as she spoke.

Her eyes had become glazed at the horrors in front of her. She blinked to try and clear her eyes, as she did, tears ran down her cheeks.

She closed her eyes, took a breath, wiped her face with the back of her hand, composed herself, then carried on walking.

"What you can see in front of you really is just the tip of the iceberg, Syd. Sadly, due to the barbaric sterilisation methods carried out by the incompetent, corrupt veterinarians that the manager of this dump calls in to assist, many dogs frequently die from infection after they have been released back onto the streets after surgery."

"What the hell? These people are sadistic, pure evil."

Knowing that they had an immense task ahead of them Susan needed to get things moving.

"Right Syd, we need to get our initial inspection over and done as quickly as possible. This is far more than the two of us can handle alone. We are going to need plenty of backup. In my opinion, I doubt that many of these poor dogs will survive another day."

They hurried through the rest of the compound, scribbling notes and taking photos on their mobile phones of the horrific conditions before their eyes.

Susan rang Elizabeth and told her of the horrors.

"Right Susan, I haven't got anyone available today. You and Syd head back and write up a full report, and we'll get a team over there first thing tomorrow. Before you hang up, are there any emergency cases that need immediate attention?"

"What are you talking about? They are all bloody emergency cases."

Susan closed her eyes. Her head started to spin, and she was struggling to catch her breath. She could feel the onset of a panic attack. In an attempt to try and ward it off, she started taking controlled heavy breaths, breathing in deeply through her nose and slowly out through her mouth.

"Liz, I'm sorry, I didn't mean to shout."

"Don't worry, darling."

Susan ended the call on her mobile, but she was still struggling to catch her breath. She called Syd, and they headed back towards the Portakabin offices.

Just as they were getting close to the makeshift office, Susan heard a loud furore coming from the main brick-built kennel block.

"Before we leave, I just need to check in there," she said to Syd.

"OK mate. Listen, while you're in there I'll have another quick wander around to see if we missed anything. If you need me, just holler."

Susan walked over to the kennel block and pushed open the door. She gave her eyes time to adjust to the bleakness, then slowly walked in. She retched at the overpowering fetor of urine, rotting food, and the distinct, pungent stench of malodor, the necrotic dead tissue and bacterial infection from untreated open wounds.

The deafening, echoed sound of dogs barking and snarling initially startled her.

Susan had to cup her hands over her ears to try and catch a moment's respite from the commotion.

It didn't take long for her senses to become accustomed to the vile smells and sounds, then she ventured further in.

On the far left-hand side of the block, a pink and white candy stripe tarpaulin had been crudely cable tied to the external bars, offering a mediocre form of protection from the elements. The cell's inhabitant lay dead on the floor.

The next cell had an injured dog, it dragged its bloodied hind left leg behind it as it continually limped around in a circle.

The next two cells had crazed dogs that leapt, barked and tore relentlessly at the iron barred fronts of their enclosures.

Next, Susan spotted a very small, frail dog, cowering in fear, in the far back of its cell.

Rusting metal bars prevented it from being harmed by the dogs constantly growling and snapping at it from the adjacent cells. Susan walked over to the pen and could see the barred front door was securely locked by a padlock.

There was hardly any roof covering to protect the dog from the severe harsh winter's weather. A meagre covering of sodden, faeces-covered straw strewn across the floor offered the sole form of comfort. An old dirty plastic ice-cream tub with a smidgen of mouldy, maggot-infested food lay at the front of the cell, next to an oil can with its top crudely cut off, which contained the only source of drinking water. Sadly, due to the freezing sub-zero temperatures, the mucky contents were iced over.

Tears filled Susan's eyes as she stood glaring at the pitiful sight in front of her.

She knelt down in front of the cage door that imprisoned the poor dog, having to waft her hand in front of her nose to try and diffuse the vile putrid stench.

With a gentle voice, trying to be heard over the barking from the other dogs, she tried to beckon the little dog to look towards her.

The dog appeared to be petrified. It remained sitting at the back of its cell, doing its utmost not to turn around and face Susan, and make any form of eye contact.

Susan took out her mobile phone and tried to snap a few photographs. She knew that potentially one day, these pictures could be the dog's passport to freedom.

After what seemed an eternity, and with a huge amount of gentle coaxing, the dog eventually started to turn its head, and look out of the corner of its eye in the direction of the kind young woman trying to befriend it.

As an element of trust slowly developed, the dog shuffled itself around. It was now almost facing Susan head on.

After a few minutes, it slowly took its first tentative steps towards the kind human outside of its cell.

It soon became obvious to Susan that the dog was in pain, as it slowly hobbled towards her. Susan could see the pronounced deformity in both of its front legs.

A sudden outburst of barking from the two neighbouring dogs caused the little dog to quickly scurry back to the safety at the back of its cell.

"You poor, dear little thing."

Susan could feel the muscles in her chin tighten, and then start to tremble. Not for the first time during this visit, and probably not for the last, tears trickled down her face.

She briefly looked up through the gaping hole in the roof, hoping that a glimpse of sunlight would somehow soothe her. She shook her head and brought herself back to her senses. Now that she was composed, she again started to offer the little dog words of comfort.

"I am so sorry on behalf of whoever did this to you. I promise that I will help you, and no one will ever hurt you again. One day, and hopefully very soon, you'll have a home to call your own, where you will know no fear. You will be dry and you will be warm. You will always have enough to eat, and rest assured that when you sleep, your dreams will all be sweet."

The plight of this disabled little dog was worse than Susan had prepared herself for.

She had now made the poor wretched dog a vow, but could she honestly offer it the chance of a new life?

Tall, slim and attractive, with shoulder-length blonde hair, Susan had grown up in Hoxton, close to London's East End. A lifetime's love of animals had spurred her on at secondary school not to follow peer pressure and become a rebel, but to work hard to gain the five GCSE grades that she required to apply to the Royal College of Veterinary Surgeons to study for a level three diploma in veterinary nursing.

Susan landed on her feet when she left school. For three tiring years, she burnt the candle at both ends, studying on a part-time basis at an RCVS-approved college, whilst also working at a large veterinary practice close to Finsbury Park, which luckily for her, was also a registered RCVS training practice.

She passed all her exams with flying colours and gained the qualification that allowed her to treat small animals, such as dogs, cats, rabbits and guinea pigs.

Although still only in her mid-twenties, she was far more streetwise than any of her friends back home. Due to her dedication to her career, Susan was a free agent, with no relationship or property commitments.

She had taken a year out from nursing to go travelling around Eastern Europe, putting her hard-earned qualifications to good use helping wherever she could with the plight of the stray dog population.

Susan loudly called out to Syd to find a member of staff.

Up until when Susan called him, Syd had been filling up any containers he could find with fresh water from the standpipe, which luckily for the first time in days was not frozen solid. He knew that the very least he could do was provide the free-roaming dogs in the compound a chance to fend off dehydration.

Syd was shocked at the emaciated state of the dogs he encountered. Some snarled, and a few bared their teeth at him, but most of them just lay there, unable to move. Many were close to death, struggling to keep themselves warm and hide out of harm's way from the bitterly cold wind that howled through the compound.

Syd knelt and stroked an elderly dog. He ran his hand gently down its side. The dog's ribs protruded through a thin layer of skin. For some strange reason, as he stroked the dog, memories came back to him of sitting on his late grandfather's knee, learning how to play the washboard.

The dog repeatedly shook its head. Syd lifted one of its ears. Never in his life had he seen a mass of ticks like it, there must have been hundreds of them, stuck together and slowly working their way down the poor dog's ear canal.

"I'll be back very soon, my old son," he said as he patted the dog and got up to find out what Susan wanted.

"What's up mate?" he shouted as he entered the cell block.

"Bloody hell, it pen and inks in here."

Syd waved his hand in front of his face as hard as he could. He gagged and almost vomited as his lungs filled with the putrid, ammonia-smelling air that filled the kennel block.

"Can you imagine trying to survive in here? Now please, try and find out where the key to this cell's padlock is. I urgently need to get in to try and attempt to carry out a physical examination."

If she was to have any chance of examining this dog, Susan was going to have to establish some form of trust and bond.

Susan had come prepared. From her small canvas backpack she pulled out her stethoscope, rubber gloves and a thermometer. Again, she knelt and held her medical equipment out in front of her, showing them to the little dog whenever it glanced over in her direction.

From where she knelt, Susan began to carry out a visual examination.

Taking a small notepad and pencil out of a side pocket in her bag, she put down her medical equipment and began to scribble down brief notes of her initial observations.

'Estimate the pup, a female GSD to be approx. 2 years old. Deformed front legs are causing discomfort when attempting to move. Teats appear to be enlarged – litter of pups? Sits slightly leaning towards the right. To carry out an in-depth skeletal examination at the surgery. She is breathing heavily and showing signs of anxiety. Have tried to socialise. The dog is fearful but doesn't appear aggressive, no snarling or showing of teeth, hackles down. My main worry on initial distant observation is that she may be suffering from both malnutrition and dehydration due to no obvious signs of fresh drinking water or food. Body shows signs of trauma, with areas of dried blood, but no apparent open wounds.'

Syd headed off over to the office to try and find the key to the kennel's padlock.

He soon returned, followed by another member of the compound's staff.

"Right Susan, I couldn't find the two blokes we met earlier, but found this muppet skulking around. His ID badge says 'кучкàр'. I did a quick online search on my mobile and apparently that means that this idiot is the on-duty dog handler."

Syd walked over and stood next to Susan, followed slowly by the man.

The man stood looming in front of Susan. A half-smoked slim Karelia cigarette hung from the corner of his mouth, and slowly a perverse smile crept across his face as he looked down on the pretty girl kneeling in front of him. He didn't speak a word of English, and Susan had only managed to grasp the basics of Bulgarian.

She stood up and attempted, unsuccessfully, to engage in some form of communication.

Susan gave up, and reverted to the age-old global means of communication, via manic hand gesticulations.

Eventually, she managed to get across that she wanted the door unlocked.

The man took a final drag of his cigarette, grunted, laughed, coughed and in a snorting sound drew the phlegm from the back of his throat and spat it on the floor, just missing Susan's foot.

He turned and started to walk away, mumbling to himself in his gruff ineligible voice.

"Oi, come back here you vile pig!" screamed Susan.

She had been incited with rage. The sight of the poor pitiful dog had aroused many emotions within her. She grabbed the man's right shoulder and spun him around so that he was now facing her head on. Susan drew back her right arm and slapped the worker as hard as she could straight across the left cheek of his grubby unkempt face.

He reeled back in shock, more than pain.

"Good girl," Syd thought to himself as he quickly stepped forwards, taking up an evasive stance. He strategically positioned himself closer to where the worker was standing. Syd stared menacingly at him, and he had already mentally planned his hand-to-hand combat moves to defend Susan if the need should arise. Mind you, from what he had just seen, it appeared that Susan was more than capable of taking care of herself.

Syd's plan was a swift left-handed extended four-finger gouge to both eyes, followed by a right-hand punch to the throat, hard enough to momentarily prevent his foe from breathing, but not hard enough to break the trachea. This would be followed by a full-powered left hook to the right cheekbone. Then for a grand finale, and for the sheer fun of it, he would systematically break several limbs of his immobilised adversary.

Sadly, Syd didn't get the chance to beat the living daylights out of the worker.

Like all bullies, the man was a coward; women, children and dogs were his forte, they posed no threat to him, they couldn't fight back or defend themselves. However, the imposing man staring at him frightened him.

As he wiped his face, his fingers made a scuffling sound as they rubbed through the two days' worth of stubble on his chin. His cheek had already begun to redden from Susan's well-directed slap.

Either defiance, anger or nerves caused him to laugh out loud.

He looked back in contempt in the direction of the dog constrained within the shed and rummaged through the pockets of his threadbare, tattered camouflage army jacket.

Eventually, he pulled out a small bunch of keys, crudely tied together with string. He threw them down onto the cold, muddy ground in front of Susan.

"Syd, we're getting this poor little dog out to a place of safety, and now."

"We can't, you know the rules," Syd replied.

"Surely you must know by now that you can't get too

emotionally involved with individual dogs."

"Well, I am emotionally involved, so stuff the rules. This little dog is in danger and believe me, she won't survive for much longer in this hell on earth. So, one way or another, with or without your help, she is coming with me. I need to examine her and get her away from this hell hole. We can make room for her at the hostel. Are you going to help me, or do I have to do it alone?"

"What about rabies?"

"Pack it in Syd, we have both been inoculated with every possible vaccine available, neither of us is going to catch anything. You know the risks are bloody minimal. Anyway, for your information, there hasn't been a reported case of any human contracting rabies in this country for over forty years. Why are you putting up so many boundaries? I thought we were here to save dogs?"

"I am here to save dogs. Just look around, there are sodding dozens in this compound that need our help, why is this one so special?"

"Come and take a proper bloody look for yourself, damn it."

The exchange between Susan and Syd was becoming uncomfortably confrontational. Mentally her emotions were running high, but she knew that she must not act irrationally. Susan closed her eyes, took some deep breaths and calmed herself down.

She knew that she needed to get this dog out and to a place of safety immediately, and for her to be able to achieve that, realistically she was going to need Syd's help.

Syd moved closer to the cell imprisoning the little dog. He was also met by the horrific sight of the poor little dog trying to survive in its vile, squalid conditions.

"Poor little mite."

Syd was a seasoned volunteer at overseas animal rescue work. He had seen, or at least he thought he had seen, everything when it came to the disgusting atrocities inflicted on animals. However, the pitiful sight of the deformed dog right there before his eyes really struck a nerve.

Tall, and thickset in stature, Syd had spent years serving Queen and Country in the army, before having to be medically discharged due to the severe disabling injuries that he had sustained fighting on the front line in Afghanistan. A permanent reminder of his distinguished military career, and the subsequent injury that had ended his career, were permanently carved deep into his face.

A scar ran from the top of his left eyebrow down his cheekbone to just above the top of his jawline. A prosthetic eye now replaced the one he lost when the burning hot shard of shrapnel hit him. He had also been diagnosed with Post Traumatic Stress Disorder and suffered regular, recurrent flashbacks to the moment he, and his mate, took a direct hit by the mortar shell. His brother-in-arms was instantly blown to pieces. Syd never could comprehend how a man standing just six feet from him could have been obliterated, and he somehow escaped with just a shattered face.

Well, the truth was Syd did know, he just couldn't come to terms with the fact that by taking the full impact of the shell, his mate had protected him, his life had been sacrificed. When the medical team brought Syd around, his body was covered in blood and flesh, Syd's dead mate's flesh. He could still taste freshly torn-off skin in his mouth, his nostrils full of the metallic smell of his departed mate's blood. Syd lay there in agony, in searing pain from where his face had been torn to pieces. A burning hot shard of metal embedded where his eye once was.

Hailing originally from Islington, North London, Syd wasn't a man to be messed with. An accomplished amateur boxer, he had worked the doors of most of the clubs in and around The Angel and Upper Street and had earned himself both a notorious and violent reputation in the pubs around Islington.

Syd detested and hated most of the human race. 'I hate people' was the mantra he lived his life by. At the top of his ever-growing list were animal abusers, closely followed by sex offenders, bullies and liars. He had no time for those who displayed vanity and despised one-upmanship. He constantly tried to avoid getting into a conversation, when treating himself to a pint, or if he had the cash, a Negroni, with the sad, usually lonely men who didn't have a life of their own, the 'me too ers' he called them. They would make up tall stories, or compete with any topic of conversation, by saying 'me too', hence 'me too ers', always trying to go one better, or having a 'mate' who had done it bigger and better.

However, Syd's compassion for dogs knew no bounds. His lonely street urchin upbringing had given him an empathy with the strays, the forsaken dogs that he had now made his personal mission to offer help and salvation to. His feelings had been ignited even more witnessing first-hand the plights of the displaced dogs he had encountered when he was actively seeking out insurgents in the bombed-out city warzones he'd been deployed to.

"Open the cage, Susan."

Susan started rummaging through the random selection

of keys that had been thrown onto the ground. Behind the bars, the little dog just sat inquisitively watching.

"Sodding hell, none of these bloody keys fit this lock, Syd."

"Let me have a go."

Syd tried every key as well. Susan was right, none of them fitted the lock.

Syd looked around the cell block and spotted a small iron bar, a discarded part of one of the cells, lying close to the main door.

"I'll jemmy it with this. Stand back, Susan."

Syd wiggled and forced the bar into the padlock's hooped shackle and managed to position it just enough to give him some leverage.

Once satisfied that the bar was secure, Syd pulled down on it with all his strength, and as he did so, he grumbled a few choice words under his breath. There was a crack as the clasp of the lock snapped and Syd fell unceremoniously to the ground.

Susan, for the first time since she had arrived at the compound, laughed, then tried to help him up.

"Get off, will you? I'm OK."

With his pride having taken a knock, Syd got up and wiped the muck off his jeans.

Susan pulled at the door.

"Help me, Syd."

"Move over."

Syd pulled at the door. The hinges creaked as the metal joints started to open.

Susan's emotions again started to turn to anger.

"These people are sodding barbaric."

She handed her minimal medical kit and bag to Syd as she squeezed through the gap and entered the cell.

She moved slowly, not wanting to scare the pup any more than unnecessary. Then reached behind her and pulled the door closed, just in case the pup should try and make a desperate run for freedom.

Syd tried to shoo away the dog snapping and growling at them from the cell next to the little dogs. In the end, he picked up a bucket of water and threw it toward the dog.

"Now please, be bloody quiet, will you?"

Susan dropped to her knees. The sodden straw, a mixture of stagnant water and urine soaked through her jeans. Slowly she raised her now mucky hands out in front of her, showing the petrified pup her grubby palms.

Syd remained outside, silently observing, trying not to frighten the dog any more than necessary.

"Good girl, I mean you no harm, come to me sweetheart."

The pup both wanted to and kept trying to make tentative movements towards the saviour in her cage, but her past experiences at the hands of humans forced her back into the safety of her corner, the sanctuary of the corner that she had hidden in for weeks.

Susan again placed her hands onto the dank straw, and very slowly and cautiously, she moved slightly closer to the terrified pup.

"Good girl, good girl."

Her voice remained soft and calm, and she made as much eye contact as possible whenever the pup looked at her. Susan remembered reading somewhere that raising your eyebrows at a dog was apparently a sign of respect. She was prepared to try absolutely anything to gain the pup's trust, so in between her words of encouragement, Susan raised her eyebrows in an exaggerated manner.

"I must look like a right bleeding idiot," she thought to herself.

At last, after an arduous fifteen minutes of gentle coaxing, Susan seemed to be making some headway. The pup had risen to its paws and had voluntarily turned so that she was now facing Susan head-on.

Patiently, Susan kept slowly moving ever closer to the pup. Frequently she would stop, to allow the little dog to accept her; Susan did not want to run the risk of scaring or freaking her out. Her knees hurt, the damp straw covered a gravel floor, and small stones had embedded themselves deep into her kneecaps. But she was not going to let the pain get in the way of the progress she had made.

Now within touching distance, Susan raised her right hand, with her palm facing upwards. Very slowly she moved it towards the dog's lower jaw. With her index finger extended, she tentatively stroked the dog's chin in a beckoning motion. Beyond all belief, Susan had managed to make physical contact with the little dog. Slowly the dog lifted her head upwards, although her eyes remained firmly fixed on the kind human in front of her.

Syd discretely wiped a tear from his one good eye as he watched the beautiful scene unfolding right in front of him.

Over and over Susan stroked the little dog's chin. She then slowly moved her hand upwards, continually soothingly rubbing the dog's right cheekbone with the back of her index finger. Susan turned her hand and began to caress the little dog's ears, then gently started to stroke her head. She moved her hand down to the scruff of her neck and gently stroked her matted damp fur.

Apprehensively the little dog now manoeuvred herself into a sitting position. Susan moved in as close as she could and started to gently run her hand down the dog's spine, all the way to her tail. Long gentle strokes, over and over again.

"Good girl, beautiful girl."

Susan continuously offered soothing kind words of reassurance.

After taking several minutes to establish the dog's trust, Susan slowly rose to her feet, remaining bent over the dog, stroking her all the while.

"I'm gonna try and pick her up, get ready to open the door, Syd."

Susan bent down and carefully tried to lift the trembling little dog. She let out a small high-pitched yelp as Susan's hands initially touched her, through fear rather than pain. Gently Susan slid her right hand, then arm under the dog's chest enabling her to continue to reassuringly stroke her left shoulder, her left arm cradling the dog's rear end with her legs hanging forward. Once happy that she had her securely, she started to raise her up, continually offering gentle words of comfort.

When she was fully upright, Susan started to move slowly towards the door. She stumbled on the damp straw but managed to steady herself.

Syd slid the clasp and opened the door, the rusty hinges creaked. The little dog initially appeared startled, but she soon relaxed.

Susan followed Syd, who had picked up her rucksack, out of the main door of the kennel block and out into the daylight.

"Wait here, I won't be a mo," Syd said as he ran towards the shelter's dilapidated Portakabin offices. He kicked open the feeble door, then soon re-emerged.

Syd's right hand firmly grasped the scruff of the worker's tatty shirt collar, and his left hand had the man's arm bent up his back, as he frogmarched him towards Susan.

"What's your name?" shouted Syd at the terrified man.

"Me Butler."

"Right Me Butler, one wrong move and I'll snap your arm," whispered Syd into Butler's ear.

"Hurry up Syd, she's getting heavy."

Syd was now shouting at Butler, who pointed to a rusty, beat-up old lime green Skoda.

Syd ran over to the jalopy, pulled open one of the rear doors, and went back to Susan to help her carry the dog over.

"It's alright Syd, I can manage."

Susan carefully carried the little dog over to the car.

"Right, now give her to me while you get in."

"She's terrified, she might bite you."

"Just do it."

Syd reached forwards and slid his hands under Susan's.

"Got her, now get in the car."

The little dog, bewildered as to what was happening to her, just looked up at Syd.

"Are we taking her straight to the charity's shelter, Susan?"

"No, Spencer the vet is out neutering in the mobile clinic today. We'll take her back to the hostel and I'll do her initial health check there. I'll give you a list and you can collect them from the compound's stores for me. I'll ring Elizabeth and give her the heads-up. It'll give her time to prep a kennel for her and we'll take her over later on."

Susan climbed into the back of the car, she brushed the seat; a mass of fag ends and empty beer cans fell into the footwell.

Syd carefully lowered the dog onto her lap.

"Right you, get over here," he shouted to Butler.

Syd handed Butler a business card from the hostel, with the address on the front.

"Now get in and drive us here, dickhead."

Butler clambered into his car and tried to insert the ignition key, although through fear he couldn't stop his hand from shaking. Eventually, he managed to engage the key, but he had to turn it several times before the beat-up old banger sparked and spluttered back into life.

As soon as the engine started, Belle became unsettled. She started panting and her head rose. She wriggled and twisted, trying to escape from Susan's grip.

"Calm down darling, you're safe with me."

But for Belle, horrible memories had come flooding back to her of the last time she was in a mechanical beast. The clanging and clumping sound and smell of the burning oil reminded her of the night of her capture.

Susan manoeuvred Belle so that she was sitting upright on her lap and able to see out of the window.

"There you go. We'll soon be on our way. You'll never come back to this hell, darling."

All the while, Susan caressed Belle's head, soothing strokes that eventually helped to calm the pup down.

"Sorry Susan, something I've quickly gotta do."

He reached over, turned off the engine, and pulled out the key.

"You wait here muppet. Understand?"

"Yes boss."

Syd quickly walked back over to the Portakabin. It didn't take long before another one of the compound workers appeared. Headfirst out of the door he flew, landing straight in a muddle puddle, slicing his hand on a shard of flint embedded in the mud.

Syd reappeared, grabbed the man by his neck and dragged him to the little dog he had sat with earlier.

All Susan heard were several life-threatening threats made that if every tick wasn't removed, and the dog given a warm bath and meal, Syd would pull the man's ears off and feed them to the dogs first thing in the morning.

Rubbing his thumb and forefinger together, Syd shouted at the petrified worker.

"Money, where's your money?"

The man slid his bloodied hand into the rear pocket of his combat trousers and pulled out his wallet. Syd snatched it from him, opened it and took out the man's driving licence.

"Right knobhead, I've got your address. Make sure the dog is taken care of, or else I'll be paying you a visit. *Comprende?*"

He threw the wallet down into a puddle and slid the driver's licence into his pocket.

Rubbing his hands together, he winked at Susan as he walked over and opened the compound's main gate.

As he did, Oz and Carter drove in.

"What going on here?" Oz shouted from the van's window.

"What's it gotta do with you, muppet?" Syd shouted back.

Oz stopped his van, leapt out, and started stomping towards Syd.

"Think that you're man enough, do you? I'll let you throw the first punch, then I'll rip you to pieces."

Oz laughed at Syd's threat.

"I do to you what I do to these vermin dogs every night, old man."

From his drinking sessions with English tourists, Oz had picked up the basics of the language, mainly how to ponce a drink, corny chat-up lines and threats of violence

"Oh, so you're the brave bastard responsible for all this suffering, are you?"

Carter was now heading over to his mate, shouting in Bulgarian, while looking over at Syd.

"Syd, please leave it. I really need to get this pup out of here," shouted Susan from the car.

"Ha, do as the lady says, old man," growled Oz.

Syd glared at Oz and Carter.

"We'll meet again, mark my words."

Annoyed that he had to walk away from the situation, Syd headed over and got into the car. Without saying a word, he handed Butler back the key.

"Drive."

"This really is a very bad day," Butler said.

The engine started, and Syd banged his fist on the dashboard.

Butler was in a state of panic as he pulled out of the Municipal Animal Control Centre's main gates, and just narrowly missed a passing motorbike. The rider shouted some abuse and Syd gave a few hand gestures back in return.

"Do you feel better now?" Susan asked sarcastically.

"Just leave it."

After a few minutes, Syd had calmed down enough to take out his mobile phone and call Elizabeth to update her of the atrocities, and the plight of the dogs that they had witnessed.

"Thanks Syd, I'll send a couple of volunteers over. Will they have any problems with the staff?"

"Maybe with a couple of them. I think it would be best to leave it till tomorrow and let me tag along, just in case, but I think I've made myself understood."

Elizabeth laughed and set about arranging getting a team together to head over to the compound in the morning to start getting the weaker dogs out and into temporary foster care.

Susan and Syd were staying at the Bedford Hotel, an attempt by the owner to bring an air of Manhattan chic and sophistication to the bleak, grey city. In stark reality, it was nothing more than a rundown hostel, with a few faded and torn posters showing some of New York's famous landmarks hung on the walls. The floors had a covering of mismatched, heavily soiled, threadbare carpets. The air had a consonant stench of boiled cabbage and stale cigarette smoke combined with an undertone of sewerage, a plumbing problem that the owner decided was too expensive to fix for his guests. The charity that Susan and Syd volunteered for had secured rooms throughout Sofia for its volunteers; they got a slightly cheaper rate, on the understanding that they would always give five-star reviews on advisory travel websites.

Apart from a scratched Barry Manilow CD playing on the stereo, the atmosphere in the car was sombre. He could take no more, Syd hit the eject button and the shiny silver disc slid out. Syd chucked it out of the window.

"Bloody Copacabana, what a load of crap."

Syd knew he had upset Susan and tried to lighten the mood in the car.

"Sing us a song, Susan."

"Syd, will you just shut the f …"

Susan refrained from a full-blown outburst, the last thing that she wanted to do was to upset the little pup sitting on her lap.

"Please, for once in your life Syd, could you just try to be quiet?"

Poor old Syd just couldn't help himself.

"I wonder what culinary delights they are serving up tonight. Oh, I know, it'll be that sodding kavarmarama, again."

He had a ravenous appetite and could easily eat for two. Every night the hostel chef, who just happened to be the owner's wife, served up the same watery kavarma, a staple of Bulgarian cuisine, a pork and vegetable stew. Without fail, the evening feast would be unceremoniously slopped into a bowl and served with a stale slice of bread.

"Look, we've just spent a morning helping poor starving dogs, just be thankful for whatever crap you get."

Susan was not in the mood for Syd's ramblings. Her concerns were solely concentrated on the little dog shivering on her lap, and certainly not on Syd's empty belly.

She relented, knowing full well that Syd was trying to say sorry in his own unique style.

"Come on Syd, from the stories you have told me. anything has got to be better than that gruel that got slopped in your bowl in the army."

Syd moved the inside rear-view mirror and looked at Susan, she smiled at him.

"On a rare serious note, when we get back to London, I'll treat you to a slap-up meal, as a thanks for helping me with this poor dog."

"No need to thank me, it's the reason I'm here darling."

Although initially reluctant to put all their efforts into the welfare of this one little dog, Syd knew that Susan was right with her concerns. Anyway, they would be returning back to the compound the next day to help with the rehoming and medical care of some of the other incarcerated dogs.

"Right Syd, then it's a date. I'll take you out for a double, double, single with a side order of jellied eels?"

"A what?"

"Come on Syd, I thought you knew all about P and M."

"Erm, that sounds a little bit kinky, Susan."

"I'll make it simple for you, dopey. Pie and mash."

"Oh right. And the double, single or whatever you said?"

"Double large pie, double mash and single liquor."

"Now I get it, just a single mash for me please."

They both burst out laughing.

To carry on with the banter, Susan decided to reignite an ongoing dispute with Syd.

"But I'm afraid you're gonna have to hop on a number 394 and head to Hoxton Street, you can't beat Cooke's, the smell of the fresh sawdust on the floor, the chilli vinegar. Bloody hell, my mouth is drooling. The only trouble we'll have will be finding you somewhere for a beer afterwards. Shoreditch is well trendy now, none of your warm beer, darts and a good old punch-up type of joints are left anymore."

Syd laughed at Susan's passion for the part of Hackney

that she had grown up in.

"Don't you think I'd look good in a pair of skinny ripped jeans? But no chance on the grub darling, Manzes or nothing, Chapel Markets, no I'd go as far to say London's finest."

Susan and Syd were both passionate about their local manors back in their beloved home city. The unlikely twosome had forged a firm friendship over the last few days and took immense pleasure in winding each other up with friendly banter, mainly used as a defence mechanism against the awful sights they encountered daily.

"Right, back to tonight's dinner. I could really go with a greased tea."

"Syd, what the hell is a greased tea when it's at home?"

"Sorry mate, I had a girlfriend from up north for a while. Basically, a chippy dinner, fish and chips, battered sausage, you get my drift?"

"Oh please do tell, how many traditional British chippies have you seen since you've been here?"

"Fair point Susan. Bloody kavarma it is then," grunted Syd.

To while away the journey, Susan started reflecting on a dilemma that had been bothering her over the last few months.

Mentally she had been wrestling with her conscience over the fact that she spent her life saving and helping animals, but strangely she chose to eat their flesh. Beef, lamb, pork and poultry filled her plate daily. Her next goal in life was to start on the road of becoming a vegetarian, and hopefully in time, a vegan.

The sudden sound of a car blaring its horn brought Susan back to her senses. She looked down at the little dog, who appeared perfectly relaxed in her company.

"Syd, you know what? I'm going to name her Sheba, after the mother of my parents' dog, Noel."

"Sorry, now I'm really confused. You're naming her Sheba after your parents' dog Noel?"

"Bloody hell Syd, listen to the words that I say, will you? I'm going to name her Sheba, after the mother of my parents' dog Noel."

"Oh, sorry. Now it makes sense."

In early 1983, eight years before Susan was born, her father Phil had returned home one Sunday morning from Club Row market, in the heart of London's East End, with a small Schnauzer bitch. Soon after, the government outlawed the sale of live animals in street markets, and centuries of tradition were lost when London lost its only live animal market. Susan's mother, Lil, was thrilled with her new fur baby addition, and initially named her Maria, mockingly, after the landlady of their local pub.

"Nope, I've made me mind up and am gonna call her Sheba."

Phil didn't like the idea of upsetting the governor of his local watering hole.

"One of my mum's favourite films was all about the Queen of Sheba. The actress who played her was beautiful."

Lil relented.

Sheba had a litter of pups on Christmas Eve 1987. Sadly, she suffered uterine inertia, a condition that sometimes happens at the end of a canine pregnancy. The problem occurs when the uterine muscles cannot contract and push the puppies from the uterus. Urgent medical attention didn't arrive in time for Sheba.

Sadly, along with three of her pups, she passed away.

The only survivor of the litter was a boy, who was born blind. Susan's parents decided it best to keep him, and they fittingly named him Noel.

For weeks they hand-reared him, feeding him around the clock.

Noel had been Susan's constant companion when she was young, never letting his disability hinder him in any way.

The story of Noel's birth, which her parents told her when she was young, was Susan's inspiration in wanting to work with dogs. As a young girl, she dreamt of one day becoming a veterinary surgeon.

Noel passed away aged ten in 1997 when Susan was only six.

Her parents were devastated and couldn't bring themselves to ever welcome another dog into their family.

They pulled up at the hostel. Syd reached over and turned off the engine. He removed the key from the ignition, picked up Susan's bag and climbed out of the car.

"Is your room key in here?"

"Yes, the left-hand side pocket."

"Right, I'll go and check if the coast is clear. Not sure they will be too happy about fleabag running loose in one of their pristine rooms"

"Her name is Sheba, and the sodding rooms are rank. Help me out with her."

Syd opened Susan's door and carefully lifted Sheba out. Susan climbed out and Syd passed the little dog back to her. Sheba now seemed more than happy being handled by her two saviours. At long last, her life's dream had come true, she had been shown mercy.

"Stay here Me Butler, I won't be long," Syd said before he turned and walked towards the hostel's front door.

He soon reappeared and beckoned to Susan.

"The managers in the khazi, do you want me to carry flea … sorry Sheba up the stairs?"

"I'm fine carrying her, just run up and open my door please."

With Sheba snuggly cradled in her arms, Susan carefully negotiated the stairs, being careful not to trip on any of the snags in the well-worn carpet. They reached her room, luckily unnoticed by anybody, and Susan carefully lowered Sheba to the floor.

"Blimey, you are heavier than you look. You're safe now poppet. Syd be a darling and nip downstairs for me. I need some sugar, salt and a bone china bowl. Only the very best for Sheba."

"Has it got to be bone china? Not sure they'll have one in this dump."

"No, you prat I was joking. Any food bowl will do, so long as it's clean. Oh, I need a spoon as well please."

Syd headed down to the dining room to collect the items Susan had asked for. The dining room was already laid out for dinner, and it didn't take Syd long to find a bowl, the sugar and salt.

Bemused by her new surroundings, Sheba started to investigate the room, thoroughly sniffing every single part of it. It all proved to be a bewildering new experience for her. Susan knew that she had to remain calm and contain her own excited energy.

Respecting Sheba's initial nervousness, she moved back and decided for the first few minutes not to touch her, talk to her or make any direct eye contact.

Once Sheba appeared to have relaxed and covered every square inch of the room, Susan clambered down onto the floor; she was now at Sheba's eye level. On all fours, she started to move in closer, from the side so that she didn't appear too menacing. Susan stopped, and Sheba then in return started to approach her, when she was directly in front of Susan she sat down, all of her own free will.

"Good girl."

Susan slowly placed her arms around her neck.

Syd reappeared.

"Right, what do I do with this lot?"

"I want to make Sheba a rehydration drink. If you can pour a pint of cold water into the bowl, and before you ask, the cold tap is in the bathroom, then add two tablespoons of sugar and half a teaspoon of salt. Then stir it up please."

Syd had poured the salt and sugar into two paper napkins in the dining area of the hostel and couldn't remember which was which.

He looked over at Susan, with a vacant look on his face.

"For fu …"

Susan closed her eyes and took a deep breath.

"For Christ's sake, you know what Syd? You could give a bloody paracetamol a headache. Just try one of them, it won't kill you, then you'll know which one is which."

"Oi, who are you getting shirty with? You're getting your knickers all in a twist over nothing."

"OK, I apologise. If it's too difficult for you, I'll do it."

"No, I'll do it, but I ain't no bleeding chef."

"Syd, the fire has gone out, let us not reignite it. Just make the bloody drink for Sheba."

"Sorry mate, you've got me confused. What fire?"

"Speaking metaphorically, you wally. Our disagreement or your stupidity was the fire. Let it go, and let's not pour petrol on the embers and reignite it. Understand now?"

"Erm, I think so."

Susan and Syd both burst out laughing.

Syd dutifully made up the drink for Sheba and handed the bowl to Susan. She placed it in front of the little dog and moved away.

"Right Syd, you're going to have to pop over to the dog shelter for me. I'll give you a list of what we are going to initially need for Sheba. Do you think you can manage that for me?"

"Get stuffed."

Susan shook her head. She wasn't going to take the bait and get into another tear-up with Syd.

She took a pen from her bag and using one of the hostel's notepads she started frantically scribbling down a list of all the basics that she would need for Sheba.

She spoke out loud as she wrote, in the hope that Syd would interject and remind her of anything that she may have missed out.

"Two tins vet diet food, flea and tick shampoo, brush, food and water bowls, leads, collar, towels. Erm, there's also the chance that she's got roundworms, hookworms and tapeworms, so we'll also need a course of all-in-one medication for her. I think that's it for tonight."

Susan looked over at Syd, who was nodding in agreement at her list.

"Right mate, I'll call Elizabeth and Spencer while you're gone to let them know what's going on and where we're up to.

The more that we can get done now, the easier it will be for the team tomorrow when we drop her off."

Syd took the list from Susan and scribbled the address of the charity's shelter onto the back.

"OK mate, leave it with me. I'll hopefully be back within the hour."

Syd returned to the car and found Butler screaming and shouting at someone on his old mobile phone.

Butler was totally confused as to what was going on. Syd snatched the antiquated phone from him, slung it to the ground and stamped on it. He grabbed Butler by the scruff of his jacket, then frogmarched him back to his car.

Syd opened the driver's door.

"Get in muppet and drive me here."

Syd showed him the shelter's address, climbed in the passenger seat and handed back the car's ignition key.

Again, it took a few turns of the key until eventually the old banger splattered and sprung back into life. A loud bang was followed by a cloud of grey smoke that billowed from the exhaust.

Susan had already called Elizabeth, who was waiting outside with everything Susan needed when Syd pulled up.

"Here you go, Syd. I've already spoken to Susan. Good thing that you're keeping Sheba at your hostel tonight, we are at full capacity here at this moment in time. We have had an emergency case, sadly we don't think there's much we can do for little Tom. Bless him, he hasn't got much time left. We'll have a kennel ready for her in the morning. Spencer will give her a thorough check-up when she gets here. We'll pick you up in the van at ten."

Elizabeth had a natural excitable nature about her. Syd

wasn't given the opportunity to respond as he was quickly handed a canvas tote bag, adorned with a fluffy pink teddy bear's head protruding from the top. This was going to be Sheba's first ever toy.

"Right chop chop, off you go, see you in the morning."

It didn't take long for Syd to get back to the hostel. He hopped out of the car, told his reluctant chauffeur to clear off, and then headed back up to Susan's room.

Luckily Susan had made one specific request when she had arrived at the hostel, a room with a bath.

She ran a lukewarm bath for Sheba, to prevent her body from overheating.

"This is going to be fun."

Since arriving at the hostel, Sheba had barely left Susan's side and she now sat staring bewilderedly at the large white porcelain bath. Susan reached down and picked her up. Initially, Sheba wriggled, trying to break free from Susan's grasp.

"Come on poppet, calm down. No one is going to hurt you. In fact, I think you're going to enjoy this."

Sheba stopped struggling and carefully Susan lowered her into the shallow warm water.

Sheba initially kicked and tried to clamber out of the bath. The slippery porcelain stopped her from escaping as her paws slid down the sides.

The sudden shock soon subsided, and Sheba began to relish the new strange sensation. She relaxed and sat down in the warm water.

Syd and Susan used their hands to cover her body and neck in water. Clumps of freshly shed black and tan fur filled the water.

"Pass me the shampoo, please."

Susan lathered the flea and tick shampoo and thoroughly worked it into Sheba's fur, paying extra attention to the area around her neck. In theory, this would prevent any escaping fleas from gathering close to her ears and eyes, where it would be difficult to shampoo safely.

Syd and Susan then covered the rest of Sheba's body with more copious amounts of warm water, and then Susan applied even more shampoo. Together they gently rubbed her all over, forming lathery white bubbles that covered the little dog. They left the bubbles to perform their magic for a few minutes then rinsed them off.

Throughout, Sheba just sat, her eyes gently closed, enjoying every moment of the affection being showered on her.

Susan lifted Sheba out of the bath. Syd grabbed two soft towels and together they gently began to rub her down.

Sheba was engulfed by a feeling of serenity.

She had almost lived her entire life in fear. She, up until just a few hours earlier, had never trusted, nor let a human get so close to her.

Once Susan and Syd had rubbed her as dry as they could, Susan picked up the double-sided brush Elizabeth had put in the bag. Firstly, she ran the pin side over the pup, more fur was discarded.

"Blimey, at this rate you'll end up as bald as Syd."

"Very funny, Susan."

"I thought it was."

"Just get on with the spa and beauty treatment, will you."

Susan laughed, turned the brush over, and then gently brushed Sheba with the soft bristles.

"Is there a fine-tooth comb in the bag, Syd? Now I've got all the knots and clumps out, I want to comb out any dead, unwanted guests."

Syd handed Susan the flea comb.

"Well, that's got rid of any unwelcome visitors, and you certainly smell a damn sight better now, Sheba. Maybe we will give Syd what's left in the bottle to make him smell nice."

Susan planted a gentle kiss on Sheba's forehead.

Syd went into the small lounge area of Susan's room, opened one of the tins of food and put about a quarter of it into one of the bowls. He had also secreted the worming tablet amongst the soft meaty mixture.

The food was put on the floor next to the other bowl that he had already filled with fresh cold water.

"Right Sheba, grub's up."

Susan patted her legs.

"Come on Sheba, follow me, we've got a treat for you."

She carried on speaking in a high-pitched voice, patting her legs.

Sheba got the hint and followed her.

"Come on Sheba, look what uncle Syd has made you. Eat your food, darling."

The little dog looked on in bewilderment. She had never been given fresh food before. Her nose twitched inquisitively as the enticing aroma of mixed meat filled her nasal passage.

She got closer to the two bowls. Syd and Susan moved back to give her space. Sheba lowered her head into the bowl of fresh food but backed off. She raised her head, her eyes stared suspiciously at Susan.

"Come on Sheba, I promise you'll enjoy it."

Sheba looked back at the bowl, lowered her head and

cautiously took a small nibble of the meat in a jelly mixture. Her taste buds went into overdrive, this was her first proper meal in months.

She recoiled. As she eagerly lapped at the food, the sound of the metallic bowl, as it moved across the ceramic floor tiles startled her.

Susan walked over and tipped the contents of the bowl onto the floor.

"There you go, darling, no more nasty noise."

Sheba looked down, tilted her head, and then took a bite. Happy that there were no more sudden surprises, the hungry little dog set about finishing her meal, and wolfing the whole lot down, she licked her lips, not wanting to waste a single morsel of the feast.

"Right, she's had her first dose of worming tablets. They'll kill off any worms living within Sheba's intestine within twelve hours, but they won't kill off any eggs left behind. She'll need a follow-up dose in two weeks to kill off any worms that subsequently hatch. I need to make a note of the date, so Spencer knows when he can do a microscopic faecal examination. Bloody hell, don't I sound like a pro."

Syd knew that Susan was a qualified veterinary nurse, but nevertheless, he was genuinely impressed with her medical knowledge.

He took the little teddy out of the bag and placed it in front of Sheba.

Bewildered at the little pink bundle of fluff she tilted her head to one side, sniffed it, then barked at it. The teddy just lay there. Sheba nudged it with her nose, but still no response. She looked around at Syd.

"Bless her heart, she hasn't got a clue."

Syd got down on all fours and crawled over to Sheba, and moved his head towards hers, and then picked up the teddy with his teeth. Acting as if he was a dog, he shook his head from side to side, while making some strange growling noises.

Both Susan and Sheba were shocked at the sight in front of them.

Syd spat out the teddy, and then pulled some pink fluff out of his mouth. Susan had to look away as she tried as hard as she could to stifle a laugh.

"Blimey, I wish I'd had my camera ready. That will live with me forever."

"Oi, what happens at the hostel, stays at the hostel."

Sheba edged herself forwards and cautiously picked up the teddy. She was curious as to what the little bundle of fluff's purpose was, but nevertheless, she mimicked Syd and began to shake her head.

Susan placed Sheba's water bowl onto a small hand towel, to prevent it from slipping on the tiled floor and scaring her as the food bowl had done. Sheba walked over and took a few sips of the fresh cool water.

"Right mate, I'm blooming starving, what do you fancy to eat?"

"To be honest Syd, I'm emotionally drained. I'm going to have a bath and turn in for the night."

"Erm Susan, silly question, but where's Sheba gonna sleep?"

"Where do you think? On my bed, of course silly."

"Oh of course. Silly me," Syd tutted.

"But first, we're going to have to smuggle her out and let her do her business. I just hope that she doesn't make any noise tonight, or mess on my nice clean bed sheets."

Sheba rose to her paws, lowered her front end, raised her bottom into the air and stretched her front legs out as far as she could.

"Oh, what a big stretch," said Susan, as she moved closer and tickled Sheba under her chin.

"What did you say?" Syd asked.

"I have always believed that if your dog stretches and you don't say 'Oh big stretch' every time, then you are a psychopath, and I don't want to know you."

"And you've got the cheek to say that I'm weird? You're a bleeding nutter."

Syd laughed, shook his head, turned and walked towards the bedroom door.

"I'll pop down and cause a distraction, I'll get the manager to knock me up a cheese sarnie. Give it a couple of minutes then bring Sheba down."

Susan retrieved the leather collar from the carrier bag of items Elizabeth had sent over.

"Here you go, look at this pretty collar."

Susan spoke in a reassuring voice, allowing Sheba to look at and sniff the collar.

When Sheba seemed comfortable with the collar, Susan moved in closer and gently placed it around her neck.

Sheba initially felt uncomfortable at having the collar placed around her neck. Thoughts of the rope nooses that had been forced onto her when she was captured, and later being incarcerated in the death camp, came flooding back to her. Although it didn't take long for her to settle down, for the first time in her life, at the hands of the kind lady, Sheba knew that the strange object wasn't there to garrotte her.

The collar was a little too big, so Susan adjusted it so that it would not slip over Sheba's head. There was already a metal dog tag attached to it, with the rescue compound's details engraved onto it. She then attached the pink nylon lead to the metal 'D' ring on the collar. Luckily there was also a slip lead in the bag, which Susan also placed around Sheba's neck.

Susan was anxious about taking Sheba out for her first walk and knew that she had to be 'belt and braces'; she couldn't run the risk of Sheba escaping when they exited the hostel.

"Well look at you, a future Crufts champ if I ever saw one."

Sheba looked up at Susan. She didn't understand the strange words that came from the human's mouth, however she picked up on and felt the love that radiated from her.

Susan gave Sheba a gentle reassuring, yet soothing pat on her head, accompanied by yet another loving glance.

Sheba was confused. One of her once feared humans was now softly saying a strange new word over and over, a word that was always combined with loving gestures.

"Sheba, Sheba."

The word flowed gently, and Sheba had already started to respond to it.

Was this now going to become the norm? Had kindness and compassion towards the little street dog now become a reality? In just a few short hours, Sheba's life had been transformed beyond her wildest dreams; that's not true, the dreams that she had harboured for months had all come true at once, she had at long last been shown mercy.

Susan bent down to lift Sheba, only this time there was no backing off in fear. The pup knew that she did not need to be afraid. In fact, Sheba almost hopped up as she was gently lifted, and then she snuggled soundly into Susan's arms.

Susan opened her bedroom door and quietly carried Sheba down the stairs. Syd was blocking the doorway to the kitchen area, trying to make small talk with the manager; neither of them had a clue what the other was saying, but the diversion worked and Susan sneaked past with Sheba.

The cold January air was bracing as Sheba and Susan exited the hostel, the sun was just dipping below the city's horizon, and the deep blood-red colours of dusk were just beginning to slowly fade away.

Susan, although still cradling Sheba, firmly grasped the loop handles of the two leads in her right hand. She took a deep breath and then gently lowered Sheba onto the pavement.

"Good girl, Sheba."

Susan started to walk, but Sheba had plans of her own.

Sheba gazed up at Susan and refused to budge. The lead tightened and the collar shifted up to behind her ears, then Sheba pulled back.

"Come on Sheba. Walk with me, you have nothing to be afraid of. Not with your Aunty Susan looking after you."

Sheba was having none of it. Either out of fear or defiance, she laid down on the cold, damp concrete slabs, refusing to move an inch. A few passers-by had to quickly sidestep to avoid tripping over the little dog.

Susan knelt beside her and gently stroked her head.

"Come on Sheba, I know you're confused, but you're safe now poppet."

Tentatively, Sheba rose to a sitting position, not once taking her eyes off the lady next to her.

Susan stood up and patted the outside of her left leg.

"Come on Sheba, heel, walk with me, darling."

Somehow the command miraculously worked. Slowly Sheba started to walk alongside Susan, constantly scrutinising her strange new surroundings.

Her senses were being bombarded by a whole array of peculiar smells and sounds.

Sheba stopped walking; something bothered her. She sat down and looked all around. Then it dawned on her, there was a sound missing. For once there wasn't the usual commotion of dogs howling and barking.

"What's up now, darling?" Susan asked. "Come on, it's not far now."

Susan patted her leg again.

Just as she was about to get up and start walking, something caught Sheba's eyes.

She leapt up onto all fours.

Walking towards them was a man with a small dog trotting daintily by his side.

The dog looked at Sheba.

"Who are you staring at?" Sheba barked. She bared her teeth and fired off another warning shot.

The man shouted something at Susan, picked up his dog, and hurriedly crossed the road.

"Now there was really no need for that, was there? That little dog was minding its own business and you go and cause a row."

Susan laughed, again patted her leg, and together they headed off down the street towards a small park.

Passers-by, wrapped up snuggly from the cold, glanced over and nodded at Susan. As they hurried past, they looked down and smiled at the disabled little dog who was now happily trotting along by her side.

Sheba cowered away from the strangers that loomed above her, she was petrified of them. Dogs were no problem to her, she'd scrap with them all day long. Humans, on the other hand, they were a different story. How was she to know that they wouldn't hurt her? Time would be a healer, and she would eventually learn.

Soon they reached the small park. As they entered, Sheba started sniffing the strange surroundings.

She then sat and stared upwards. For the first time in months there was no gloomy cell ceiling bearing down on her, just the starry sky above.

She got up, shook herself, then started to follow Susan.

Continually Sheba squatted to scent mark, and overscent areas already claimed by other local dogs. She passed small amounts of urine, making claim to her new domain. After several minutes, they walked on a bit. At a small grassy area next to an empty flower bed, Sheba stopped and began to circle, sniffing the ground. Backwards and forwards she scampered, then she found the spot she was looking for. She gazed up at Susan, squatted then defecated.

"Good girl. Bloody hell, nobody will ever believe me that you're already house trained."

Susan rummaged through her pocket, but she had forgotten to ask Elizabeth for one vital piece of equipment, poo bags.

"Bloody hell. You'd have thought she would have thought of sending over a roll of poop bags."

Susan tutted and looked around for a makeshift poop scoop.

"They'll have to do," she said out loud as she picked up some nearly rotted leaves. She layered a few in her hand and scooped up the poop, then discarded it in one of the park's bins. She looked back at her hand, gagged, then knelt and wiped a small piece of poop off her hand.

"Right, that's enough adventures for one day. Let's head home."

As they walked back to the hostel, Susan gazed down admiringly at the little dog who was now walking confidently by her side. Her crippled front legs flopped about awkwardly below her wrists. However, she was extremely mobile, not allowing her disability to hinder her ability to trot along in any way.

Susan initially walked past the hostel and glanced in. Luckily Syd was still talking to the manager. His burly frame blocked the kitchen doorway. His left elbow was resting on the door frame. Susan could see he was still munching on his sandwich, every now and then he would emphasise what he was trying to say by waving his arm about, causing the two slices of bread to flap together.

"Right little lady, no noise. You hear me?"

Susan again bent and carefully scooped Sheba up in her arms. She walked over to the heavy swing front door and shoved it open with her right knee.

"Evening Syd."

"Hello darling, had a good day?"

Syd had intuitively realised the reason for Susan's loud interaction.

They were both talking in slightly exaggerated raised voices just in case Sheba decided to let out a sudden bark. Before the manager had got a chance to look past Syd to see who he was talking to, Susan had already begun heading up the stairs to her room.

She hadn't long settled Sheba down when there was a knock at her door.

"Open up mate, it's Syd."

Susan opened the door.

"I know you're gonna be stuck in here tonight. I got the chef to knock you up a cheese and onion sarnie. There's also a bag of crisps, a bar of choccy and a couple of cans of beer. If you should need me, just shout."

"Thanks, Syd you're a darling. Sheba is nicely settled on my bed. I'm going to eat this feast you've brought me, then get an early night. I'm exhausted. See you in the morning, mate."

Susan blew Syd a kiss, closed the door and sat down on one of the wooden chairs in her room.

She let out a huge sigh, rubbed her eyes and then shook her head.

"What a bloody day," she mumbled to herself as she tucked into the snack Syd had brought her.

Susan ran herself a hot bath and picked up one of the cans of beer.

"Well, it's not quite prosecco, but it'll have to do."

Susan suddenly awoke, the water in the bath was freezing cold.

"Bloody hell, how long have I been asleep?" she thought to herself.

Carefully, so as not to disturb the cold water too much, Susan moved her left foot towards the plug, hooked the chain between two toes, and tried to pull the plug from the waste trap. Eventually, it gave way and the ripples of cold water that covered the parts of Susan's body that had already dried caused her to shudder. Once all the water was gone, she climbed out of the bath and grabbed her towel off the radiator.

It didn't take her long to dry herself and slip on her grey towelling tracksuit bottoms and bedtime t-shirt. As Susan entered her bedroom, Sheba lifted her head. She yawned and then lay her head back down on Susan's pillow.

"Cheeky little madam."

Susan carefully climbed under the duvet, so as not to disturb Sheba, and tried to settle down for the night.

As hard as she tried, she just couldn't fall asleep. She tossed and turned for an hour or so, her mind in overdrive, thinking about the events of the day.

Then there was the next hurdle that they had to cross, trying to get Sheba to the safety of the UK. She knew all too well that it was going to be a huge undertaking to help Sheba, and in the end, would there be a family out there who would be prepared to adopt her with her severe disabilities?

"Sod it," Susan said out loud as she threw off the duvet and clambered out of bed.

Again, Sheba lifted her head, but she soon went back to sleep.

Susan's room was cold, she always slept with the window open, the sounds of night-time city life normally helped her sleep, reminding her of her small flat back in London.

"Right, there's no time like the present. Gotta start sometime, let's find Sheba her furever home."

Susan cracked open the last can of beer Syd had given her earlier, fired up her laptop and quickly set about trying to put together an urgent appeal for Sheba.

To start with, she uploaded and added the distressing photos she had taken of Sheba the first time she had seen her locked in her cage at the compound. Then she typed a quick message.

WILL YOU PLEASE HELP ME PLEASE????

The disabled pup's name is Sheba. She is approximately two years of age, and she has been rescued from a state-run shelter, a very 'loose term' indeed in Bulgaria. We would like to raise the funds to get Sheba to the UK. Now her main problem is that she potentially has rickets that has never been treated. Her nature is wonderful. I have spent time with her, and although she is disabled, when walking, she is extremely mobile. This site is about Sheba getting to the UK and getting the care and a home she so deserves. Will 2015 be Sheba's year for a chance of happiness?

"Sounds alright to me," Susan thought to herself.

She pressed the send button, and instantly launched the appeal on both her personal and the charity's social media sites.

Sheba's name and profile were now out there, on the world wide web. Potentially millions of people would get to see her harrowing photos. Now it was a waiting game to see if an offer of a home in the UK would miraculously come in for her.

Susan climbed back into bed, snuggled up against Sheba, then slowly drifted off.

At bang on 10 o'clock the next morning, one of the nurses from the rescue pulled up at Susan and Syd's hostel. She gave three blasts on the animal ambulance's horn. Syd checked that the coast was clear, and in a well-practised manoeuvre, Susan carried Sheba down the stairs and out to the awaiting van.

There was a sombre atmosphere at the compound when they arrived. Sadly, little Tom had passed away. He had been brought in the previous day after he had been found slung into a refuse bin.

His body was riddled with dozens of 50 mm nails that had been fired into him from a nail gun. He had also been beaten so ferociously that his eyes had literally popped out of their sockets. There was nothing that Spencer, the compound's vet, could do for the little dog, the horrific internal damage he had sustained was beyond repair.

As Spencer administered the Pentobarbital, the seizure medication used to end a dog's life humanely, five volunteers gathered around stroking Tom's frail body, giving him lots of cuddles and trying to use their happy voices to tell him what a good boy he was, even though this was the hardest thing for them to do. The drug quickly rendered him unconscious and shut down his heart and brain functions. The blessed little soul now had to make his lone journey over the Rainbow Bridge.

Susan and Syd spent some time consoling the volunteers before introducing them to Sheba.

After about an hour of playing with Sheba, and settling her down, Susan and Syd got ready to leave, they had some more urgent work to carry out at the shelter they had rescued Sheba from.

"Right little lady, you be a good girl, you hear me?" Susan said as she bent down and kissed Sheba on her forehead. She stood up and pulled a few strands of fur from her mouth.

Sheba, in a state of confusion, looked up at Susan, who had by now handed the lead to Spencer. She also gave him the preliminary notes that she scrawled down at the compound.

"Take extra care of her, she is one very special little lady."

Spencer nodded.

"I can see that. Right missy you're coming with me. Time for a check-up."

During her health check, Spencer had taken a small blood sample and carried out a pre-anaesthetic blood test. He had also weighed her and had calculated the exact amount of anaesthesia that would be required.

Sheba had been starved for the previous twelve hours to hopefully prevent any vomiting when she would wake up after her procedure.

Sheba was led into the small makeshift operating theatre. Bewildered by the room she now found herself inside, she grasped at her lead, which was being held by one of the nurses, and tried to pull her backwards, out of the room.

The nurse knelt and stroked Sheba.

"Don't be afraid poppet. Once this is all over, we can look at getting you to your new home."

Reluctantly, Sheba dropped the lead and tentatively followed the nurse.

Spencer entered the room, holding Sheba's teddy bear. He sat down on the floor and started to play with the toy. Sheba shuffled over and joined in.

Once he was happy that she had calmed down, he lifted her up onto the operating table. Initially she struggled, but she soon relaxed when given her toy back to play with.

One of the nurses took over distracting Sheba, while the other picked up the hair clippers. She switched them on, away from Sheba. The sudden click and buzzing sound alarmed Sheba, she tried to back away, but there was nowhere for her to go, the other nurse was still holding tightly onto her collar.

For a couple of minutes, the nurse with the clippers kept switching them on and off, every time moving them ever closer to Sheba.

"Hold her tightly I'm going to try and shave her fur now."

She moved in and gently started shaving Sheba's fur from the middle of her tummy, the area where Spencer would be performing the surgery.

"There's a good girl. All done."

The nurses cleaned the freshly shaved area with an iodine mixture and called for Spencer.

"OK little lady, one small prick then you'll drop off into the land of nod."

He retrieved the hypodermic needle that contained the pre-med. Swiftly, he parted some fur on Sheba's front right shoulder and carefully inserted the needle containing the combination of several drugs.

Sheba looked around at him startled. She quickly calmed down as the concoction started to make her feel sleepy.

The cocktail he had administered would also ensure that the pain relief she would be given when she awoke would be as effective as possible.

Spencer and his team had already preliminarily cleansed the operating theatre. The two nurses conducted a final full sterile clean, and then gathered the sterile wrapped set of surgical tools Spencer would require.

With Sheba becoming drowsier, Spencer prepared to administer the accurately measured dose of anaesthetic to fully sedate her.

"Nurse, can you double check the dosage for me, please. Sheba weighs eighteen kilos. I am using Diazepam/

Midazolam and have calculated 0.4 mg/kg IV. Due to the state of her front legs, I am opting for a four-inch jugular catheter."

The nurse checked and confirmed his calculations. Spencer drew the liquid from the phial and injected it into Sheba. Within a minute she was fully sedated. A tube was placed into her windpipe to allow the correct level of anaesthetic gas and oxygen to be continually administered throughout the short procedure.

"OK nurse, are we all ready?"

"Yes Spencer, good to go."

Spencer patted Sheba on the head.

"Well little lady, this is the first step to your new life."

Spencer covered his mouth and nose with a surgical mask. "Right ladies, if we are all happy then I'll begin."

The two nurses who were monitoring Sheba both nodded.

"Scalpel please."

Spencer was handed the surgical tool and carefully sliced through several layers of flesh. He parted the incision he had made with his fingers and found the first of Sheba's ovaries. He tied off its blood vessels and then carefully sliced it off. He cleared the area of blood, then found her second ovary, and repeated the process. He then tied off the uterus, cut it free and removed it. He checked and then double-checked for any signs of bleeding before cleaning the incision area one last time. Then he began to sew the layers of stomach tissue back together. Finally, he carefully closed the incision area with a row of neatly stitched sutures.

"Right, nice job if I do say so myself."

Again, he patted Sheba on the head.

He pulled off his mask and looked down at her badly deformed front legs.

Gently he lifted her left paw, which hung limply below her metacarpal bone. A bulbous callus had formed where her leg touched the ground. He ran his hand down to her paw. Sheba's black claws had grown extra-long and thick and were curling back into her pads, due to them never coming into contact with the ground because of her deformity.

Spencer shook his head.

"You poor little thing. I know that somewhere in the UK there is a skilful surgeon who can mend your poor legs," he whispered to Sheba.

As he stood in silence, gently caressing her body, his mind wandered back to his five years as a student at the Royal Veterinary College, London. He thought about the complex lectures he had sat through, listening intently to the skeletal makeup of dogs.

"How on earth would you even begin giving this poor little dog two straight legs? One thing is for sure, if it does happen for her, she'll be no stranger to the surgeon's knife for the next year or so."

Without realising it, he was speaking his thoughts out loud, and unaware that one of the nurses had walked into the theatre.

"Were you talking to me, Spencer?"

Startled by the sudden intrusion, he spun around.

"No sorry. Miles away. Is everything alright?"

"We are going to have to move Sheba into the recovery area. We have just received two separate calls within minutes of each other, we have two separate emergency cases en route. The mobile team in the north of the city have caught a dog who is suffering from a botched castration. His wounds are badly infected and the stitches have burst. A team in the south has found a Belgian Shepherd. His legs are bound together with gaffer tape, and it appears his teeth have been ground out. He is understandably very distressed, very angry and in a lot of pain."

Spencer looked at the nurse.

"How the hell would you grind the teeth of a Mali? They'd rip your hand off."

"I don't know, Spencer. Obviously, we won't be able to fit a muzzle if you have to try and repair the stumps he has left."

"We'll cross that bridge when he arrives. Obviously, once we've calmed him we'll sedate him and do whatever we can."

He gave Sheba one last stroke.

"No rest for the wicked."

He looked around the operating theatre and started mentally preparing the kit he was going to require for the two dogs heading to the rescue. Then he turned his attention back to Sheba.

"Right young lady, you're going to have to stay inside for a week or so. No running around for you, I'm afraid."

Daily, Spencer would look in on Sheba to check on her operation wound for any signs of infection. Although, if the truth be known, he enjoyed the thirty minutes of peaceful respite from the atrocities he had witnessed throughout the course of the day.

Sheba had been given a dreaded 'buster collar' to wear. Naturally, she would have wanted to lick the scarred area, in her mind helping with the healing process. There's a myth that dogs' mouths and tongues have antibacterial properties. The scientific fact is that dogs' mouths also contain harmful bacteria that live alongside the good bacteria, that if Sheba had licked her wound could have caused an infection.

As the days passed, Sheba's scar started to itch. The torturous collar annoyingly prevented her from giving the aggravating irritation a much-needed lick.

Away from the convalescence suite, at long last things were starting to look positive for Sheba. The initial profile Susan had done of her had received a lot of attention, and a trickle of donations had come in. But, as of yet, there had been no offers of a home, however, the rescue team remained optimistic.

A few days later, back in England, things took a turn for the worst for European dog travel.

Elizabeth was sitting with a cup of tea going through the rescue's inventory of food and medical supplies, or more to the point, the lack of them when her mobile phone rang.

She didn't recognise the number, usually, she would have rejected the call, but for some reason, she answered.

"Hello?"

"Hi Elizabeth, I'm really sorry to trouble you. I was given your number by Wilson. I'm not sure if you've met him, he runs a small rescue just outside Sofia. My name is Polly, you don't know me, but I'm involved with a team who arranges transportation for street dogs to the UK."

"Hello Polly. Yes, I know of Wilson, him and his team rounded up a lot of strays a few months ago. How can I help you? Or are you ringing to help me?"

"Neither really. I've only just arrived back in Bulgaria. I helped transport six dogs to a sanctuary in the UK that already had adoptive families lined up. The reason for my call is while I was in the UK a vet friend of mine rang me regarding an outbreak of babesiosis."

"Babesiosis in England? There has never been a recorded case over there as far as I am aware."

"You're right. That is until a couple of weeks ago. This really is not good news for us trying to get dogs over there. Not just from Bulgaria, all of Europe is under the spotlight."

"Bloody hell. Have you got more in-depth details? Save me having to trawl through the internet."

"Two dogs, not living with the same families, became infected, strangely they live, and were exercised in the same area. A town in Essex was identified as the common denominator. As a precaution, two large fields have been cordoned off, with warning signs put up advising dog walkers not to enter. There have since been other cases, luckily, they were saved, but all of them required blood transfusions. This is really serious."

"Oh Polly, let's not worry too much yet. I have an old acquaintance, a lecturer in veterinary sciences at Cambridge. I know he has been working on, along with a zoology expert friend of his, an article for the *Vet Times*. For some time now he's been gathering data relating to tick-borne diseases. I'll give him a call."

"To be honest Elizabeth, I doubt he'll be able to help. The local vet, who just so happened to have treated both the initial cases, carried out some detective work of his own. He sent his data to the RCVS, they passed on the info, and now two specialist government agencies are working in the area. They will take whatever actions are necessary."

"Where does this leave us?"

"I'm not sure. Initial findings state that potentially it could prove impossible to stop the spread of the disease, caused by a single-celled parasite."

"You have gotta be kidding. From memory, the parasite finds its way into the bloodstream and that's why it's so dangerous."

"Yes, from what I have learned, and been told, then it enters the cells and in the process of trying to kill the parasite the dog's natural defences would in fact destroy its own blood cells. A bloody painful death."

Polly paused, then continued with the potential problems the relocation charities would now face.

"This is the worrying bit for us. The expert's main concern is that it could spread throughout the country."

Elizabeth shook her head then butted in.

"How is this worrying for us? Surely our dogs can hopefully still be taken to the UK and stay in the rescue sanctuaries?"

"I have it on good authority that the experts have serious concerns about the outbreak, and these are going to be published in veterinary journals. They will potentially highlight that if it spreads quickly throughout the country, then it is going to be a very significant problem. So far there is not enough gathered information to predict how quickly this will happen. Also, it is highly unlikely that the problem will disappear, now that both the vectors and pathogens have been firmly established. At present, there is a very well-defined area of contamination. The problem in the future is that every female tick will lay a couple of thousand eggs, and all those offspring from that disease will carry the disease. As mammals move around, they will start spreading the disease. Although dog walkers can be advised not to go there, foxes and other animals may transport these ticks countrywide."

Elizabeth stared vaguely at her phone, almost imagining that it had transformed into Polly, who had somehow just sprouted a second head.

"I'm still lost. You've dazzled me with all the scientific gobbledygook, but I still just don't get how it will affect us."

Polly could feel herself becoming more frustrated in trying to make Elizabeth grasp the severity of the situation.

"In a nutshell Elizabeth, it is without a doubt that the deadly strain of tick has been brought to the UK by a dog that had recently returned from an overseas family trip. The bit that causes us concern, there is talk that it could have originated from one of the dogs brought over from an overseas dog rescue facility."

The penny dropped.

"Oh, sod it. Will they stop our efforts then? What about all the dogs we have saved, we don't have the facilities to keep them all here. Do they expect us to give up on them and leave them to die?"

"I'm hoping that they won't stop the import of rescued dogs. But one thing is for sure, we are going to have to expect a lot of negative press over the next few weeks, until something else makes the headlines."

A week after Sheba's surgery, Susan popped back to Elizabeth's office to check up on her recovery.

She also needed to go over the necessary requirements to finally get her to the UK.

"Hi Susan, how are you?"

"All fine and dandy thanks."

Elizabeth instinctively could see that Susan had something on her mind.

"Come on then, out with it."

"Out with what?"

"Something is bothering you. Tell Aunty Liz all about it."

"Why do they do it?" asked Susan.

"Who and do what?"

"People, why do they hurt the dogs?"

"I think it would be easier for me to describe colour to a blind person than answer your question."

"I'm not sure I can carry on with this rescue work, Elizabeth. I can't stand seeing the pain and suffering those poor dogs have been subjected to."

"We all have days like that, Susan, but you have to carry on, you were put on this planet to help them."

Elizabeth knew she had to change the subject, and quickly turned it around to all that Susan had done for the little disabled dog she had rescued.

"You did right in getting Sheba out of that hell on earth, you saved her life. Isn't she a gorgeous little doggy? We have all fallen in love with her. To be honest, we'll be sorry to see her leave. Anyway, I've printed off the GOV.UK travel requirements for dogs, and I've added the basic costs. Hopefully, your fundraising page idea will strike a nerve with some of our supporters back home. Give my love to the brute when you next see him."

Susan had soon forgotten about the negativity that had engulfed her, her mind was now fully focused on Sheba

"Thank you very much, Liz, and thanks for taking care of her. Slowly but surely donations have started trickling in. I've copied a few dog rescues back home into the fundraising page, and hopefully one of them will pick up on Sheba's plight and be able to step in. Oh, and I take it by the 'brute' you mean Syd?"

The two ladies chuckled.

"Have you got the list I need for Sheba?"

Liz handed Susan the A4 piece of paper. Susan sat down and started reading through the necessary requirements:

'The dog must be treated against tapeworm before travelling. Treatment must be administered by a vet not less than one day and no more than five days before the dog's scheduled arrival time in the country of destination. Treatment date and time must be recorded by the vet on the pet passport or official third country veterinary certificate.

All dogs would need a passport. This will have to have a unique ID number, their given name and a detailed description of the dog, showing the gender and breed of dog if known, and colouring and any distinguishing features. The passport will also have to be filled out with a full and detailed vaccination record, including all the small stickers from the vaccines stuck in the relevant pages.

A medical certificate for the dog indicating its origin, if this was known and health status, which will have to be issued by an authorised veterinary doctor, and which verifies that the dog has undergone a check no more than twenty-four hours before the expected date of travel and the check has not shown any clinical symptoms of a disease.

If over three months old, the dog has received a rabies shot with an inactivated vaccine containing no less than 1 UI, measured by applying the activation method described in the existing European pharmacopoeia, no less than thirty days and no more than twelve months prior to the date of travel, and that the certificate bears an indication of the vaccine's brand name and serial number.

The implanting of microchips in all captured dogs.

Microchips are now mandatory within the UK, and these details are also to be included on the passport.

All female dogs will have to be spayed and male dogs neutered.

List of requirements and estimated costs Sheba will need to get her to the UK:

Neutering £19

Rabies vaccination £32

Microchipping £15

Dog passport £18

Travel costs £150

Total, approximately £230 to get Sheba safely to the UK.'

"To be honest Elizabeth, we're not far off that total now. If we are lucky enough to raise above the basic costs, we can allocate those extra funds to chip in with Sheba's ongoing boarding fees until an adoptive family can be found. There will also be the additional costs of a thorough veterinary medical examination by the designated vet of the charity who eventually takes care of her."

"Just a thought Susan. The £150 travel fees are for a shared transporter van. There's no way Sheba could endure a couple of days cooped up in a cage, surrounded by other dogs. She'll end up doing herself, or one of the other passengers, a right mischief."

"Bloody good point. Are the transporters independent or charity funded?"

"Charity funded, and as you know money is sparse. Leave it with me, I'll see what I can do."

"Thanks Liz, I'm pretty sure that's everything covered."

"By the way Susan, did you see the online articles about the tick problem not far from London?"

"Yes. A girlfriend I was at college with works at the RCVS. She messaged me a few weeks back when she first heard. I didn't want to worry you."

Elizabeth shook her head.

"You should have told me."

"Why? I didn't want to add to your problems, you've got more than enough on your plate as it is. Anyway, it was a lot of nothing at the end of the day, and it has all blown over now. As long as we can prove all necessary precautions have been taken, we can carry on finding homes back in the UK for our dogs. The problem can be controlled by regular monthly flea tablets, the one's already recommended and administered by vets. All the negative and damning fake news reports were on the whole ignored and treated with the utter contempt that they deserved. Yes, a few lowlife ignorant upstarts did offer their worthless, uneducated opinions. You know the type, nonconformists, typical attention-seeking social outcasts. Their lifetime ambition is to appear on daytime TV to get their fifteen minutes of fame boasting of their illegal substance and alcohol abuse. They get their kicks humiliating themselves and their families, bragging graphically about their relationship problems. Who gives a damn about their opinions?"

"Well, I consider myself well and truly told."

"Sorry Liz, these wan ... I mean idiots, really do piss me off. Right, time for me to pop in and see Sheba."

Susan left Elizabeth and headed to the hospital block.

Sheba leapt up at the cage door of her kennel as soon as she heard the voice of her human friend.

Susan knelt in front of her.

"Right little lady, I've brought a nice treat for you. But

I'm warning you, leave the other doggies alone. Do you hear me?"

Susan slid the metal clasp and opened the door. Sheba walked out and stared all around the room. Just as Susan was about to take the gift that she had brought for her out of her pocket, Sheba pelted across the room.

A red mist had descended over her, she went potty, snarling and barking at a dog recuperating in his kennel after having one of his hind legs amputated.

"No Sheba, leave it!" Susan shouted as she ran across the room after her. She grabbed Sheba by her collar and pulled her away from the kennel. The small dog tried to shuffle to the back of his pen, well out of harm's way.

"Naughty doggy. What the hell was that all about? That poor little sod has lost a leg, and the last thing he needs is you gobbing off at him."

Susan, grasping firmly on Sheba's collar, frogmarched her back across the recuperation area and put her back in her kennel. She tutted and shook her head.

Sheba shuffled forwards and tried to poke her nose through the metal bars.

"What the hell have you been through in the past? Why are you so afraid of other dogs?"

Susan couldn't stay angry at her for long. She tickled Sheba's nose, and as she did, Sheba tried to lick her hand.

"There's something so very special about you, poppet. Even when you've been a little mare you still always manage to tug at my heartstrings."

She reached into her pocket and pulled out the special treat she'd brought, a tin of sardines in tomato sauce. Carefully, so she didn't slice her fingers on the sharp metal edge, she peeled back the lid and pulled out one of the sardines. Sheba's tongue lapped at the bars as Susan poked the oily fish through. It didn't take Sheba long to devour the whole tin.

Susan reached into her pocket for a tissue to wipe her fingers but couldn't find one.

"Sod it, you haven't got germs," she said as she licked her fingers clean.

A week passed. It was late afternoon, and yet again, Susan had had a day from hell in another one of the city's so called 'dog sanctuaries'.

Ordinarily, she would have headed back to the hostel and locked herself in her room.

Once within her little place of peace and sanctuary, she would have picked up her beloved travelling companion, a jet-black Fender acoustic guitar, and tried to play a few chords. After thirty minutes or so, she would grab her bottle of cheap, nasty local vodka and drown her sorrows. But not today, she needed much more consoling than booze and a guitar alone could give her.

Instead, she decided to pop back over to the rescue sanctuary to see how Sheba was doing.

Liz was clearing out a kennel when Susan arrived. Instinctively she knew why Susan was there. She knew that the compound Susan had been working at had a grotesque reputation and that mentally, the day would have taken its toll on Susan.

"Hi Susan, be a darling. Would you take Sheba out for a walk for me please?"

"That's just the tonic I need. Is she fully healed now?"

"Yup, all healed and ready for transportation. And she has had most of her jabs. Listen, as a suggestion the keys to my van are on my desk. Get her out of here. She is going stir crazy and needs a break from this place. Why don't you take her for a walk in the forest at the Borisova Gradina. It'll do both of you the world of good, get right away from rescue sanctuaries and the hustle and bustle of the city for a little while."

"Bloody good idea. We've got an hour or so until sunset. You know what it's like, after dark, the local druggies and idiots take over the park."

"Can't you take Syd with you?"

"I'll tell him you called him a druggy idiot."

"I didn't say that, I meant take him with you for company."

"Not today, he's dealing with a couple of the workers at the compound we were at earlier."

"Bless him."

They both laughed, knowing full well that Syd had his own unique ways of dealing with anyone who harmed dogs.

Sheba started twirling in excited circles as soon as she saw Susan approaching her kennel.

"Come on missy, we're going out. Now, no repeats of last week, you leave the other sick doggies alone. Hear me?"

Susan opened the kennel door, and after a cuddle, stroke and a face full of sloppy kisses, she attached Sheba's new pink lead, a gift from one of the nurses, to her collar and led her out to the van. Sheba grumbled at a couple of the dogs on her way out, but a firm word from Susan calmed her down.

Susan lifted Sheba onto the passenger seat, secured her to the seat belt, carefully closed the door and went around and climbed into the driver's seat.

Susan took a CD out of her small rucksack and slid it into the van's stereo.

She had made herself a disc before she had left the UK, a collection of her favourite music, ranging from her childhood to her time at nursing college.

"Right Sheba, do you like 'Les Bicyclettes De Belsize'? It's my favourite Engelbert Humperdinck song, it reminds me of when I was a little girl."

Susan cranked up the volume and set off on the short drive. As she drove, she sang, rather badly, along with the CD.

All the while Sheba sat quietly, with a contented smile on her face, looking on in wonderment at the passing cityscape as it hurtled past.

Whenever she spied a fellow street dog, scurrying along the pavements, Sheba would strain her head to get a better look, hoping that it may have been one of her siblings. Once she had again been left disappointed that it wasn't Duque, Tess or Sam, she'd let out a loud, angry, warning bark, which always, without fail, made Susan jump.

Susan pulled up and parked the van in a side street just outside the main entrance to the park.

She climbed out of the van. In the cold late afternoon air, Susan could feel a fine misty rain. She closed her eyes, and bent her neck back, so her face was facing skywards. She smiled; the rain felt as if sparkly champagne bubbles were gently hitting her skin.

After a few moments, she opened the passenger door and carefully lifted Sheba out.

"Oh Sheba, life right now feels so good being here with you. Come on poppet."

Susan looked down again at the little dog, with her tail wagging in excitement, looking back up at her. Susan patted her thigh with the palm of her hand and off they set together, at a nice slow gentle pace.

They walked past the empty flower beds, a few bulbs were just emerging through the frozen, solid soil. The once carefully manicured lawns had been churned up into muddy quagmires by the dogs that had run over and dug at them when they were in the park having their daily exercise over the wet winter months.

It took them about five minutes before they reached the forest, a peaceful oasis set within the bleak grey city.

Together they walked through the woods. On their stroll, they encountered a few other dog walkers, and every time without fail, Sheba would bark at the dogs. Was she warning them off or protecting Susan?

"Leave it," Susan would command her firmly, but Sheba took no notice. It was as if an angry red mist had descended and enveloped her.

Continually she growled at any dog she spied, those walking off lead who dared to venture over to say hello were met by a ferocious show of teeth. The dogs, without fail, always retreated to the safety of their handler. Duly, the handlers would glare at Susan and mumble some profanities under their breaths.

"Get stuffed," Susan would shout. Sheba would look up at her, and Susan would wink back at her.

They carried on walking through the woodland, amongst the vast variety of oaks, sycamores, birches and ash trees that had all been imported. Many were still bare of their leaves, but in a month or so the forest would be blooming and springing back into life.

As they ventured on deeper, the carefully thought-out

planting scheme radically changed. Up ahead, standing tall and proud in the slowly fading daylight, were the various species of deciduous trees and ferns that had been specially brought in from the city's neighbouring forests, along with the coniferous black pines and spruces from the mountain region of Rila. The forest had now taken on an eerie, almost Jurassic appearance, Susan half expected to be met by a hungry tyrannosaurus rex.

The ground underfoot was covered with decaying leaves, and the air was full of an earthy aroma. Sheba's nose twitched continuously as she tried to pick up on the array of strange new beautiful scents that surrounded her. One of Susan's lessons, when she was training to be a veterinary nurse, had focused on the importance of allowing dogs to sniff their surroundings when on their walks. Susan knew that for Sheba, sniffing was calming, mentally engaging and therapeutic, and by allowing her the time to explore the world around her provided her with some much-needed mental relaxation.

Susan plucked up the courage to walk even deeper into the forest, why should she be scared? She had her faithful German Shepherd dog next to her for protection.

The dense evergreen tree canopy prevented almost all traces of daylight from ever reaching ground level, and where wildflowers should sprout, the soil and decomposing leaves, and discarded bark were completely covered by a soft moss floor. The thick damp, small flowerless green plants underfoot made it feel as if Susan and Sheba were walking on a thick, soft woollen carpet.

With the sun now rapidly retreating and the temperature dropping, Susan turned and started to lead Sheba back to the van. In the distance she could hear screaming and shouting, some of the city's lowlifes and drug addicts had now started to emerge to come out to play.

They arrived back at the van and Susan unlocked the doors, opened the passenger door and carefully lifted Sheba up.

"Good girl, now hang on while I get in."

Susan closed Sheba's door and headed around to the other side of the vehicle and climbed in.

"Sod it, silly cow. Just can't get used to the steering wheel being on the wrong side."

Susan laughed to herself as she got out of the van and headed back round to Sheba.

The pup looked bemused as Susan opened the door, lifted her out and carried her around to the right-hand side of the vehicle.

"It's probably safer for me to drive."

Susan shut the passenger door, walked back around and this time clambered into the driver's seat. She locked the doors, put the key in and turned on the ignition. The van was cold and Susan blew into her cupped hands to try and warm them up.

"Bloody hell it's freezing," she said as she reached for the fan blower control. She turned it up to full, but the engine wasn't warm enough yet to throw out any warm air. She turned the knob on the heater to the window demister.

"We'll just let it warm us up a bit and clear the window before we head off.

Right, while we're waiting, do you want to listen to another song on my CD, 'Mr Blue Sky' by ELO or 'Bless You' by Tony Orlando?"

Sheba looked at Susan and tilted her head to one side.

Slowly, the temperature inside the van began to rise, and the window screen began to clear from the bottom up of condensation.

Using her woolly gloves, Susan wiped the van's windows to remove the droplets of water that had formed and that were running down the glass.

"Right, if you don't pick a song then I will. Are you sure you have no final requests? Your loss, I'll choose then, and don't moan."

Susan opted for 'Bless You'.

She slid the CD back into the player, selected the tune she wanted to hear and pressed 'play'.

As the song began to play, Susan looked over at Sheba and stroked her head.

"You know what poppet? This song could have been written just for you."

Susan began to sing along.

"Oh, darling, bless you. Bless every breath that you take. Yeah, bless every move that you make so perfectly. And bless your little heart for loving me. Oh, bless you, bless you, child."

Sheba sat staring, her head tilting from side to side.

"I know, I know, don't give up the day job."

She laughed out loud and wiped the windscreen one more time with the back of her hand. Once she had cleared enough for her to be able to see out of, they set off on the short drive back to the dog rescue.

CHAPTER NINETEEN

Ann picked up her freshly made cup of strong sweet black coffee, gathered her cigarettes and lighter, then headed out of the reception area to the shelter of the large oak tree.

The biting cold January air hit her hard, and she wrapped her arms tightly around herself. Her waxed jacket may have been waterproof, but it didn't offer any protection against the cold.

She propped herself against the wooden fencing surrounding the paddock. She could see that the ground was still frozen solid.

The frost was beginning to retreat as the winter's sun rose in the sky. Slowly it displaced the shadows that spread out from the oak tree and stable blocks. Before Ann's eyes, the Hertfordshire countryside slowly became swathed in a warm winter's glow.

She laughed at the antics of the two donkeys noisily playing in the paddock they shared with a handful of rescued sheep. The boisterous pair, a jack and jenny called Dolly and Bailey, had been rescued from a breeder in the Provence region of France, they were destined to become salami meat and had to be purchased for the value of the meat that their bodies would have yielded. Ann took out and lit a cigarette;

she took a much-needed, long hard drag.

She cursed out loud as she took her first sip of coffee. Annoyingly for her, it was still far too hot to drink. It was her morning break working as a kennel maid at the dog rescue, a job she loved and had done since she left school thirty-five years earlier. She reached into her pocket for her mobile phone and logged into her social media account.

Saturday night had been spent at a music venue in Cambridge, The Damned, a London-based punk rock band were on a reunion tour after nearly forty years performing together. Ann had luckily managed to get herself a ticket and had spent the evening reliving her youth, pogoing to the loud music, drinking a few pints of snakebite, a combination of cider, lager and a dash of blackcurrant juice, her drink of choice in her younger days.

She had posted some obligatory photos before the evening's festivities had got into full swing, with the obligatory accompanying comments about how great it was to relive her misspent youth and to get to see her heroes again. Fans had travelled far and wide for the gig, and Ann had managed to meet up with and reminisced about the good old days with a couple of faces she had known from the punk movement in the late 1970s.

Now she was eagerly checking on how many responses she had received from her post, accepting new friends' requests and replying to some of the comments about how good her evening had looked.

After reading the updates to her status she started to scroll down to check up on any new activity from her family and friends.

Ann stopped scrolling. Glaring back at her from the

screen was a photo of a poor little dog, accompanied by a desperate plea to try and raise the urgently needed funds to help it, and to find it a furever home in the UK.

Ann's compassion for all animals had no bounds, and she regularly subscribed to many animal welfare sites, making regular charitable donations to assist the charities with the associated costs of rehoming and relocating dogs to the UK.

The previous year she had been part of the rescue team that had helped to bring a severely disabled German Shepherd dog, named Tammy, over from Egypt.

Consequently, Ann had worked round-the-clock shifts to help nurse her back to health after major corrective surgery had been performed on her two deformed front legs. The image now staring at her from her phone bore a remarkable similarity to the deformities that Tammy had once endured and suffered from. She logged onto her online banking and sent a £10 donation to the charity to help with the fundraising appeal for the little dog.

Throughout the day, the image of the little dog kept appearing on Ann's phone. She could see that the donations to her appeal to rescue her and get her to the UK had exceeded the amount needed. There had been dozens of messages of support left on her online appeal page, but as of yet, no offers of a home for her had been made.

Ann's many years in working with rescue dogs had taught her that people naturally tended to bypass any dog who was elderly or one with deformities. Another issue that Ann was mindful of was that the little dog could potentially be blind or deaf. Often these disabilities were not mentioned in the uploaded profiles of the strays. They were not visible defects, such as missing or deformed limbs, and, as Ann knew only too well, would not impact on the appeal for the dog in the photograph.

It was 6 o'clock, and the end of Ann's shift. The Hertfordshire countryside night sky was pitch black.

Before she left to go home, Ann called Elsie, the owner of the sanctuary to update her on the progress of two dogs that had been saved, and recently brought over to the UK from a 'Killing House' in Spain. At the end of her update, she mentioned the little dog that was gaining a lot of public interest and support on social media.

"Miraculously they have reached the total needed to bring her over in less than two weeks, now there's just the small issue of trying to find her a safe haven in the UK until she is adopted."

"I know exactly where this is leading, Ann," said Elsie.

"Do we have enough space at present to take her?"

"Yup, we've got two boarding kennels vacant, and as it's winter I doubt we'll be getting many boarders in for a few weeks yet."

"Give me all the details that you've got about her so far."

"No worries, I'll send you the link to her online appeal and profile."

"You know that I can't make any promises. But in my forty years of running this rescue, I have never turned a dog in need of sanctuary away yet, and I don't ever intend on doing so. I'll have a good look later on. I need to know exactly what we're up against, and what specialist care she will need. If it's not too late when I've finished, I will even try to get the ball rolling and make some calls."

Elsie sat down. She was exhausted, having just finished yet another eighteen-hour day.

Yet again, a cheese and raw onion sandwich and sweet cup of tea would have to suffice for dinner. She started to look at the profile of the little dog Ann had sent to her earlier.

"From what I can see from the photos, her disabilities do look exactly the same as Tammy's."

It was midnight and Elsie was sitting with four of her own dogs, all rescues whom the rescue had struggled in finding homes for due to illness or other health problems. Syska, a Malinois, looked addled at Elsie as she mumbled away to herself.

"I'll ring the orthopaedic surgeon first thing tomorrow morning. I know that we can help this little dog. We will do what we do best, step in and offer her a place of sanctuary."

Although it was very late, she decided to get the ball rolling and sent an email to her acquaintance, who was a specialist veterinary orthopaedic surgeon, with some photos from the internet of the little dog.

"I know he can fix her," she thought to herself. She glanced over at Tammy, fast asleep on her soft bed.

"First thing in the morning we'll put a plan of action into place. As long as the charity has taken care of everything at their end there's no reason why she can't be here with us within a fortnight."

Elsie was awoken the next morning by her mobile phone ringing. Yet again she had fallen asleep on the couch, her neck ached due to the awkward position she had slept in.

She looked at the caller ID. It was Bill, her orthopaedic specialist friend.

"Hi darling, I'm guessing you saw my email then?"

"Morning Elsie. Yes, I saw it this morning. I'm just driving to work and thought it'd be a good time to have a chat. Well, I'm guessing that you are bringing her over. Are you going to keep her, or have you got a home lined up for her?"

"Yes, to question one, no to part one of question two, and as of yet, no to part two of question two, if that makes any sense. In all fairness Bill, I've only just agreed to step in. I haven't even been in touch with the overseas rescue team yet. So it's all still up in the air, so obviously we've not put her on our dogs need rehoming page yet."

"I sort of understand your answers. Well Elsie, there's no time like the present."

"You'll help her if they agree to us taking her?"

"Of course, and yes, before you ask there'll be no fee."

"Oh Bill, you are a darling. I owe you one."

"Actually, Elsie you will now owe me two, you've forgotten about Tammy."

The pair of them burst out laughing.

Elsie hung up, and then dialled Ann's number.

"Morning boss, is everything OK?"

"Yes Ann, all's fine and dandy. Just ringing to let you know Bill has kindly offered to operate on Sheba, if she comes to us. I know it's your day off, but could you contact the rescue team looking after her? I've got to take Peggy back to the vets for a check-up after her operation. If they're in agreement to let us take care of her, can you add her to the rehoming page? We need to get the ball rolling ASAP in trying to find a family willing to adopt her. Use the photos you've downloaded from the Bulgarian charity. We'll add our own if and when she gets here. Oh, also, while I think about it, send the overseas team a copy of our rehoming application form and our criteria for adoptive families, it's important that we let them know how we operate."

"Ah, that's the best news I've heard all day, mind you, it is only half seven. I'm just gonna take Rupert out for his morning walk, then I'll get straight on it. If you think of anything else, send me a text. And thank you for agreeing to help Sheba."

"Don't thank me darling, it's what we do. Thank you for alerting me to her plight. Take care and give Rupert a big hug from me. Speak later."

Ann went to her freezer and took out a bag of frozen peas, and put a couple of handfuls into a sandwich bag. Every day she stopped on Rupert's walk and fed the ducks on the local pond. She then grabbed an apple, her daily treat for the small horse they passed that was tethered on the common land.

She put Rupert's collar and lead on him, then they headed out on their morning's stroll.

Once home, after an hour's walk in the bracing cold, Rupert was rubbed down and dried, then Ann made herself a strong black coffee. She sat down and sent a message to the social media page that had been set up for Sheba.

'Hi, we are a small dog rescue sanctuary, established for over thirty years, based on the Herts/Essex border. We primarily used to take in local abandoned dogs from the two local authority dog warden teams, once the compulsory seven-day deadline for euthanasia had been reached. Over the last year or so we have been assisting overseas rescue teams with the rehoming of street dogs. Please see attached links regarding a street dog who had what appears to be the same disabilities as Sheba. I have also attached press releases regarding the corrective surgery Tammy received. We have everything in place to offer Sheba the chance of a new life and the surgery she needs. I have also attached a few of our rehoming documents. Best wishes, Ann xx'

Susan was out shadowing a team rounding up street dogs to take them to a newly set up neutering centre when her mobile phone pinged for the umpteenth time.

Sheba's page had received hundreds of goodwill messages. Regular posts kept appearing saying 'Oh what a gorgeous girl' or 'I wish I could adopt her, but …'.

People meant well, but, as kind as their messages were, none were offering Sheba a home.

Out of courtesy, Susan would always press the 'like' button, but she was becoming increasingly frustrated that no positive response had yet come through.

She took her mobile out of her rucksack and looked at the latest message. Susan couldn't believe her eyes.

"Bloody hell, we've done it!" she excitedly cried out.

One of the volunteers, who had been trying to catch an elusive small dog, spun round. As she did, the dog ran off again.

"Is everything OK?" the volunteer asked.

"Everything is more than OK. Right, I need to find a café so I can sit down and do some quick research into this rescue, then ring Liz. I'll be back and explain everything as soon as I can. You carry on, I'll ring you when I've finished."

"OK, there's a lovely little coffee shop just down the road who have the most delicious pastries."

"Thanks. Catch you in a bit."

Susan found the café, ordered herself a double espresso, and an apple Banitsa, then set about doing an online search of the rescue sanctuary who had messaged her.

"Wow, these guys sound amazing," she said to herself, as she scrolled through the search engine's results. The articles about Tammy's surgery had been published in the national press and there were links to radio interviews.

"Well Sheba, I think you've certainly landed on your paws, beautiful girl."

Susan dialled Liz's number.

"Hi Susan, I know why you're ringing, I saw the message. Well, have you done your research?"

"Oh Liz, they are more than perfect. We've done it."

Susan's voice quivered, she was overwhelmed and couldn't take it all in. She covered her mouth with her hand, then the tears of happiness flowed.

"No darling, you did it. Where are you at the moment?"

"In a café just up the road from the round-up team."

"Right, I'm going to send the van over with one of the nurses to take over from you. I need you back here to arrange everything for Sheba. Give us about half an hour to get to you. And once again, well done darling."

Susan quickly finished her coffee and cake, then headed back to where she had left the volunteers. They hadn't moved on; they had spent the last half an hour still trying to catch the little dog who had already escaped several times.

She heard a bib and looked over as the rescue centre's van pulled up.

Ada, one of the nurses, got out.

"Oh Susan, well done girl. Liz told me the amazing news."

"Isn't it brilliant? I still can't believe it. Right, this lot have so far only managed to catch one dog. It's in a cage in the back of their van. You know the drill, make sure it's well cared for, plenty of water, but no food. Give them a couple of hours then head over to the neutering centre, and monitor any procedures carried out. Tell them we will visit the dogs in two days, and please reiterate to them that none are to be released without our say so."

"Don't worry Susan, I've worked with them before. Now you clear off and give Sheba her good news."

On the drive back to the sanctuary, Susan sent a social media friend request and private message to Ann.

'Thank you very much for offering Sheba a home in the UK. If it's OK, could you please message me your mobile number and I'll call you within the hour x'

"Blimey I'm so excited, yet nervous," Susan said to Reg, the driver.

"I bet you are. Let's hope that Sheba is the first in a long line of pups we can get to the UK," he replied.

Susan's mobile pinged twice. One was Ann accepting her friend request, the second was a short message, just a mobile number and two kisses.

As soon as they arrived back at the sanctuary, Susan headed to the small admin office and dialled Ann's number.

"Hello."

"Oh, hi Ann, it's Susan. I really don't know where to begin but thank you so much for your amazing offer to help Sheba. She really is adorable."

Ann butted in.

"Calm down, darling. We've seen Sheba's profile you put up, you're right, she is adorable. Have you got everything in place at your end? We're good to go, as I said in my original message, we have an orthopaedic surgeon who has agreed to do the corrective surgery, and we have all the facilities to take care of her. All we need to do is start finding Sheba her furever home, but we're sure that a family will come forward soon. Who wouldn't want to adopt this beautiful girl?"

"That's fantastic, once again thank you so much. I need to check with our vet to see where Sheba is up to with her inoculations and organise a passport for her. She was spayed a couple of weeks ago, so that'll speed things up a fair bit."

"Brilliant. Keep us updated please, Susan."

"Will do. Bye Ann."

Susan wasted no time. She logged onto the office's computer, found all the relevant information that she needed and downloaded the documents to get Sheba's passport processed.

Once she had printed off everything she needed, she headed off to find Spencer.

"Hi mate, sorry to disturb you, but have you heard the brilliant news?"

Spencer was writing some notes up on an emergency case he had just dealt with.

"Hello Susan. Yes I did hear from one of the nurses. Best news I've heard in a long while."

"I've started gathering everything together to organise Sheba's passport."

"No need Susan. I've been keeping a file with everything logged about Sheba. She has her microchip and the unique number is on her documents. All her jabs are now done, including her rabies one. All the phial stickers are in her notes. She's good to go. I'll submit her passport to the Municipal Veterinary Clinic, who will then issue her certificate to travel."

"Blimey, looks like I've added to the deforestation of the planet for nothing printing all this off."

"You weren't to know, Susan. You crack on and do what you need to do and leave the forms up to me. Oh by the way, I needed to add a date of birth. You wrote in your first appeal that she is roughly two years old, so I opted for the 3rd of March as her birthdate, in honour of the anniversary of my great grandfather's death in 1943 during the Bethnal Green tube disaster."

"That's perfect Spencer, we'll never know for sure exactly how old she is. Although to be honest, looking at her now I'd guess she's probably just over a year old. Anyway, a minor detail, I'll get on with looking into transportation. With any luck, her new life will begin before Valentine's Day."

Days of frantic emails and phone calls followed, and finally a date was arranged for Sheba's life-changing journey to England, Friday the 13th of February.

CHAPTER TWENTY

It was a bitterly cold February morning. The air was full of excitement as Sheba's saviours gathered together to bid her farewell and wish her well on the arduous 1,500-mile journey that lay ahead of her.

She was about to undertake the next stage of her relocation. Hopefully, very soon, she would have a family, and home, to call her own.

Cliff and Charles, the two drivers, went through their final vehicle checks. Oil, water, fuel level, tyre pressure, snow chains, lights and wipers. They double-checked their provisions and gathered the cash they had been allocated, their passports and all of Sheba's required documentation.

Liz pulled up in her van.

"Morning darlings. How are we all? And how's my little Sheba, all fine and dandy I hope?"

She couldn't hide the excitement in her voice.

"Right, where are Sheba's drivers?"

"Morning, I'm Charles, Cliff has just popped to the gents again."

"Morning Charles. Be a love will you and help me get a box out of the van."

Charles followed Elizabeth over to her van, picked up

the box of provisions, then took it over and placed it with the rest of the kit needed for Sheba's journey.

"Right, there should be everything Sheba will need in there. I'll just quickly go through it with you. OK then, we have several tins of dog food, I must add they are Sheba's particular favourite brand, a small bag of kibble, several litre-bottles of spring water, two stainless steel bowls, a bag of emergency medication, just in case, a few treats and a small box of poo bags."

"Anything for us?"

"No dear, you are big enough and ugly enough to pack your own stuff."

The group laughed. Liz could always be relied upon for a quick-witted putdown.

Without any major hold-ups or breakdowns, the journey should take about thirty-six hours. Although allowing for unexpected delays, Sheba could end up being locked in the back of the van for almost forty-eight hours.

Gifts of a few toys had already been placed in her cage to try and offer some form of mental stimulation during her trip to the UK.

The route they were going to take was via the E70, passing through Serbia, hugging the Bosnian border before cutting across Slovenia and then on to Austria. The final stretch would take them across Germany, then through France. They would then board the cross-channel ferry at Calais, arriving at the port of Dover, England within two hours.

Then it was a final one-hundred-mile drive to Hertfordshire.

Cliff returned from the toilet, for the umpteenth time.

"It's the cold, goes straight through. Right, if we're nearly ready I'll fire up the jalopy and get it warmed up," he said.

As the van burst into life, Sheba, who was getting a farewell cuddle from one of the nurses who had taken care of her, spun around and barked.

"Bloody hell, that made me jump!" the nurse shrieked.

As Sheba stared at the van, rage surged through her body.

The sudden unmistakable, rattly sound of the diesel engine, and the pungent stench of kerosene that stank worse than a trump, combined with the grey smoke that had been emitted from the exhaust had initially alarmed her.

But that distinct smell also brought harrowing memories flooding back. Her mind flipped back to the awful night that she was captured, the night that her mother had been slaughtered, the night that she had seen her siblings for the very last time. Her anger soon turned to sadness.

Her train of thought was suddenly interrupted by a kindly voice.

"I'll never forget you, sweet Sheba. Please, don't you forget about me. Enjoy your life, and let your love flow freely."

Sheba looked up and there looming above her was Susan, her saviour.

Sheba's anger and sadness drifted away.

Susan kissed her on the forehead, then threw her arms around her neck.

Syd was standing in the background. He knew his macho image would be destroyed if he gave Sheba a farewell hug; there was no way he would let the little group that had gathered for her farewell see him cry.

He called out Sheba's name. She looked over at him, Syd winked, blew her a kiss, then discretely wiped a tear from his eye.

Charles looked at his watch.

"OK folks, if you've all said your goodbyes, it's time we were heading off.

If you can please get Sheba into her travel cage, we'll load her onto the van."

Susan gave her little dog one last hug and led her over to Cliff.

Liz stood back; she hated goodbyes. Plus, she would hate anyone to find out that she had a gentle side. When no one was looking, she wiped her eyes on the cuff of her coat.

With a little gentle coaxing, and a few freshly cooked sausages as bait, Sheba was soon locked safely in her cage.

She looked excited, yet terrified at the same time.

Charles and Cliff carefully lifted the cage and slid it into the cargo area of the van.

"Blimey, she's a lot heavier than she looks," grunted Cliff.

As the van door was gently closed in preparation for the long journey ahead, Susan closed her eyes. Tears streamed down her face, but for once, happy tears.

Both drivers had had a late night, and neither of them fancied taking the first shift, driving along Bulgaria's treacherous, ice-covered roads. A severe weather warning had been issued of a severe snowstorm approaching. They decided that the only fair way to pick who was to drive first was to toss a coin.

Cliff took a two-leva coin from his pocket and flicked it into the air, it landed on the back of his hand.

"Go on, you call. To be honest with you mate, I really don't want to be behind the wheel today. You know, Friday the 13th and all that. Why couldn't they have arranged it for tomorrow? A day wouldn't make any difference."

"A bit superstitious are we Cliff?"

"Just call will you?"

Charles called heads. Luckily for him he won, and unsurprisingly, he opted to let Cliff drive for the first eight hours.

One of their main worries was the noncompliance of the long-haul HGV drivers, returning to Bulgaria from England.

Due to the drivers' desperation to meet their deadlines, or face losing their jobs, many drove their huge wagons in a state of sheer exhaustion.

The vast majority of them did not observe the strict driving regulations they had to adhere to in the UK, which had put them behind schedule. Often their tachographs had been tampered with or were faulty.

Accidents were an all-too-common hazard that Cliff and Charles witnessed daily. The dog-tired truckers would momentarily fall asleep at the wheel of their HGVs. Without warning, up to forty-four tonnes of metal and cargo would veer across the road. No mercy was afforded, nor prisoners were taken, as they crashed into, and obliterated any unfortunate oncoming vehicles, annihilating their inhabitants. Along with the treacherous weather, the first day of driving was going to be a white-knuckle ride getting Sheba to her new home in England.

Cliff sounded the van's horn.

Susan, Syd, Liz and the rest of the group clapped and let out a rousing cheer.

Sheba's final, happy memory of Sofia would be the shouts of good luck, as the van slowly pulled away.

CHAPTER TWENTY-ONE

Syd and Susan's temporary voluntary rescue work in Bulgaria had come to an end, and they were heading back to the UK.

Their flights from Sofia to Stansted had been booked, and they were leaving the following evening. Their cab had been pre-ordered for the twenty-five-minute transfer journey.

As he returned to the hostel after his last day shadowing a neutering team, Syd spotted a letter in his key cubbyhole. He retrieved his key and stuffed the letter into his pocket.

Once he was in the solitude of his room, he tore open the brown envelope. Crudely scribbled on a small notelet was all the information that he required.

'Tuesday evening Kinko Bar Tsar Simeon Street'

"Looks like I've got myself a date for tonight then. Thanks Butler, you snivelling little grass," he mumbled to himself.

A few days earlier, Syd had stopped by the compound where they'd rescued Sheba from. Butler was on security duty and had been given a simple ultimatum, let Syd know where he could find Oz and Carter, or have several teeth extracted with a pair of pliers. Butler opted for the painless option and sold his mates down the river.

For Syd it was perfect timing, what with him flying home the following evening. He would have hated not to have been able to say goodbye to Carter and Oz in person.

There was a knock at his door. He opened it to be met by Susan standing there.

"Do you fancy a final night out, Syd? My treat."

"Sorry darling, I've got a date."

"You what, you've got a date? You sly old dog."

Susan was bemused, and if she was totally honest with herself, slightly jealous. Syd had not once mentioned that he had met someone, and why take his new mysterious lady friend out on his final night in Sofia?

Susan said goodnight, and with a wink of her eye wished him 'luck' on his night out.

With her plans for the evening dashed, Susan decided to spend the evening alone in her room swotting up on the atrocities inflicted on street dogs in Romania. A girlfriend, who had been on the same veterinary nurse course as Susan, had already started volunteering in a remote village close to Bucharest. Susan had already messaged her to arrange accommodation. After a two-week break back home in London, Susan was flying out to Romania for three months. She often wondered if she would ever get to use her hard-earned qualifications and one day become a veterinary surgeon, her main dream in life. But for the moment she was happy dedicating her time in helping with the ongoing plight of street dogs.

Syd headed off for a shower and shave, in preparation for the evening ahead.

When dressed, he popped downstairs to the small office in the reception area of the hostel.

"Evening mate, I'm leaving tomorrow, along with the young lady who is in room seven. Sorry but there's been a small bit of damage in my room, any chance I could borrow some tools and do some minor repair work?"

"My English no good boss."

"Bloody hell, here we go again. Tools, tools, you know, bloody tools."

Syd started making some ridiculous sounds and manic hand gesticulations trying to emulate power tools. Although his military career had taken him all over the world, Syd never bothered trying to learn the local lingo, his attitude was that they would have to learn his native tongue. Mind you, he had learned to order a beer and swear fluently in several foreign tongues, something that had got him both out of, and into trouble many times in the past.

Stifling his laughter, the duty manager got up from his chair and led Syd into the communal kitchen. He unlocked a wooden door and tugged on the grubby old pull cord.

The strip light begrudgingly flickered into life.

A familiar frowsty smell, a combination of old tins of paint, varnish and dirty hand tools that had been locked away in the airless larder filled the air.

Syd looked along the rows of ramshackle shelves that strained under the weight of the junk piled up on them. On the bottom shelf, he spotted a tatty canvas army holdall, with a selection of hand tools protruding from its broken zip.

Syd pulled an old 2 lb ball peen hammer from the bag, and gave it a swing, slapping the hammerhead into the palm of his left hand.

"Perfect, just the job. Just need to grab a few nails squire."

He put the hammer down on one of the shelves and carried on looking.

On one of the top shelves was a row of old biscuit tins.

Syd reached up and lifted a couple down and prised off their lids.

One was full of rusty old ironmongery. Syd tipped the contents out and luckily found exactly what he needed – a handful of four-inch nails.

"Thanks mate. I'll give the hammer back first thing in the morning, guvnor."

Syd quickly shoved the nails into one of his coat pockets, he didn't want the manager to see what he had taken, then he slid the hammer into his belt.

The manager looked bemused. He shook his head, turned off the light, locked the cupboard door and then headed back to his office, mumbling something under his breath.

Syd followed him and pretended to head back upstairs to his room.

Loitering in the darkened hallway, Syd heard the manager get into a loud argument with his wife on his mobile phone. The office door slammed shut.

"Perfect timing and I've got an alibi," he thought to himself.

Syd did up the toggle wooden buttons and pulled up the faux-fur-lined hood on his khaki parka.

When he was sure that the coast was clear, he quietly crept through the kitchen, opened the back door and headed out under the cover of darkness.

Syd shivered as he met the cold night air. He clambered ungracefully over the hostel's small rickety wooden fence, the days of him charging around assault courses were long behind him. If he had got his timing right, it should only be a brisk twenty-minute walk to the bar on Tsar Simeon Street.

The grotty bar that he had reliably been informed Oz and Carter would be drinking in.

As Syd reached his destination, he heard two familiar voices. Luckily for him, Carter and Oz had just been thrown out of the bar by two of the bouncers. They had gotten a bit too over-friendly with the new pole dancer, who just so happened to be the owner of the bar's girlfriend.

Music blared from the club that Syd had stopped next to. He propped himself against the front window and watched as his intended victims staggered off along the street. Ironically, one of his favourite songs, 'It'll Be Me' by Jerry Lee Lewis, was playing on the CD jukebox.

"Oh, it'll be me all right," he mumbled to himself.

Oz and Carter were completely inebriated and blissfully oblivious to the brute who stood glaring at them from the opposite side of the road.

Syd's distinctive battle-scarred features were eerily illuminated by the multicoloured lights emitting from the club's neon sign that hung above him. His prosthetic eye glistened brightly as the garish lights every now and then reflected in it.

The unfortunate twosome swayed and staggered, arms across each other's shoulders for support, along the footpath.

Poised and ready for action, Syd started to follow them.

Carter stopped walking, and turned back, looking, with one eye shut to help him focus, on both sides of the road to see if they had already passed the gyros shop he was looking for. Syd darted into a darkened shop doorway to avoid being spotted. He waited for them to head off again, biding his time, in readiness to make his move.

He dodged the traffic and ran across the street, all the

while keeping a safe distance.

It was nearly time, slowly Syd began to move in closer for the kill.

Aimlessly the pair stumbled into the Holy Trinity Park.

Carter was trying to light a cigarette, while Oz had stopped and was emptying his bladder up against a large old oak tree.

In his drunken state, Carter didn't see, nor hear his attacker approach. From out of the darkness a huge, clenched fist flew towards him.

Carter felt an almighty clump on the left side of his jaw. The heavy blow was accompanied by a sickening crack, like the sound made when you step on a fallen stick in a forest. Unfortunately for Carter, in that split second his jaw had been shattered.

Instantaneously his head spun around and snapped back, rattling his brain inside his cranium. A flash of darkness enveloped him, as the senses within his body rapidly shut down. The damp evening grass softened his impact as he keeled over.

Oz, who was in mid-flow, spun around to see what had caused the sudden noise from behind him. He turned back to quickly try and finish urinating and zip up his jeans.

He was too late.

Syd had already ran over and grabbed him from behind by his left shoulder and a clump of his lank greasy hair.

Syd slammed Oz's face forward into the rough bark of the tree. His nose burst and split open. His eyes started to stream from the pain. He sniffed to try and clear his nasal passage. The metallic taste of gore filled his mouth, then his warm blood trickled down the back of his throat. Stunned by the swift, painful severity of the initial attack, he hadn't been able to raise his hands to defend himself.

Dazed, he felt himself spun around, his back now resting against the tree.

Just at the point he was going to pass out, a burning sensation brought him back to his senses.

Syd grabbed both of his ears, his fingernails easily sank into the mastoid. Syd twisted Oz's ears to the point they were almost torn off, then using them as handles, he started to pommel the back of Oz's head into the clammy husk of the tree. Syd spun Oz around again, then rammed his face back into the bark.

Oz blacked out.

In his time working as a bouncer, the thing that Syd despised the most was the increase in ladies and men having their drinks spiked by perverted low lives, with the intention of making their victim vulnerable to assault, rape or robbery.

Syd had taken the time to learn about the warning signs displayed by an unfortunate, would-be victim. He knew that they could have slurred speech, be feeling extremely drunk, even if they'd only had one drink, feeling dizzy, have loss of muscle control, nausea, confusion, blackouts, vision problems, seizures and a slow heart rate.

While patrolling the club or bar he was working at, if he ever saw anyone displaying any of the warning signs of having their drink spiked, he would get them to a quiet area and continually talk to them to try and keep them conscious, then call for an ambulance.

If he was to ever manage to find the perpetrator, well, they would certainly have some severe mobility and eating issues for the next few months, with a broken jaw and two broken legs.

A few days before his planned attack, Syd had gone to the seediest bar he could find in the city. It didn't take long before he found a dealer and decided a small bottle of chloroform would be better than a couple of Rohypnol tablets. Once he had done the deal in an alleyway next to the bar, Syd beat up the dealer, took the remainder of his illegal drugs and threw them down a drain, and took all of his ill-gotten cash, which Syd put into the charity box at the rescue centre run by Elizabeth.

Retribution and pain were Syd's sole intention, and to enable him to carry out his revenge on Oz and Carter, after knocking them both out, he covered their mouths and noses with a rag soaked in the chloroform. The vast quantity of alcohol they had consumed would add to the effects of the drug.

"Wakey wakey, come on Sleeping Beauty, time to rise and shine."

Oz felt a stinging pain as his face was continually bitch-slapped from side to side.

"Come on, snap out of it my old son."

Syd's gruff voice paired with his cockney accent mocked Oz in time with his continuous fore and backhand slaps.

Oz slowly came to his senses, but the effects of the chloroform left him in a dazed state.

His head thumped. He coughed, spluttered and spat out a mouthful of cruor. He tried to open his eyes, they stung from the continuous flow of sticky blood that ran into them, pouring from the gaping wounds on his forehead. Fragments of bark were embedded firmly into the thin layer of skin that covered his skull. His nose bones had been shattered, forcing him to breathe through the salty bitter taste of blood that had congealed within his mouth. He coughed again and spat out another mouthful of blood.

"Make one sound and I'll rip your sodding jaw off. Understand?"

Oz did not respond, so Syd punched him just below his chest bone, two ribs cracked. With the air knocked out of him, he tried desperately to gasp for a breath, causing him to swallow even more blood. Syd slammed his head back into the tree.

Oz blinked, trying to clear his eyes of blood, and to try and focus on his assailant.

He was confused, what with his violent reputation and less than savoury accomplices, who would be brave or stupid enough to have done this to him?

Oz attempted to move his hands to wipe away the blood from his face. But he couldn't, his shoulder joints had both been dislocated and were awkwardly bent skywards, supporting the full weight of his body. He slowly regained semiconsciousness, only to be confronted by a searing, agonising pain coming from his hands.

Turning his attention to Carter, Syd repeated the same process and started slapping him around the face to revive him.

Syd's actions were far more sadistic towards Carter. The power of his punch had caused a mandibular fracture, resulting in his maxillary artery being severed by fragments of the sharp edges of his shattered jawbone.

His head hung draped forward, and his lower jaw, now unattached from the temporomandibular joint, swung precariously. Blood poured down his t-shirt from his opened mouth.

For the Gruesome Twosome, there was no escape, they had both been nailed to the imposing tree.

There they stood, helplessly impaled to the mighty woody girth. Blood poured down their arms, which had been extended above their heads. Syd had hammered two four-inch steel nails through each of their palms. He had purposely misdirected some of the heavy hammer blows, avoiding the intended target of the nail's head, instead, smashing the head of the heavy hammer onto their palms and slender jointed digits on both of his victims' hands. The human hand is made up of twenty-seven bones. Carter and Oz's hands had been obliterated, every single bone shattered, probably beyond surgical repair.

"Teach the child right from wrong, then you won't have to punish the man," Syd thought to himself.

Carter remained in a semi-unconscious state as Syd stood in front of them and began to deliver a short sermon. His distinctive scarred features were eerily illuminated by the silvery moonlight.

"Right you pair of heartless bastards, do you remember me? Sadly for you, the young lady isn't here to save you tonight. Look lads, no hard feelings, take tonight's lesson on the chin, pardon the pun, Carter. We all know that you're both vile, worthless, cowardly scum and someone, in this case me, has had to be a voice for the voiceless. Only on this particular occasion, my actions have spoken far louder than words. Now chaps, from this day on, please be nice to the doggies. If there has to be a next time that I have to come calling because I've received word that you've been misbehaving, well let's put it this way, next time I will do you both some serious damage."

Although she would never know it, Sheba's retribution on Oz, the vile two-legged being she hated more than anything on earth, that she had vowed would one day happen, had been finally carried out.

Syd's violent torture session had been perfectly executed in less than fifteen minutes, and very luckily with no interruptions. Sadly for them, any potential witnesses would have needed to have been silenced.

"Right chaps, I'm off now. But I've got you one last present before I go."

He reached into the pockets of his duffle coat and rummaged around for the pair of pliers that he thought he had borrowed.

"Bloody idiot," he said out loud. In his haste to borrow the tools he would need, he had forgotten the pliers.

"Look lads, really sorry, it's my mistake. I wanted to give you a manicure as well. A Syd special. You don't mind if I owe it to you, do you? I promise, the next time we meet up I will rip your fingernails out as well."

The pathetic twosome impaled to the tree would never know just how lucky they had been.

In his heyday, for an added encore, Syd would have slit their top eyelids open with his trusted flick knife.

His beloved companion, a gift passed down to him by his father, went everywhere with him. The mechanism in the top-quality Italian Stiletto was as quick today as it was the day it was purchased by his father, the standard sidearm for the Teddy Boys, from a back-street shop in Kings Cross, North London, in the 1950s.

A simple press of the silver side button sent the five-inch, razor-sharp stainless-steel blade flying out.

Syd sniggered out loud as he walked away from the bloody carnage he had just inflicted. Although for his own sake, obviously rather than theirs, Syd hoped that Oz and Carter's battered bodies would soon be discovered; they were both haemorrhaging vast quantities of blood.

The damp, green tussocks of grass beneath his victims' feet had been flattened and were rapidly taking on the hue of decent full-bodied claret.

Knowing that their assailant had left, Oz began to wail out in anguish, trying to summon help.

Syd glanced back at his handy work. The grotesque scene eerily illuminated by the light of the silvery moon, resembled a scene from one of the late 1970's gory psychopath horror films he had enjoyed so much as a teenager.

"I'd love to watch whoever finds that pair of rats trying to pull those steel nails out of their hands. That is seriously going to bloody hurt," he chuckled to himself.

Pleased with the fruits of his evening's labour, Syd started to head back towards the Boulevard Slivnitsa. Deep down he hoped that when he arrived back at the hostel Susan would still be awake.

He had already planned the final part of his evening with military precision.

After he had wiped the hammer clean and given it back to the manager to put back in the cupboard, he'd shoot up to his room, have a quick shower to freshen up and remove any blood that may have splattered on him, then slip on the change of clothes he had already left out on his bed.

A quick splash of aftershave, then he would pop and tell Susan all about his disastrous evening.

Obviously, he would have to lie to her. Although Susan

would probably have been proud of what he had done, the fewer people that knew the truth, the better; he had had his fingers burnt in the past.

Instead he would tell her how his date had stood him up. He knew full well that Susan would laugh at him. Hopefully, if his plan came together, she would kindly offer to take him out for a nightcap, mainly to let him lick his wounds and drown his diminished macho pride.

Freshly booted and suited, Syd banged on Susan's door. The knock was far more aggressive and much louder than he had intended. It was his signature knock, the one he would use when doing his debt collection rounds in London.

"Who's there?" came the slightly nervous reply from behind the heavy wooden barrier.

"Sounds like the beginning of a cheesy dad joke," laughed Syd. "You lucky girl, get your coat on, you've pulled," he continued, with his usual air of arrogance.

The door was unlocked and opened as far as the security chain would allow.

For an added comedy effect, Syd had popped out his prosthetic eye and was standing in his best Quasimodo stance.

Syd was met by a pair of dark brown eyes peering at him. The usual nocturnal sounds of the hostel were blocked out by the Indie music blaring loudly out of the android phone sitting on the small dressing table in the corner of Susan's room.

She removed the security chain and fully opened the door. Her face became engulfed with a wry smile as she stared mockingly at him, soon followed by her roaring with laughter as Syd started shouting

"The bells, the bells!"

"Well, go on, tell me Casanova, or Quasimodo, what happened then?"

"Sweet FA, the bitch never bleeding turned up did she. Not to worry, it's her loss anyway."

Syd smiled as Susan again started to laugh at him. The cheeky cow was ridiculing him, but deep down she was pleased that she was going to get to spend her last night in Sofia with her mate.

"Give us a minute. And Syd, please put your bloody eye back in."

Syd did as he was told, and pulled his eyelids apart then slid his glass eye back into its socket.

Susan switched off the music and put her phone in her pocket, popped on her ankle boots, grabbed her coat, and matching purple woolly gloves, hat and scarf that her nan had knitted for her. She took the key out of her purse and double-locked her door. She paused, then turned to Syd.

"Before we go out, tell me the truth Syd, second best, am I?"

"Not at all darling. To be honest mate, I didn't think you'd have come out with me on a date if I'd asked you."

"Good answer."

They headed off together, arm in arm, out into the cold night air for a few final farewell drinks at the local bar. Ahead of them lay an evening of drinking, laughing and reminiscing about the success of their voluntary mission in Bulgaria.

During the course of the evening, they spoke of their future plans for helping the planet's brutalised canines. They also spoke openly of their pasts.

Susan told Syd about how she had yearned to be a vet

from a young age, although now a fully qualified veterinary nurse, she hoped to one day continue her training and eventually become a fully qualified veterinary surgeon.

Syd spoke of his teenage years hanging around in Soho, where he had made the acquaintance of a couple of 'working girls'. The girls didn't have the luxury of a room to offer their clients any form of comfort as they plied their trade, so they used the West End's dingy back alleyways.

Syd had met the girls in the only pub in Soho where the landlord allowed them to drink, without judging them on their source of income. For Syd, in his studded leather biker jacket, twelve-hole oxblood Dr Martens, and lime green Mohican hairstyle, it was also the only pub that allowed punks to enjoy a beer or six, as long as they behaved themselves.

One winter's day, over a late afternoon drink, they told Syd of their repulsion at some of the men that they had to 'perform' with, and some of the degrading acts the men asked them to do. Syd was sickened and came up with a cunning, foolproof plan, which they sprang straight into action.

Syd told the girls of the specific clients that they needed to seek out.

They didn't have long to wait, before the Friday night's stream of black London taxis swarmed into the West End.

Soon their cargos of gormless, chinless wonders were hopping out of the taxis in eagerness of the night of vice that lay ahead of them.

Proudly wearing their satin bowler hats, and no matter what the weather, a gentleman's umbrella always hanging off their arm, and their hand clasping a black briefcase. A dark grey overcoat covered their pinstripe suit, the standard antiquated uniform from a bygone era of the city gent.

The girl would move in closer and listen to the fare.

"That'll be £1.75, please guv."

Two-pound notes would usually be handed over.

"Keep the change, old boy."

Perfect, the girl knew that the punter had made roughly a three-mile journey, probably from the wealth and debauchery of the square mile.

Now it was time for her to move in for the kill.

"Hi, handsome, fancy a bit of action?"

Of course, the dirty old sods did, that was the reason they were there. It didn't take long for the deal to be struck.

The girls shuddered as the creepy old men would put their arms around their waist, pulling them in tight, so close that the girls could smell the booze that lingered on their breaths from the lunchtime drinks in one of the square mile's wine bars.

Little did they know as they eagerly trotted along Wardour Street that they were lambs to the slaughter.

Soon they arrived at the preselected alleyway.

Discreetly the girl would scour the area to make sure they hadn't been followed, and that there were no police officers about. Their main worry was the police vans, known as 'Meat Wagons' crammed full of bully boy SPG officers, who patrolled the streets of Soho.

Syd, with his trusted 1942 War Department issue MK2 BC42 brass knuckle duster gripped firmly in his right hand, would be hiding in the shadows at the back of the dead-end passageway.

The girl would bring her eager punter into the alley and commence doing the dirty deed.

Just before proceedings could go too far, Syd would leap

out and slap the gentleman about a bit.

To carry on the charade, the girl would let out a faint scream and run. If the guy really repulsed Syd, his brass knuckle would come in handy for the swift and painful removal of a couple of front teeth.

Syd would then rob the hapless punter of their jewellery and money. The best thing for muggers in the late 1970s was that just about everyone carried cash. The punter, only slightly battered or a bit toothless, would be allowed to run. This was always a hilarious sight, the city gent, often his head adorned with a tightly spun rabbit fur bowler hat, scarpering along Wardour Street trying to pull his trousers up.

Now came the clever part.

"They couldn't go squealing to the gavvers," Syd said.

"Gavvers?" Susan looked confused

"The old Bill, you know, the police. I usually call them a lot worse, but spared your lug holes due to you being such a refined young lady."

"Thank you, kind sir. Please do go on."

"Anyway, the chinless creep would have phoned earlier on in the afternoon and lied to his missus. He would have told her that he was working late, or had an urgent meeting he had to attend, so he had absolutely no reason, or plausible excuse to have been in my stomping ground, the heart of Soho, London's fun, yet notorious red-light district."

Susan shook her head and Syd smiled as he momentarily harked back to his happy, yet misspent youth.

"I would share the proceeds of the crime with the girls."

"That was kind of you."

"I know," replied Syd sarcastically.

"I always kept the cash. I would spend it later on that

evening on a few pints, a packet of fags, and hopefully a ticket for a gig, the Stranglers, Damned and Siouxsie, were my favourites, but to be honest, any punk band would do. The girls kept the jewellery, which they would pass on to one of their fences."

Although she knew what he had done was wrong, Susan couldn't help but look on admiringly at Syd as he reminisced about his good old days.

"Proper little Robin Hood, weren't you?"

"You could say that. Although actually, I think I may have been more of a marriage counsellor."

"And how, may I ask, did you come to that conclusion?"

"I'll tell you why. In my stopping those men from having their perverse, wicked ways with the women, just imagine how many couples are now celebrating milestone anniversaries. All the parties, the kids and grandkids looking on adoringly, not knowing the seedy lives that their dads and granddads once led. And that's all thanks to me."

He laughed out loud, then looked remorsefully at Susan.

"I'm not proud of some of the things that I have done in my life, but I wouldn't change a thing. I know that I'm old, but I'd like to think that I'm wise. And you know why? Because I was young once, and yes, I admit, incredibly stupid. Dogs have now become my salvation though. In rescuing them I may have lost my mind, but I found my soul. In fact, I'll go even further, until one has loved an animal a part of one's soul remains unawakened."

"Bloody hell, that's very spiritual and philosophical Syd."

"Full of surprises, aren't I? But I'll tell you now, if you ever tell anyone that I said it, I'll deny it."

"Your secrets are safe with me mate. Deep down you

really are a bleeding big softy. I knew from the start that we would be mates, Syd. I have lived my life with the mantra that I never trust a person that doesn't like dogs. However, I always trust a dog when it doesn't like a person."

"Right Susan, that's more than enough of the philosophical hippy shit, get the drinks in."

They both burst out laughing. Susan decided to really push the boat out and ordered herself a Balkan 176°, the lethal 88% abv vodka that came in a bottle with thirteen different health warnings (including one in Braille), Syd opted for a pint of Kamenitza Dark, with a port and brandy chaser.

Susan had already made up her mind that after a couple of weeks of catching up with family and friends back in London, her next port of call was going to be to head back to Eastern Europe, this time Romania. Sadly, the atrocities inflicted on the stray dog population there easily matched, or may have even exceeded, anything she had witnessed in Bulgaria.

Syd was casting his net further afield, and he was off to China. He had been in contact with a UK-based activist group and was off to offer his services and try to help thwart, as best he could, the vile Yulin Dog Meat Festival.

CHAPTER TWENTY-TWO

Easter Monday, 6th April 2015.

Sheba had spent nearly two months at the rescue sanctuary.

Her journey over in the transport van had gone without a hitch. In the end, Cliff and Charles had completed the drive in just under forty hours.

Sheba's right leg had successfully undergone surgery, hopefully, very soon she would go under the knife for her final operation to straighten her left leg.

"Right Sheba, now you listen to me, little lady. I want you to be on your best behaviour. You have some very special visitors."

Intrigued by the words that had just been said to her, the little dog became excited in her kennel. She had a fresh scar running down her right leg from the surgery she had undergone a few weeks earlier. Her left was still deformed, but it didn't stop her from leaping up at the cage door of her kennel.

She heard the distinctive rattling sound of a lead and chain collar, which excited her even more. Usually, it meant that it was her turn to go out and play in the paddock, but the lady's words were not the familiar ones.

Sheba was still excitedly running in circles and jumping up at the kennel door.

"Come on Sheba, back up. I can't open your door if you're pushing at it."

Sheba eventually backed away allowing the lady to slip the securing bolt and enter. She slipped the collar and lead around Sheba's neck, gave her head a little stroke and ran her fingers through her fur to tidy her up a bit.

Sheba was led out into the passageway. The rest of the rescue dogs housed in the other kennels became excitedly animated. In unison, they started barking and jumping up as they watched the little dog pass them.

Sheba kept on looking up at the lady. She had learnt her way to the play paddock, yet today she was heading in a different direction.

She was led down the small passageway, then through the reception area.

Together with the kennel maid, they walked through the front door out into the warm spring sunshine.

On the other side of the car park, next to the paddock where the two donkeys lived, Sheba could see two humans, a lady and a man.

They both knelt when they saw her. Sheba glanced up at the lady holding the lead, then back over at the two strangers. Intrigued, and for reasons unknown, she dragged the kennel maid towards the two strangers.

"Hello, gorgeous girl," the man said to her.

Sheba looked at him. He was kneeling at her eye level, directly in front of her. Slowly he outstretched his arms, just as the lady who rescued her from the compound back in her distant home country of Bulgaria had done many weeks ago.

Instinctively she leapt straight into his awaiting, open arms. Sheba started licking his face as he gently embraced her. She then looked towards the lady next to him. Sheba shuffled over and clambered up at her.

The man looked down at Sheba's legs. He knew all about her history and her operation. Now up close, he could see the state of Sheba's poorly deformed front left leg and the fresh, angry-looking scar that ran the full length down the front of her right leg.

The couple took it in turns cuddling her, all the while saying her name, over and over.

"Sheba good girl, Sheba beautiful girl."

After an hour or so of playing with and being showered by kisses from the lady and man, Sheba was reluctantly led back to her kennel.

Over the coming weeks, the man and lady visited her every day. Together they would go for walks around the paddocks and fields within the boundaries of the rescue sanctuary. They would sit on the grass, Sheba resting her head on their laps, and they would talk to her.

Sheba never understood the words that they said to her, but she was being told of the plans that they had for her. Of how her life would be, and the adventures they would go on together once her operations were all over, and she had finally been allowed to move in with them.

They also spoke to her, with tears in their eyes, about their dog Shane.

Shane had crossed over the Rainbow Bridge a week before they had met Sheba.

In the spiritual world's grand scheme of things, wouldn't it be amazing if Shane had met Bevan, and they spend their days playing together and looking down upon Sheba.

Bevan and Shane, waiting patiently for the inevitable day when they will both be reunited with their four- and two-legged, loved ones.

CHAPTER TWENTY-THREE

Thursday, 23rd April 2015.

Sheba arrived, rather unexpectedly at her new home.

Things had not quite gone to plan that day. She was meant to have her final operation, but upon arrival at the surgery, it was discovered that she had broken her leg that had already been operated on. An emergency plan was sprang into action, and she was now moving into her new home, two months earlier than planned.

She was carried gently from the car into her new home and gently lowered to the floor.

"Go on Sheba, you're home now darling. Go and explore," said the man.

She looked up at the two humans. Although they were smiling, Sheba could sense that they were sad.

Off she scampered, excitedly investigating the place that was now to be her furever home.

She ran into the lounge, her plaster cast clumping awkwardly on the wooden flooring.

With her tail frantically wagging and wafting the air, a small clump of soft fur blew from under one of the couches. Sheba looked down and sniffed it, she picked up on the distinct scent of a dog.

She turned and started sniffing the air. Strangely, she could sense that there was a presence.

She turned and set off to find it.

She followed the scent trail, which led to a glazed wooden cabinet in the lounge.

The scent overpowered her. She closed her eyes and pushed her nose against one of the small glass panels. A patch of condensation from her expelled breath formed on the glass.

The aura made her shudder. She opened her eyes and stared at a small wooden box. She sat and felt compelled to lower her head. She didn't know why, but she needed to show the little box her utmost respect.

Sheba looked up at her new family.

They stood staring at her, with tears streaming down their faces.

She looked back at the box, then back at the two humans.

The man knelt in front of her, and around her neck he lovingly placed a pretty pink collar that he had purchased a few days earlier. Elsie from the rescue sanctuary had already etched a name tag, which the man secured to the collar.

"There you go my beautiful girl. That's your special ID tag, with your name and home address on it."

Little did Sheba know of the significance of the shiny little metal disc. It clearly had her new, furever home etched on it, a home that will be eternally filled with love and joy.

"I am so grateful to you for showing me mercy, for showering me with love and for giving me a home. But I'm confused, and for some strange reason, and I know that I shouldn't be, I am also scared. Please, I wish I could make you understand that I have spent my life sleeping on the cold, dirty ground, or damp soiled straw. I have had to fight for food and gobbled it up as quickly as I could. Do not be sad if I am frightened of your loving touch, many people have beaten me. Please be patient with me, I am new to your world, but I will come to accept the love that you give me. I will grow to trust you, but I have nothing to give you in return except for my heart and unconditional love. I hope that these small gestures will go some way in repaying you for all that you do for me."

Sheba knew that her family didn't understand her gentle guttural grunts but hoped that they would pick up on her body language, the way that she snuggled into them, licked their faces and bowed her head.

The man's hands embraced her, and he kissed her on her head.

"They understand," Sheba thought to herself.

"We will always love and protect you, little lady," said the lady.

With his hands still stroking her neck, the man spoke to Sheba.

"I know that you are bewildered and that it will take you time to accept the changes. You may wish to test the boundaries, that's fine, you'll soon settle down. In time you'll work it all out for yourself, together we'll sort out a routine, and in a few weeks, you'll let your guard down and we'll see your true personality. You have months of surgery ahead of you, and believe me, we will be with you every step of the way. Together we will build a bond, you will get to trust us, and feel secure with us, your new family, here in your very own home."

Sheba licked his wrist. The words he said were alien, but his gestures and body language told her all that she needed to know.

Sheba thought back to Hamish's words of warning

regarding betrayal, however, she instinctively knew that her new family were not shepherds, and they would never betray her.

Sheba awoke from her first night in her new home just as the sun was rising.

Her right leg ached. As she tried to manoeuvre herself into a more comfortable position, she caught her nose on the bulbous bandaging that protected her broken limb.

She could feel a strange sensation, a human hand was gently stroking and caressing her body. She had not slept so peacefully, nor deeply, since she was a pup, nestled up against her dear, late mother.

Before she had fallen to sleep the previous evening, she had let out an enormous sigh, a sigh of relief, a sigh of contentment.

She now knew that she was safe and that an almighty weight had been lifted from her poor little shoulders. She instinctively knew that this was her home, and her new family, her place of sanctuary and love.

For her, peaceful nights, sleeping in safety and comfort were now going to be a thing of reality.

She watched as her human drank from his mug. After a while he put it down on the floor next to him. Intrigued, Sheba moved over and sniffed the brown liquid.

"That smells nice," she thought to herself, before lapping at the remnants. Wow, it tasted so good.

The man burst out laughing. Sheba wagged her tail.

"Cheeky little madam. So you enjoy a morning cup of tea do you?"

Sheba again wagged her tail.

The man broke off a piece of the digestive biscuit he was

eating and gave it to her.

"Well darling, looks like I'll have to share my tea and biscuits with you every morning then."

She had a few more months of corrective surgery ahead of her, but with her new family's support, and her resilient nature, Sheba would get through it.

As the days passed, Sheba learnt a whole new language. Her loving human's facial expressions and the words they repeatedly spoke to her, that were always accompanied by loving hand gestures, and their unique body language. She noticed their aroma changed depending on their emotions, and Sheba soon understood the sudden rise in their adrenalin signalled anxiety in them. This would be her signal to shuffle over and kiss them, letting them know not to worry and everything would be OK.

In return, her family had to try and learn her unique ways of communication. They soon came to realise that dogs do speak, but to only those who know how to understand them. They soon picked up on the little gestures she would make, such as an exaggerated stare at the patio doors, meaning if she needed to be carried out to relieve herself, or her struggled movements, accompanied by a little whimper, that told them she was uncomfortable, or that her broken leg was hurting.

"At last, the stars have aligned. Although I have lost those dearest to me, I know full well that one day we will be reunited. For now, I have been given all that I have ever desired. I no longer live my life in fear and suffering, I have at last been shown mercy."

Sheba xxx

Read the powerfully emotional story of Sheba's ongoing journey and adventures in the true-life sequel …

Shane, Sheba and Sky

Printed in Great Britain
by Amazon

26871140R00189